The Two Mary-Beths ©

A Regency Romance
by
Adelaide Jolley

Storytelling at its best. Romance. Long kept secrets. A sinister villain. A great story equals a great read. Readers won't be disappointed. I cringed. I laughed and I kept on reading.
I loved it!
JMc.

With thanks to JMc. for all her encouraging service, and to Annie P who willingly jumped in to help.

Most of all, my sincere and loving thanks to my amazing patient husband, Chris, who remained calm, yet supportive when I nearly gave up.

A very special shout out and a big thank-you to artist, Jeremy Carling for creating and designing the lovely book cover for, The Two Mary-Beths. His patience was endless. Thank you, Jeremy!

Prologue

'Darling,' Miss Elizabeth Chetwode gave her younger brother, Jamie a warm smile. 'It is only for another two years.'

Jamie, now nearly nineteen years old, and no longer the green youth who joined Longton's as a junior clerk five years ago rubbed a sturdy hand through cropped dark-brown hair.

He looked so handsome dressed in the latest style. His rich honey-coloured eyes clouded as his well-defined top lip sank from a capital 'm' shape to a frown. His fingers skimmed the lace-covered table.

'You know I want to work with horses; Rutland sounds perfect.'

Elizabeth put a hand over his, 'when you qualify and have your own patrons you can do exactly that.'

Maroon-clad shoulders, broad and muscular from his days at the brewery heaved.

'You are going away.'

'Only for six months, Jamie.'

'Supposing you then decide against a London Season?'

Withdrawing her hand, Elizabeth straightened. 'Then I shall buy us a house with enough land for your thoroughbred racers.'

Hope sprang across his face. 'So, I can join you directly?'

Elizabeth wavered. 'Surely weekly letters will be enough for now?'

'So, you get the countryside, while I slave away in the London smog?'

Elizabeth sighed. 'Foregoing a Season means I could live in modest circumstances and be a teacher for those who do not have a chance to learn and wish to do so, for the rest of my life. You, however, can do your part to fulfil Mama's wishes. Then, when you have taken your Articles, the Quality will vie for your services. You will have wealth and prestige, and then you too, could be of help to those who are treated unjustly, yet who cannot afford to fight that injustice.'

Jamie sniffed derisively. 'Mr. Longton is not exactly wealthy, and he certainly does not help anyone who cannot afford his fees.'

'His wife is sometimes rather extravagant,' Elizabeth countered.

Jamie's jaw clenched.

Elizabeth knew what annoyed him. It was that Mama had entrusted *her* with the significant fortune, and not him. He had been far too young to handle such a sum. Besides, Mama wanted most of it to be used for her Season. If she complied that was.

Although longing to carry out their late Mama's wishes, the thought that she was expected to find a husband among the *haute monde*, appalled Elizabeth. She wanted live in quiet contentment as a generous caring spinster rather than be at the mercy of a man.

Jamie's jaw unclenched and he changed tact. 'Promise you will work as a companion for six months only?'

'Yes,' Elizabeth, relieved by his change in attitude smiled. 'After all, I cannot leave Lady Bucklow's, home as one of her penniless protégés then instantly launch myself into Society as a modest heiress, can I?'

Jamie frowned. 'I still do not understand why you had to rely on her benevolence for so long.'

Elizabeth sighed. 'Dearest, you know why. It was the solution to my dilemma. Now, though, this position as a companion to Miss Wybrow will give me a foothold in Quality drawing-rooms.'

'The *ton* might reject you.'

Deep in her heart, Elizabeth already knew this and was relieved. She did not want to be a part of, 'Society'. She wanted to be able to offer to teach children, whose parents could not afford to pay for such a luxury, to read and write and do basic arithmetic.

'Not if they get wind of my dowry.'

Jamie's honey irises darkened again as he looked at her in concern. 'I hope you know what you are doing Sis.'

'Promise not to do anything rash, Jamie?'

His usual easy humour had returned. 'I promise. Come, let me escort you to your coach.'

As he rose, larger than life to take up her heavy, but modest portmanteau, several admiring feminine lashes fluttered in his direction. Purposely ignoring, or not noticing, Jamie ushered her out into the bustling London, street.

Chapter One

The portmanteau thumped onto the grass verge at Elizabeth's feet.

'Thistleton is about a mile yonder beyond Hooby Lodge.' The coachman pointed across the fields. 'Once over that stile, just there, stick to the footpath and ye'll not miss it. Sorry about the long delay Miss.' Then slapping the reins, he whisked the coach off.

The words echoed through Elizabeth's mind. Although it was not the coachman's fault that an axle broke, and everyone had to stay an extra night and half a day at an inn until it was repaired, the journey that should have taken two days, had taken three and a half. As there was no way of getting in touch with her future employers, the Wybrows, all she could do, was hope they still wanted to employ her as a companion to their daughter. What if they did not though? What if they deemed her unreliable?

It was a peculiar confusion of thoughts, that on the one hand it would not put her in dire financial straits, but on the other, she would either have to find something else similar in order to appease Jamie or else he would use her failure to follow Mama's wishes, as an excuse to do the same. She felt a bit guilty, because she had what Jamie wanted, which was the open countryside, while he was stuck at Longton's learning to be a solicitor.

She had reminded herself so many times, that she *was* doing what Mama wanted, but perhaps not in the exact way Mama wanted.

Then there was Lady Bucklow to consider. Lady Bucklow had been so kind and considerate throughout the last few years, and then made such an effort to secure the right kind of employment with a good family, and in what was thought of as a good area for her, that it might seem as if Elizabeth was not grateful for all the kindness and care shown to her.

If there was such a thing as miracles, then Lady Bucklow was the very pinnacle of miraculous intervention. For Lady Bucklow had suddenly appeared at the exact time she was needed the most. Elizabeth had often wondered what would have become of her if Lady Bucklow had not been there. Elizabeth knew without a doubt, that the secret inheritance, she and Jamie only recently found out about, would have been appropriated, or more to the point misappropriated, by their permanently inebriated father Charles Westernbury. A father who only showed up once a month to demand money from dear Mama. How Mama, managed to have money to give him, Elizabeth and Jamie never knew. Although they lived a decent enough life, in a respectable part of London, all they had was the money Mama earned through giving private lessons to children in various subjects. Charles Westernbury only took money; he never gave them anything in return. The truth was, his drunken abuse meant that none of them wanted him to stay. Mama said that giving him money kept him appeased enough to stay away.

Wafting the rise of dust from her face Elizabeth turned her thoughts to the job in hand and studied the expanse of hedged-up countryside. Never had she seen so much land with so little on it. As for her destination being only a mile away, that was a joke surely? Apart from the shrubby tree-lined path on the other side of the stile, all she could see over the hedgerows, was an expanse of green and brown hedged fields.

Resolutely smoothing her indigo pelisse with gloved hands, adjusting her light blue bonnet to a sober angle, she set her reticule firmly over one elbow, hauled up the portmanteau and staggered toward stile.

Heaving the portmanteau over the stile, she then climbed over it. Then hauling the portmanteau back into her arms, she tottered forwards. The ground was uneven, the shrubs needed cutting back, and she was facing the late last day of August's afternoon sun. Only the slightest thread of coiling breeze made it bearable.

Determined to eradicate those dreadful memories of the now distant past from her mind for the umpteenth time since beginning what turned out to be an arduous journey, she turned her mind to other matters. This was a new chapter, another part of her life to savour; another part to conquer, even; just a means to reach her goal.

Fifteen exhausting minutes later she thumped the portmanteau onto the ground for the fifteenth time and sat on it.

She was hot, sticky, and unusually for her, growing frustrated.

Taking a deep breath, she stretched her arms to relieve her aching limbs before removing her gloves. To cool down a little more, she took off her bonnet and slipped off her pelisse and placed them beside her. Then, closing her eyes, she lifted her chin to the sky to savour the fresh air.

A few moments later, she opened them to study the way ahead.

The path curved ahead slightly allowing sunshine to stream through the overhead branches. Mossy mounds nestling against the base of brawny barks looked luxuriously green and comfortable. The trees to her right thinned out making the fields gloriously visible. It was as pretty as the London parks, but larger.

No wonder Jamie wanted the countryside.

The agreeable sound of distant voices drew her attention to the fields, so leaving the portmanteau, pelisse and gloves where they were, Elizabeth strolled to a thinner stretch of shrub and gazed inquisitively toward them.

She smiled.

Two fields along, whole families were tying hay into bundles. The pleasant harmonious sounds drew her closer to the thinned-out barrier, and without thinking, she squeezed herself through to get a better look. This was her first real taste of rural life.

She watched entranced, as two immense greys pulled a cart. Gently leading them was, her own dear brother, Jamie.

Her heart stopped for a second before immediately thumping into frantic action.

Oh no!

How could he?

Now, she knew why he was so compliant just before they parted. He had planned to follow her all along! He must have hired a horse and ridden like the Devil to be here before her. What was he thinking? Anger, and a sense of betrayal swept through her. Had he expected an open-arm welcome?

Her anguished cry went unheeded. The harmonious sounds, the thready breeze, and Jamie's concentration obliterated all other noise. His smooth graceful gait never faltered as he effortlessly guided the distant greys. The sun glimmering on his superfine tailcoat had darkened it to a deeper burgundy than she remembered. His beautifully polished boots threw glinting sparks into the air. He was wearing his good clothing too.

Elizabeth's mind blazed.

Jemmy! she silently screamed. *How could you*?

Forgetting her fatigue, she began running. Her nimble booted feet skipping over fields of green and ploughed earth alike; her anger gathering momentum as she ran.

Suddenly she was in his field racing noiselessly toward his broad back now bending away from her. Her mind was still silently screaming, '*Jemmy!*' over and over.

Suddenly she was directly behind him and had pounced on his shoulders before he knew she was there.

'Jemmy!' she berated furiously. 'I *trusted* you and you have betrayed me!'

Her attack and frenzied battle cry caught him so utterly off guard that James Bauval, fourth earl of Alstoe reeled sideways, and with a silent oath shook her off in one swift move. Unfurling his powerful frame, he turned with slow deliberation and complete self-control to face his foe.

The cheery harmony of his work force had abruptly stilled to a deathly hush, lurked threateningly behind him.

Every muscle in his body that had primed him for hair-trigger fight instantly leached the breath from him. His heart lurched with pain and shock, at the sight of her. His knees nearly gave way. But he stayed strong.

She gave a tiny whimper. 'Oh.'

The petite, adorable, pink-faced Boadicea in front of him immediately paled and gasped. Immense chrysolite irises widened under rapidly flickering caramel lashes.

The air that raced back into Bauval's, lungs was followed by an unexpected, intense yearning. His desire to pull her into his arms and soothe away that abashed look almost got the better of him.

Almost.

Managing to cover his tumultuous feelings, he raised a brow. 'Oh?' he echoed with absolute self-mastery.

He could not drag his gaze away from her. He stared in spellbound fascination as the floating strands of her hair that had escaped from a golden twist of waves feathered her cheeks.

His heart seemed to rise into his throat as an almost unbearable aching grief started throbbing through him.

She was utterly bewitching, yet the aching grief intensified making him feel breathless. She was the double of-

'I,' her delectable full lips parted and her chin dipped so she had to look up at him through those delicious flickering lashes, 'thought you were my-,' A creamy gloveless hand shot to her mouth, stopping her mid-sentence.

Masking the maelstrom of conflicting emotions, Bauval waited until the silent count of four before mouthing, with pounding inward turmoil, but seemingly unruffled outward calm, 'You thought I was?'

Dropping her hand, Elizabeth looked up at him and wished she had not. Something deep within her began to swirl and melt at the same time. She could not tear her eyes away from his. What was happening to her? 'I am *so* sorry,' she breathed. 'Please forgive me.'

Her blue chambray dress swirled as she stepped backwards. 'I have made a dreadful mistake. You look like my;' she blinked, 'someone.'

To Elizabeth's consternation he instantly bridged the gap she made. He was rightfully livid. How could she have been so mindlessly foolish? How could she have thought this massive, older, beast was her dear brother, Jamie?

This man's hair, although cropped exactly like Jamie's was blue-black, not darkest brown. His face was larger and stronger, his skin more tanned, his nose more masculine, and his lips, now a thin slash above a strong smooth chin were nothing like Jamie's. His eyes much darker than Jamie's, glinted onyx-black.

And his size! Jamie was considered large, but this man was a giant. He stood far taller, more authoritatively imminent, and dangerously more powerful than anyone she had ever met.

The peculiar fluid melting sensation continued seeping through Elizabeth, making her feel weak and languorous.

Still having to control his jumbled emotions and his mixed-up reaction to her, Bauval inclined his head slightly. 'Your someone?'

Her mouth opened and closed in rhythm with the two furtive steps she took backwards.

Again, he reduced the gap.

'You called me *Jemmy*,' he said ominously. 'No one calls me Jemmy except family and close friends.'

The unfamiliar deliciously mysterious melting sensations robbed Elizabeth of coherent thought. 'I-'

James Bauval's heart lurched. His mind whirled. She was incredible. Her hair swathed in sunlight glowed a rosy beige. Her flawless ivory skin now suffused with contrite pink reminded him of raspberries and cream. A pulse in her slender, taut neck flickered as she swallowed and his eyes automatically grazed the delicate cream skin below her throat, skimmed the scooped neckline of her dress and flicked for a second on her smooth white décolletage.

Was his mind playing tricks on him? Who, was this minx who rebuked him without preamble and now observed him with such complexity?

A pain whipped through him. She looked so like-,

His mind whirred. His legs nearly gave way again. No, that *was* impossible. He was being ridiculous.

Quickly marshalling his senses, he swallowed. 'Who are you?' he ground out before he made a complete fool of himself by asking her if she was a ghost. 'What is your name?'

'Mary-Be,' The old name nearly came out, but she caught herself, 'Elizabeth.'

Bauval's spine chilled spreading icy disquiet into every nerve of his body. Was he going mad? Had her attack addled his brain?

'Mary or Elizabeth what?' he bellowed more loudly than he intended.

Hell fire! Had his manners gone the same way as his wits?

'Chetwode! Elizabeth!' she flared back.

Ironic humour dissipated his tension; a smile played across his mouth, and Elizabeth watched with melting fascination as his countenance changed. Black irises transmuted to soft velvet with tiny flecks of silver flickering out. His whole face slanted into a wide soft smile. Then, when with a deep chuckle he stepped forward and took her hand in his, she nearly collapsed.

'Miss Elizabeth Chetwode of the Cambridgeshire Chetwodes'?'

Before Elizabeth had time to deny it, he raised her hand to his lips and gently kissed the back.

His touch made her feel as though fluttering velvety butterflies were sashaying along her spine and into every nerve of her body.

'No,' she managed, trying not to sound feeble. 'Not Cambridgeshire. I am from London.'

Her hand remained in his while he turned to stare in the direction of the road.

James fought for self-control. How could this little spitfire be having such an effect on him?

'London?' he deliberated, trying to quell his emotions, before sheering back to her. 'Did you *walk* here Miss Chetwode?'

She blinked up at him. 'No.'

He glanced quickly to the sky, then drawing a governing breath, turned back to her. 'Fly perhaps?'

She whipped her hand from his. 'Certainly not.'

He was ragging her exactly the way Jamie did. So, he was like Jamie after all. She did not know whether to laugh or cry.

Her sudden racked expression plunged into his being and tore into the depths of his soul. He had seen that exact look in his mind a thousand times ever since-

He stared helplessly into forlorn chrysolite irises.

'No.' His ragged sigh escaped before he could control it. 'Please,' he bowed towards her, his extended hands gently reaching for hers. Ignoring his inner tumult, he prised her arms away from her stiff body and drew her nearer to him. 'I have upset you. Forgive me.'

His complete turnabout astonished her and as she blinked up into his expressive face, she wondered how could she have thought him a beast? Gentleness flowed from every contour of his body.

'It is I who should apologise, please forgive me. Now if you will excuse me,' she attempted to regain some of her scattered senses, 'I must return to fetch my belongings then continue my journey.'

His hands remained firmly on hers. 'Your belongings Miss Chetwode?'

The tenderness in his tone flowed through her.

His heart soared as a trace smile curved her delicious mouth.

'Yes, I left them in my haste to reach,' she paused, 'here.'

He let the scant explanation go. If she did not want to tell him who she thought he was, so be it. It was not up to him to force her secrets from her and expose whoever she thought he was in front of his workers.

A voice came up behind him. 'Beggin' your pardon milord.'

Relieved at the interruption, Bauval swung round to the older man.

'Yes Felton?'

'I know the early coach from London was delayed by more than a day. I reckon they put 'er off by Smythe's Path.'

'Indeed?' Again, quashing his inner chaos, James swivelled back to her. 'Was the London coach delayed?'

'Yes.'

'Were you supposed to be collected?'

'Yes, but there was nobody there so the driver put me off as near to my destination as he could.'

James inclined his head. 'Where are your belongings, Miss Chetwode?'

Elizabeth drew a relieved breath. Soon, she would be back on track instead of bandying with this tantalising lord whoever he was.

'Oh?'

Her bafflement intrigued him. 'You have forgotten where you left them Miss Chetwode?'

Her cheeks flamed. 'No sir, I mean my lord.'

Silver flecks danced from velvet onyx irises. 'Oh no, I cannot allow such formality after such an auspicious introduction. I insist you call me Jemmy.'

Shimmering-velvet butterflies suddenly began skimming along her spine.

'No.'

'Come,' he chuckled at the commotion behind her chrysolite irises. 'Tell me where you are going and I shall drive you there.'

An astonishing elation surged through her. 'My portmanteau and pelisse are on the path.'

Crushing the aching turmoil Bauval inclined his head.

'Felton please fetch Miss Chetwode's belongings while I escort her to my curricle. Still addressing Felton, he raised Elizabeth's arm to tuck it under his elbow. 'Please look out for her bonnet too.'

Elizabeth gasped. The indecency of it! What must he think of her? Indecorous witless, shameless and hatless.

As the curricle bounced over the uneven road, Elizabeth could not keep her eyes and thoughts off him. The velvety butterflies sashayed through her every time she re-lived the touch of his fingers against her skin when he placed her bonnet on her head.

Having already mentioned the Wybrows, his expression was now one of reflection.

'I have heard of the Wybrows. Their daughter is not yet out.' He shot her a brief enigmatic glance. 'Mrs Wybrow will not be pleased you are late.'

Elizabeth's logic was instinctive. 'I am sure she will understand.'

His concern surprised her. 'She might give you a hard time all the same; send you home to your Mama,' he said lightly, 'so I shall escort you to the house myself and explain.'

'Oh, please,' Elizabeth placed a hand on his muscular arm, and immediately wished she had not. 'There is no need. Besides,' she added, unable to prevent the bleakness from creeping into her voice as she recalled Mama's last words when she lay dying on the day-bed, *Forgive, I beg you, Mary-Beth please forgive.'*

She could not help remembering too, that a second later Min, their neighbour arrived to tell them that Westernbury was hurtling towards the house in fury. 'My mama died four and a half years ago.'

Bauval's heart jumped. *Four and a half years ago?* He quashed his own excruciating grief as Miss Chetwode's obvious distress sent several conflicting emotions careering though him. His arm however vibrated at her touch and he had to fight the urge to stop the curricle, take her in his arms and kiss away her pain.

Quelling that thought with difficulty, he growled, 'An orphan? Then there is every need.' Although he concentrated on the road, Elizabeth noted his changing expressions. 'You are completely alone in a strange place. You need a champion. A word from me will give you security.' The curricle slowed as he turned to look at her. His irises had transmuted from onyx to velvet black. 'Will you allow me to be your champion?'

Her insides swirled with fluttery pleasure. 'Yes.'

He turned his attention back to the road.

'Then that is settled.' The wavy 'm' of his mouth formed a no-nonsense line. 'From now on, you will be under my wing.'

Suddenly, without warning the curricle rounded a sharp bend, and before she had time to think, Elizabeth was half-pitched across his lap.

The slippery polished leather upholstery was her undoing, because the more she tried to right herself, the more she failed.

Bauval's seriousness rapidly vanished as he chuckled with delight at her nearness and at her flurried efforts to move away. Champion or not, he was thoroughly enjoying the delectable sensation of her being so close that he did not intend to lift a finger to help her. Yet.

With jiggling, heroic effort, Elizabeth finally managed to sit upright and wedge herself back into position. No thanks to him! So, he was all talk, was he?

Had she not heard it all before whenever Papa promised to change? Empty words to suit the moment.

Lord Bauval, her champion? Hardly. She would be a fool shelter under his wing.

Her scowling face brought out the rascal in him even more. 'Shall we do that again Miss Chetwode?'

His impishness might have made her chuckle under different circumstances, but without warning, the cantering mare shot round another bend and Elizabeth lunged helplessly against him again.

The beast.

'You beast.' Elizabeth spluttered trying to haul herself upright again.

The bouncing curricle prevented her from realigning herself, but what really incensed her was feeling him give a slight chuckle.

How dare he!

With one deft movement, she leaned over and snatched the reins from his gloved hands.

The sudden change startled the mare pulling the vehicle, and the curricle careened an abrupt halt. The impact sent Elizabeth hurtling over the dash and onto the shanks.

He grabbed her and the reins just as she began to roll and pulled her back up so quickly that she landed, squirming and wriggling on his lap with an unladylike thump.

His heart was thumping with a terrible fear. 'You could have been killed!'

'Me?' she retorted, struggling off him. 'What about you?'

'I would not have been any the worse for wear.'

James felt his heart skitter with shame. What the devil was he thinking? Was he so addled by feckless stupidity that all gentlemanly traits had fled?

The answer hit him like a cannonball.

Yes!

This little spitfire not only scorched him with her flaying attack; she had scorched him with herself too. She had blazed into his being, and brightened his soul.

Every part of him tingled.

Suddenly she was back sitting upright on the squabs, fixing him with an infuriated school-marm stare that instantly stifled every feeling, but shame.

'Do you have to behave like a silly little boy?' she scolded as if addressing an unruly child. 'Perhaps you get away with immature behaviour because of your position or is it that you are so spoiled you have no idea of how to behave?'

His astonished reaction had no effect on her whatsoever.

'I suppose Nanny let you behave like a monster, Jemmy,' she paused and flicked those caramel lashes with cool disdain. 'Just what is your last name?'

James could not believe the effect her lecturing was having on him. He felt childlike, sublimely vulnerable, and in disgrace. When was the last time anyone spoke to him like that? Goodness! It was darling Nanny Renn, years ago. She always scolded him when he behaved like a monster, as he had just now.

He wanted, yes actually wanted to hold his head in embarrassment, and meekly admit his delinquency just to prolong Miss Chetwode's scolding, and then, oh heavenly bliss, allow her to take him in her arms and pull him tightly to her just like Nanny Renn did.

He swiftly marshalled his thoughts before he did the taking of her in his arms. Hell fire! What was happening to him?

Her unrelenting, 'Well?' brought him back to coherence.

'Well, what?'

'Your name?'

'Bauval.'

'Bauval?'

Delicious excitement rose through him. She was magnificent! Every nerve in his body now quivered with restraint. The temptation to haul her into his arms, kiss the haughty look from her face and feel her anger dissolve with his touch was almost too much.

Almost.

He took a controlling breath. 'Are you quite ready Miss Chetwode?'

'Are you going to behave yourself?' she riposted.

His sense of humour had not quite deserted him however. What if he refused? He suppressed a smile, curbed his thoughts, and angled his head. 'How could I not?'

'Very well,' she murmured. 'Pray continue.'

He clamped his jaw on a quick-fire retort. He had behaved badly. Yes, he probably did abuse his position occasionally. What did she expect though after her initial flaying assault? A meek-little-lambkins? Well really. Regardless of the effect she had on him, she had much to learn.

Taking Miss Chetwode under his wing would definitely have its advantages.

Mustering his thoughts, he changed the subject. 'I shall inform Mrs Wybrow that the coach was delayed,' he declared smoothly, as if the last ten minutes never occurred, 'and that you waited by Stranton Cross for a considerable length of time. I shall say I drove by, saw you with your luggage then insisted you to accept my escort. I shall then declare my intention of being your guardian.'

'But-'

'-But nothing. This is a cruel world, Miss Chetwode. As your guardian, I shall expect to call on you from time to time.' He flicked glittering eyes to her. 'Naturally, I will be the model of decorum at all times.'

'Ha,' she scoffed, completely forgetting to take him to task about his dishonesty, 'I doubt you can control your,' she was just going to say 'mischievousness' but after a swift glance at his expression, thought better of it. She certainly did not want to encourage more devilry. Besides, her own dear Jamie was more than enough to cope with on the now, thankfully, rare occasions, he ragged her.

She took a deep breath, 'Brutishness.'

Keeping the curricle steady, he turned to her.

'Brutishness?' he echoed.

Now she really had offended him. Keeping a hold on her herself she nodded. She must not let him upset her. He had behaved brutishly. Only a brutish character would chuckle as she squirmed helplessly on his knee because of his thoughtlessness.

'Yes, brutishness.'

He pulled the curricle to a halt and for one ghastly second, she thought he was going to order her off. 'And what may I ask, was your behaviour attributed to Miss Chetwode?' He made soft tutting sounds, 'Before a proper introduction too. Whatever is the world coming to?' he continued airily, 'When unaccompanied young ladies accost all and sundry on a mere whim?'

'I have apologised for that.'

A slow smile played across his lips.

'Ah yes,' his irises flecked silver. 'You did. Very noble in the circumstances.' His eyes already etched with softly defined laughter lines, crinkled merrily at the corners. 'Just imagine the consequences if you had not?'

The sight of his labourers along with the distinct impression of danger flashed through her mind, and she realised that each worker had postured in defence of their master. The consequences could indeed have been disastrous.

Her immediate racked expression felled his whole being. He advanced a fraction. 'Miss-,'

Suddenly she was a hissing, spitting, blaze of fury.

'You think it amusing?' she cried tilting away from him. 'You find merriment that your people could have,' she cast about for the right words, 'set about me?'

James stifled a relieved chuckle. He would rather have those chrysolite eyes flashing prisms of yellow-gold fury, than see them cloudy and desolate. The desolation of someone he had cared about was something he never wanted to experience again.

'You judge them too harshly Miss Chetwode,' he murmured, delighting in the absurdity of it. 'My people are God fearing folk. They believe in justice.' He pursed his lips to prevent the pleasure from showing. 'It was not you they would have set upon. The whole lot of them would have grappled me to the ground,' he schooled his features to match his tone, 'ordered the swiftest man to run and fetch the parson and,' a warm sensation tweaked through him, 'had us married us in a trice.'

Aversion ripped across her face. 'No!'

Her instant reaction flattened every ounce of his humour. There were Mamas' all over the country flinging their daughters in his direction, vying for his attentions in the hopes of ensnaring a peer. A rich one at that. Yet, here was this little minx, flashing prisms of sparking fury at the thought.

Just what bothered him about such a reaction anyway? Anyone else would consider it a firm offer. He should feel relief, not disappointment. He should rejoice at his narrow escape not stare at her like a rejected swain.

What was happening to him?

Elizabeth quickly pulled herself together. His labourers would have done no such thing. He was jesting. Placating her with humour just as Jamie did when he went too far. She drew a breath and decided to accept the olive branch he offered with a jest of her own.

'Pray forgive me,' she murmured in dulcet tones. 'I did not mean to inconvenience your lordship.' She dropped her chin to look at him through her lashes. 'Interrupting the hay making was unforgivable enough. Interrupting the hay making for a mere wedding service would be extremely uncivilised.' She swept her chin up with a dramatic sigh. 'County life is so different from town life is it not?'

He stared at her, confounded by her irony in her tone.

His dark eyes narrowed and flecked silver. He dropped the reins.

'I declare you are joshing me, Miss Chetwode.'

He started inching along the bench as he spoke. 'Ribbing me,' he said softly. 'I think you need to be taught a lesson.'

She gazed at him as a strange molten fascination held her captive. 'Me, my lord?'

He closed the gap between them. 'I thought we agreed on Jemmy.'

She looked so utterly bewitching with her eyes wide with total innocence, and her lips expectantly swelling into two glossy mounds.

His fingers suddenly flicked out to lift her chin. 'So,' he murmured, 'I shall start right now.'

His body was against hers. The scent of spicy soap and something she did not recognise caused those velvety butterflies to flutter through her. Muscles defining every fascinating contour of his face stretched taut, but not tense, under firm flesh. His mouth, she previously deemed to be thin and hard was now spell-bindingly full and soft. His bottom lip curved in a sensuous mound; his top lip formed a wavy 'm'.

As he lowered his face, tiny shards of lightning bolts prickled her mouth in a peculiar anticipation.

Suddenly, James drew right away from her.

A tiny bud, somewhere near his heart started to flower, and although he wanted to hold her in his arms, the urge to protect and nurture this audacious yet vulnerable little creature rose above all his baser feelings.

He drew a deep silent breath as his chest brimmed with an infinite and unexpected tenderness. She was everything he never knew he wanted.

Until now.

That knowing, that new revelation, seemed to elevate him to a higher plane. An inexplicable plane he never knew existed.

A plane, and an elevation he never wanted to leave.

Chapter Two

In an effort to conceal the intensity of his feelings James whizzed round the last corner. He, who did not believe in the absurdity of love at first sight, was utterly bewitched by the adorable creature beside him.

'Look to your left, and you will see Wybrow House.'

Elizabeth, trying to ignore the ridiculous tingling feeling, looked, but remained silent. What was happening to her? She had to stop these foolish sensations. His nearly kiss had turned her upside down and inside out. Why had she allowed that to happen?

Now, each time his expression changed, and each time his hands flicked the reins, her heart flipped in rhythm with his every move.

She, who fiercely vowed never to let any man except her brother Jamie into her heart, had fallen at the first fence. If she was to have the happy and unselfish life she planned, she had to bridle these nonsensical breath-taking feelings. To give in to them, would meaning end up like poor, dear Mama.

Elizabeth forced herself to focus on what he was saying.

As James threw her a quick glance his chest tightened. There it was again. That look he had seen many times before. That desolation that scored his soul. A look he never wanted to see again.

Was she a ghost sent to remind him of the sins of his past?

Now he was being irrational. Of course, Miss Chetwode was not a ghost, she was a living spitfire. His senses whirred and his body thrummed. The vigorous Miss Chetwode certainly was not an ethereal apparition. She was a vibrant, beautiful siren. The shame of the past sliced through him. If only he thought like that about dear Mary-Beth, his second cousin.

Managing to block the pain of her past by imaging her charitable future, Elizabeth turned to him. To her surprise however, he appeared impassive. Only the slackening of his well-defined top lip gave him away. He was secretly frowning exactly the same way Jamie did. How could that be?

The instant he turned to her though, his expression changed and her spirits rose. How could he be so like Jamie one second, and so different the next?

She was being fanciful. He was nothing like Jamie.

Bauval's mood brightened. Oh joy, she was now smiling. Her wretchedness had vanished. Her caramel lashes flickered over bright chrysolite irises. Her cheeks glowed, and she was smiling.

He was a whimsical fool. How could two unrelated people be so alike? The woman beside him was the epitome of health and vitality. She was not like their dear Mary-Beth at all.

Although he tried disregarding her loveliness, his mind refused to do so, and irrespective of his good intentions, a yearning coursed through him again. He wanted her in his life more than any woman he had ever met. Yet, he was confused about why she had had such an effect on him? He was twenty-nine for heaven's sake, not a green youth in the throes of first love.

With absolute self-mastery, he inclined his head to a grey stone three-storied house across the meadows their left. 'Can you see it?'

Elizabeth turned.

Even though it was surrounded by rich pasture she had expected it to be larger. Anyone employing a companion for their daughter would be of considerable means surely? She counted the windows immediately above a columned veranda. Six in all. Above the two corner windows, two attic gables with barely visible windows jutted from the roof. A strange chill slid through her, and she tried not to shudder. The house looked dark and sinister, lifeless and dejected.

'It is not what you are used to, Miss Chetwode?'

Had he read her thoughts? Nothing during the previous four and a half years was what she was used to.

She glanced at him and instantly regretted it. His jaw, set in a firm line angled down at her. His onyx irises were alive with something she did not understand yet excited her all the same. The 'm' on his top lip had levelled to a smooth line. For a second, she wished herself back in London or in one of Lady Bucklow's other equally plush houses as far away from this unsettling lord as possible.

She gathered her wits. 'What is anyone used to?' Supressing the peculiar chill, and not wishing to appear fussy or dissatisfied, she forced herself to add in a lighter tone, 'One man's palace is another's hovel is it not?'

'True, very true, Miss Chetwode.' His smile of acceptance made her stomach fall and rise in fluttery waves.

Mrs Wybrow's puce dress rustled as she bustled across the polished hall to greet them.

'Thank goodness!' she gushed. 'I was beside myself with worry.' She curtsied to James. 'My Lord.'

'Mrs Wybrow,' he tilted his chin down.

'My lord,' she continued without looking at Elizabeth, 'however can I thank you?' Without giving him time to reply, she asked, 'Will you take tea, my lord?' Again, without waiting for a response, she directed an order to the man standing behind her. 'Dabbs, please tell Mrs Hoddan to bring a tray into the Mandarin salon.' She turned back to James. 'Do please come this way, my lord.'

Her lace cap bobbed on only just-greying hair as she led them forward. 'Here,' she trilled throwing open the door of a beautifully arranged, large, but obviously little used, room. 'I am afraid there is no fire,' She waved towards the window. 'We rarely light one in here, as this room is warmed by the sun.'

A peculiar shivering sensation fizzed through Elizabeth. The room was not warmed by the sun or anything else, even though it was warm outside.

James gave no visible sign of having felt the shiver. 'What a lovely room, Mrs Wybrow. I am perfectly all right, but I think Miss Chetwode is feeling somewhat chilly after her ordeal, and may benefit from somewhere warmer.' Elizabeth felt, rather than saw, his brief glance.

Mrs Wybrow wheeled to her. 'My dear Miss Chetwode,' she spoke as if she had genuinely forgotten Elizabeth was there. 'How unforgivable of me. What a dreadful time you must have endured. When I heard that you were not at the crossroads, I was utterly distraught.'

'One of the shafts on the coach cracked.'

Elizabeth never got around to explaining anything further. Her employer was too intent on impressing a lord.

Perhaps he was right and his presence would save her from a dressing down for being late?

'The small parlour is somewhat warmer. Dabbs will escort you there, Miss Chetwode.'

She was being banished without a blink, and that hurt. Not the discourtesy of it, but the thought of being wrenched from Jemmy.

'Perfect Mrs Wybrow,' Bauval ingeniously declared. 'May I have the exquisite pleasure of escorting you both through?'

His cunning floored Mrs Wybrow for a moment. Then she rallied.

'Of course.' Narrowed eyes flicked to Elizabeth. 'How delightful.'

Elizabeth remained silent as Mrs Wybrow studied her. 'You are extremely stylish for a companion Miss Chetwode,' she said archly.

The earl had left, and Elizabeth heard to her surprise, that on their way here, he discovered a 'connection' between them. Her late Mama had apparently been a companion to his dying great-aunt Sibyl over twenty years ago. Bauval announced firmly that he therefore had a duty to Miss Chetwode. A duty he intended to uphold.

'Lady Bee must be more of a philanthropist than she makes out,' Mrs Wybrow continued, 'kitting you out in the latest fashion.'

Despite the censure in her new employer's tone, Elizabeth experienced a *frisson* of guilt. Her wardrobe was due to the money in Lombard Street and, this time, not Lady Bucklow's benevolence. She could not tell Mrs Wybrow, that though.

The springs of the Queen Anne chair creaked as Mrs Wybrow moved. 'Pamela will be terribly envious.' She gave a martyred sigh. 'Mr. Wybrow dotes on dear Pamela. Gives her anything she wants, but sadly he has his limitations.' The lace cap fluttered as she shook her head. 'Naturally we try to ensure Pamela is always in the stare of fashion.' She paused to draw a quick breath. 'I presume your bonnet is starched silk?'

Elizabeth nodded, 'Yes, Mrs Wybrow.'

'Your dress, I see is the latest cambric craze.' There was a sigh in her tone. 'Pamela will have to have a new wardrobe. I suppose we must be grateful that our daughter's companion is elegant, and that she is *au fait* with an earl.'

Elizabeth had not wanted to start this job with any extra deception. All she wanted to do, was bide her time in a respectable manner until her twenty-first birthday. After that, as far as she was concerned, the money in Lombard Street was hers do with as she wished.

Acquainted with Lord Bauval through her dear Mama? Now she had to keep up that pretence as well. The thought of extra subterfuge niggled.

Although still imperiously condescending, Mrs Wybrow changed the subject. 'Lady Bee writes that you became extremely accomplished under her care.'

Elizabeth merely nodded. How could she say that she had many of those skills before Lady Bucklow rescued her? However, she could be branded a fraud out to fleece the gullible if she said so.

Not that it was entirely her fault, Lady Bucklow was serious about her obligations and felt it her duty to pluck unfortunate girls from the streets. Her aim was to rescue them from *the social evil*. If those rescued showed willing, she trained them to an employable standard, then sent them out to various establishments to work. The families taking them on felt they too had done their charitable duty.

However, Lady Bucklow had quite literally rescued her from the streets by hauling her up, bare-foot and filthy from stagnating mixen covering the roads, into her carriage.

It was the untied bootlaces that caused Elizabeth's main problem. At first, the bootlaces lashed about, flaying her legs and getting in the way. Then as she ran, the two inside laces, one from each boot, somehow tangled themselves tightly round each other. Within seconds she could not move her legs at all. She stumbled twice before quickly stopping to tug each boot off. Then holding them at arms-length, and rushing blindly around the corner of a filthy alley, she did not see a hand reach out until it was too late. The boots were snatched from her grasp so she had no alternative but to continue tearing bare-foot through the mucky maze.

Carts, dogs, adults and children blocked her path as she ran. Her stockings were torn and threadbare. Her loose hair caught at anything and everything. Tears blazed down her cheeks as her feet dashed on hard varying surfaces. Bare feet in the mixen, was the last straw.

Then, without warning, a carriage drew up beside her, and Elizabeth too out of breath to resist or object, was pulled into it and driven off. Her father, out of sight, but definitely within earshot never saw what happened to her.

Could he run? Oh yes! Never in her life did she imagine he had wings on his feet that almost matched hers. When she had raced from the house, with poor Mama dead on the shabby chaise-longue, and with the envelope Mama gave her, sewed inside her own bodice, she thought to shake him off, double back and take refuge with Min, their next-door neighbour.

Mrs Wybrow's words came back. Bright and accomplished?

Regret poured through Elizabeth. Would she ever put her talents to use in an ordinary classroom again? Mama had tutored the children of parents who could afford such luxuries. Her deep desire to help children whose parents were not quite so prosperous, to read and write, almost hurt.

On one occasion when Westernbury was visiting them, he had ranted and raved that helping in a school was not a real job and that she should be out earning a decent wage, but Mama held firm. She told him that Elizabeth was staying put. In a fit of vengeful fury, he immediately took Jemmy out of school and took him to the brewery to work. The boy's wage went straight into Papa's pocket. Although Jemmy loved working there it was such a waste because Jemmy was a good scholar. Two more years and he would have gained his certificate with ease as she had only months before.

Mrs Wybrow's lofty tone brought her back to the present. 'I believe Lady Bee taught you to sing and to play the pianoforte?'

Elizabeth drew a silent breath. Lady Bucklow did not teach her to sing or play. Mama taught her. One day, Lady Bucklow just happened to hear her sing and play. The next minute, Lady Bucklow was avidly teaching her everything. That lesson led to others, and because Elizabeth learned so quickly Lady Bucklow soon moved her on to other things. Soon, Lady Bee had her performing in front her friends. She saw Elizabeth as a nurtured prodigy.

Mrs Wybrow took the silence as meekness, and her tone softened slightly. 'You need not be ashamed of moderate talent Miss Chetwode. Our dear Pamela is quite the musician. She sings and plays to perfection.'

Elizabeth smiled politely, wondering where the young woman she was to be a companion to, was.

'Lady Bee mentioned your gift for languages. It seems you picked up Italian as if born to it. Perhaps you can persuade Pamela to study it a little more?'

'Of course, Mrs Wybrow.'

'Naturally we would not have deemed one of Lady Bee's girls suitable as a companion. However,' her voice dropped, 'our previous girl let us down dreadfully.' Her face shadowed as her hands writhed in agitation. She swallowed and flicked her eyes shut for a second. 'Such an excellent character from her former employers too.' She then flicked her eyes open to stare straight at Elizabeth. 'Mr. Wybrow said we could not possibly do worse by giving you a chance.'

Shocked by such odd remarks, all Elizabeth could murmur was a quiet, 'Thank-you.'

'There are some who might brand us fools to take you on.' Mrs Wybrow's smile did not reach her eyes. 'Dear Mr. Wybrow is so charitable. Blue blooded you know. Not titled,' she said mournfully, 'too far back.' Her chin dipped, 'The Merry Monarch no less.' She sighed, 'One gets used to second best.'

Elizabeth gulped. If Mrs Wybrow got a hint of any of her past, second best would be an understatement.

Dashing away the memories, Elizabeth forced herself to study the room instead. It was plain compared to the Bucklow's place. Comparing it with her childhood home however, it was a palace.

The walls were painted light green. Two gilt-edged mirrors, either side of a small dresser hanging on the far wall made the room appear larger than it actually was. The other walls were bare except for a single candle sconce in the middle of each. A lone brass clock ticked bravely on the wood mantle shelf above, the now lifeless black grate. The only other pieces of furniture in the room were two matching chairs, the Queen Ann wing chair Mrs Wybrow occupied, and a chintz sofa.

The sofa where the earl so recently lounged.

A *frisson* of fluttery butterflies sashayed along Elizabeth's spine. She could see his deliciously long muscular legs stretched out in front of him. She could still hear his smooth well-modulated voice in her head. She could still smell the lingering scent of his cologne. The velvety fluttering continued sashaying along her spine and into every nerve in her body, as she forgot all her good and noble intentions, and remembered how he nearly kissed her.

Throughout his visit, she had controlled her immense desire to study and analyse him. To avoid doing so she had concentrated on Mrs Wybrow instead.

Each time he moved so much as a muscle though, she knew, and at one point found herself silently following his every breath with one of her own. She had also had the absurd desire to mirror his movements.

Mrs Wybrow was obviously captivated by him. He charmed her with small talk and delighted her with promises of returning soon.

Those butterflies continued their fluttering.

Mrs Wybrow's insincerity cut into her blissful musings.

'That is why we were more than happy to take on an orphan,' she said sanctimoniously. 'Particularly, as it appears,' she took a deep breath, 'an orphan with a titled protector.'

Ignoring the pompous tone, Elizabeth managed a smile. She needed this job until her twenty-first birthday. Then she could enter minor Society.

Or not.

It was all very well for Mama to decree she use the money for her debut, but what was she going to do afterwards? When most of the money had gone on finery what was she live on thereafter? Currently her dowry was enough for what she wanted. A home with a little land, a simple carriage, some livestock, some hired help, and funds for a small schoolroom. Enough also for Jamie to buy into a good firm. With good management she could live a contented life.

Mrs Wybrow's voice cut into her thoughts again. 'With the *coached* refinement of a gently bred girl.'

A vexing thought suddenly crossed Elizabeth's mind. If the mother was this high handed, what was the daughter like? Would Pamela Wybrow look upon her with disdain too?

She took a steadying breath. 'Thank-you Mrs Wybrow.'

If Quality and polite society behaved like this, why did Mama want her to be a part of it? Why was it so important that she go into Society? Why not Jamie as well? Mama's wish for him to become articled to a lawyer and buy into a firm was sensible. He would earn a good living, and if he worked hard, a first-class reputation.

It made sense. Jamie had a fine brain, and a capacity for hard work. Getting him to leave the brewery had been the hardest part. He loved the brewery. He loved the sights and sounds, the smells, but most of all he adored the dray horses with whom he had such an affinity. It had taken a lot of persuasion to get him to join Longton's and even more to stay.

She inwardly sighed. She had to obey Mama's wishes if only for Jamie's sake. For how could she be cross with him, if she refused to carry out Mama's wishes?

The door suddenly burst open in a flurry of fuchsia velvet. A riot of russet curls glistening with gold highlights tumbled to the girl's face as she flipped the hood of her cape back.

'Mama, Dabbs said you wanted to see me. Oh.' The cape swirled as the girl skidded to a halt. 'Hello.' A bright smile spread across her pink face. 'Mama never mentioned us having visitors.' She swivelled her slim, child-like body back to her mother.

Mrs Wybrow turned to Elizabeth with a smile. 'Perhaps my high-spirited daughter could do with some of Lady Bee's training?'

Pamela frowned. 'Lady Bee?'

Mrs Wybrow threw a hand to Elizabeth. 'Miss Chetwode is one of Lady Bucklow's girls. Did we not mention it some weeks ago? Miss Chetwode,' she threw a hand to Pamela, 'My daughter, Miss Pamela Wybrow.'

Although it was such an informal introduction, Elizabeth stood up and held out her hand. 'Miss Wybrow I am delighted to meet you.'

'Pamela, Miss Chetwode is to be your new companion.'

Pamela's eyes widened. 'Mama she is perfect.' The romping curls swung as she turned. 'When you said I needed someone mature, I had visions of a dowdy old lady.' She pulled a face and turned back to Elizabeth. 'I am seventeen,' Pamela rushed on, 'how old are you, Miss Chetwode?'

Pamela was like a breath of fresh air in the otherwise cheerless house, and Elizabeth warmed to her immediately. 'Just over twenty, and a half Miss Wybrow.'

Mrs Wybrow turned to Elizabeth. 'Sensible girls of Pamela's age are in such short supply. Her devoted Papa and I discussed the matter at length, and although our last girl was a total disaster-'

'-Mama!'

Mrs Wybrow threw her daughter a warning glance. 'We decided to put the interests of dear Pamela first.' She paused, 'You are sensible I hope Miss Chetwode?'

Although that brief dizzying nearly-kiss raced through her mind Elizabeth nodded. Every time the memory came back, that delicious feeling automatically seeped through her. She inhaled hardily.

'Yes, Mrs Wybrow.'

'Good. You will live as part of the family and when the time comes and you have proved your worth, you may perhaps accompany our daughter when she makes her come-out.'

Pamela Wybrow's come out? She certainly did not intend staying that long. 'Surely that is some time away?'

Mrs Wybrow flapped her hands. 'Less than two years, however Pamela must be measured up for the latest styles. She cannot appear in a lower light than her companion. Go along girls get ready for dinner. Mr. Wybrow will be here soon.'

Mr. Wybrow frisked tiny metallic eyes over Elizabeth as she entered the room. He did not smile, just motioned her to sit on the chair on the other side of his desk.

His study was brighter than the other rooms. For although it was not even dusk, an oil lamp glowed on the desk beside him.

He had not been in long, and supper was ready but he insisted on seeing her beforehand.

Elizabeth resisted the urge to cover the small curve of bare flesh above her bodice with her hand. Her frock was not showing any décolletage, but perhaps she should have chosen the pink-sprigged muslin instead of the dove grey and tied her hair more tightly back? One or two loose blonde waves wafted as she lowered herself onto the edge of the seat and rested her hands demurely on her lap.

He remained motionless, only his eyes moved as a dominant stare scrutinised her.

'Miss Chetwode,' the richness of his voice surprised her. 'I hear from Mrs Wybrow that you arrived with Lord Bauval.'

Just the mention of that name made her heart race. She must be strong.

She scraped her thoughts together, 'He took pity on me.'

Thick greying brows rose. Bald flesh on and above them furrowed. Apart from that, the expression on his face never changed. 'Did he indeed?'

He expected more. 'The post coach was late,' she said. 'I was alone.'

'What luck,' the flare of the lamp flickered into the hollow under his cheekbone. Light against dark. 'Such a propitious arrival,' his rich voice held more than a hint of sarcasm.

'Yes Mr. Wybrow,' she said subduing all mutiny. 'Even more so when I,' her heart skipped with absurd, and unexpected delight, 'discovered my late Mama was once a companion to his late great-aunt.'

The skin on the bald his part of his head creased deeper. 'Late?' he echoed, 'how convenient.'

Something about him made her insides squirm.

His eyes never left her as he leaned forwards to rest crêpy hands on the desk. 'Our previous girl proved most unsatisfactory Miss Chetwode.' His tongue snaked out and slicked his lips.

Elizabeth managed to control a shiver; but inside, her nerve endings quivered with a strange revulsion.

His eyes roved her face. 'I hope you do not disgrace yourself in any way, my dear.' He dropped his gaze to her mouth and let it linger.

Elizabeth willed herself into composure by steering her eyes to the base of the oil lamp. 'I will not Mr. Wybrow,' she replied with self-possession.

He studied her face before answering. 'Good.' The deep, rich drawl might have been charming on anyone else. 'Our dear Pamela so easily led, is enamoured of you already.'

'Thank-you Mr. Wybrow; I shall not let you down.'

He scraped his chair away from the desk and held out his hand as he rose. 'Come along.'

The abrupt change in his manner surprised her. A murky smile hovered across thin lips. 'Let us go into supper.'

Elizabeth breathed in silently and stood up.

He was thin, small and very nimble because in less than a second his humid hand rested on her back just below her neck. Worse though, was the horrible caressing movement his fingers made on her skin.

'I think we understand one another perfectly.'

She pivoted to face him so quickly his hand dropped. 'I am sure we do Mr. Wybrow,' she replied crisply.

The dining room table was long and narrow like the room. The four places set were on one corner. The rest of the table was bare. Only a flickering brace of candles on a dresser and the weak fire in the grate relieved the surrounding austerity. Thick brown drapes pulled across a bay window blocked out the very last of the light. Each person appeared in spectral silhouette against the gloom.

The womens' meal consisted of a small slice of cold beef, two plain boiled potatoes, a few carrots and one thick slice of bread and butter. Mr. Wybrow however, ate three times as much, and while the women sipped water, he downed two glasses of red wine.

When Dabbs came to clear away and asked if there was anything else, they wanted, Pamela looked at Mrs Wybrow.

'Please may I have some fruit, Mama?'

Mr. Wybrow huffed in a breath.

Pamela's voice became almost a plea. 'I have been out walking this afternoon, Papa. You know how hungry the fresh air makes me feel.'

'There's an obvious answer to that,' he retorted, 'but if you must, you must.' He glanced at Dabbs. 'You may bring up one or two of the bruised apples.' He turned to Elizabeth. 'For you too, Miss Chetwode?'

His tiny metallic eyes focused on her through the gloom. Her stomach churned. She was still hungry, but she had eaten far less in the past and survived. 'No thank-you, I have had sufficient.'

Mrs Wybrow gave an audible sigh. 'Very wise Miss Chetwode. You do not want to be full of ingestion so close to retiring.'

Retiring? Elizabeth darted a look at the clock on the mantle shelf. It was six-thirty.

'Ah, Miss Chetwode, Mr. Wybrow did not fully advise you of our ways I see.' Mrs Wybrow beamed at her husband. 'I fully understand your reluctance, my dearest.' She came back to Elizabeth. 'Men find it so difficult to establish the rules,' she crooned in dulcet tones. 'Mr. Wybrow is so benevolent. Our previous girl,' she explained rather too brightly, 'retired early so we could spend our evenings with each other as a loving family should.' She wafted a hand in the air. 'Naturally, there are times when this is not so. Now and then you will oblige us by attending our occasional family gatherings, and making up a foursome at cards.'

Pamela, who was informed about Lord Bauval's visit, squealed with delight. 'Miss Chetwode, we can invite your earl.'

Jemmy? Elizabeth's heart bounced.

'Pamela,' Mrs Wybrow huffed. 'Lord Bauval is far too busy to dance attendance on a mere companion.'

The word 'dance' had an instant impact on Elizabeth's imagination. Now her body was gliding with decadent rhythm across a ballroom in an even more decadent waltz.

'I doubt we shall see him again,' Mr. Wybrow scoffed.

Pamela frowned. 'Mama said he promised to call. A gentleman does not break his word surely?'

Mrs Wybrow tutted. 'Really Pamela, you should know the difference between an earl, and a gentleman. An earl will merely try to keep his word. A gentleman however,' she inclined to Mr. Wybrow, 'of your Papa's eminence, for instance, is honour bound to do so.'

Pamela's face fell.

Elizabeth dared not speak. She knew instinctively that Jemmy intended to visit. To appear too confident though, might bring on Mr. Wybrow's sarcasm.

Mrs Wybrow's stark tone softened. 'It is possible he will come once, just for appearances sake.'

Elizabeth's mind flew to the vision of the earl lounging, with devastating grace on the Wybrow's sofa. It flew to way she slid against him in his curricle, then to how near his lips were to hers. Weightless, velvety butterflies sashayed through her. No, she must not think these thoughts. She must be sensible.

'And to honour dear Mr. Wybrow naturally,' Mrs Wybrow added.

Mr. Wybrow glanced at the mantle clock. 'I shall retire to my port.' He scraped his chair back as he rose. 'Do you know the way to your room Miss Chetwode?'

A horrible thought writhed through Elizabeth. Was he going to offer his escort? 'Yes,' she forced brightly. 'Up the rear stairwell, over the gallery to the back attic.'

Pamela shot from her chair. 'No!' she squealed. 'Papa you cannot!'

The sparse lighting meshed to a comet's tail as Elizabeth whisked her head from one to the other.

Pamela's face had crumpled. 'You promised.'

Mr. Wybrow's face stilled in stark outline against the candle-light as he looked at his wife. 'Mother,' he began gravely, 'Is this true? Is Miss Chetwode in the back attic?'

'Yes,' Mrs Wybrow whimpered. 'I thought that was your wish.'

The hollow in his cheeks deepened. Metallic eyes narrowed. His voice however remained calm. 'Please see Miss Chetwode is given the front gable chamber next to Pamela's.'

Less than a second later, Pamela had rushed over and kissed her father's cheek.

'Thank-you Papa.'

Mrs Wybrow gave him an adoring look, 'Walter, you are so kind.'

She then turned to Elizabeth.

'Did I not say our dear child is his first and last consideration Miss Chetwode? Do you see how he indulges her?' Her smile was mawkish. 'Such a charitable man,' she cooed. 'As I am sure you have realised by now.'

Ignoring the slow chill creeping through her, Elizabeth dared a quick look at each face and drew a silent breath.

The strange cloying happiness laced with fear made her want to turn and run.

She slowly exhaled. The mood in this house was more chillingly unstable than the life she, Jamie, and Mama experienced at the hands of her drunk and capricious father.

Chapter Three

James Bauval tried not to think of Elizabeth Chetwode, but the more he tried, the less successful he was. He should not have nearly kissed her or offered to champion her. His heart thumped wildly. How had it happened? Since when did he fall in love at first sight? It was too ridiculous. How could he be in love with someone he did not know? Ever since meeting the delicious Miss Elizabeth Chetwode, however, his head swirled with all sorts of absurd thoughts. He imagined her sitting in the softly lit pleasant room of Alstoe Hall, bringing laughter and cheer to their home. He imagined holding balls and soirées, meeting and greeting guests, with her at his side. Most of all, he imagined the sounds of joyful children around him. His insides twanged and his breath caught in his throat.

Sighing gently, his mother, Lady Levana, put her needlepoint down and looked across at him with tender concern.

He noticed immediately. 'Really Mama,' he smiled, 'I wish you would not glare at me like that.'

Lady Levana continued studying him.

Jemmy was every inch a Bauval. His long, fawn cashmere clad-legs were stretched out in front of the hearth. His dark undone jacket revealed a cream silk waistcoat over a white, flawlessly knotted cravat. His dark hair, neat despite how many times he ran his fingers through it.

Her tone was full of concern. 'Is there something wrong dearest?'

Jemmy shifted under his mother's scrutiny. How could she tell? He had tried so hard not to reveal himself. His hands came together and steepled at the fingertips.

Attempting to quell an intense yeaning, he rocked his head forward to meet her gaze.

A sudden smile twitched at her lips. 'Is that a church-steeple you are making?'

A *church*? Was she implying he was so in love with the bewitching Miss Chetwode that he was thinking of marriage? He drew a steadying breath. How nonsensical could he get? His mother had no knowledge of the enthralling Miss Chetwode.

His mother, as perceptive as she was, had no idea that he was still reliving that first dazzling moment he saw Miss Chetwode. He had tried and failed to curb the deliciously pleasurable effect she had on him. He had recalled their conversations, her expressions, her annoyance when he behaved badly so many times, his head buzzed at the memories.

There was the way she looked at him, the way her golden lashes flickered over chrysolite irises, her luscious mouth, the devastating smile, and the innocent, response when he nearly kissed her. He was enslaved, yet he felt free. He was in chains, but they were weightless. He was caught, yet not snared. He was invigorated, yet felt a deep sense of calm. Above all else, however, was an infinite need to protect, and cherish her.

Forever.

He looked down at his fingers. Yes. Miss Chetwode was the one he wanted.

'Perhaps you are subconsciously thinking of marriage?' Lady Levana smiled.

His insides juddered. How could she possibly know that?

'Marriage Mama?' he just about managed to rasp. 'Do you think I could court a young lady without your knowledge? Even if I tried, the gossip chariot would be there before me.'

He hated lying to her, and his denial filled him with misery. Although, his mother had spoken lightly, she had, unknowingly excavated the depths of his soul.

Moreover, he saw that his swift tongue had hurt her.

'Mama, forgive me.'

He rose and moved with gentle grace to her chair. He bent close to the faded light brown curls and dropped a kiss on her forehead.

'That was ill-done of me.' He straightened up then looked down at her. 'Please forgive me.'

Lady Levana did not look up but, turned to stare into the fading fire watching the swift flames chase smoke up the chimney.

Flames of love chasing hazy smoke?

She knew instinctively that, despite his denial, she had touched something deep and raw within her son. She swallowed the lump in her throat. Had he fallen in love against all the odds? Her eyes misted. Was her perception telling her something else too? She must not be hasty. Jemmy had pride. He would rather face a lynch mob than admit to unrequited love.

He had vowed *never* to love again. Yet Levana knew that, that love was a brotherly love only. With true love, there had to be a thrilling spark that ignited on thought and on sight.

Although it was possible that love could grow from friendship to passion, in *their* case it had not. Not once had she witnessed that spark between her son and the beautiful girl she so desperately wanted as a daughter-in-law.

Sweet Mary-Beth, her late husband's cousin Elizabeth-Ann's, daughter, and therefore Jemmy's second cousin.

'Mama?' he laid a gentle hand on her shoulder.

She turned to look up into his face. 'Of course, I forgive you, dearest.'

She wanted to see the humour in his eyes. She wanted to see the wavy 'm' of his upper lip curve up. She wanted him to be happy.

A mischievous little elf nipped at her, however, and she just could not resist.

'Except when you go out into the fields and work like one of the labourers.'

The sudden intense memory of the delicious Miss Chetwode jumping angrily on his back and berating him, demolished James' self-control.

He withdrew his hand trying, and failing to mask his emotions grated, 'It is my choice how I conduct myself whether in the fields or out.' He knew he was being irrational. 'Goodnight Mama.'

He bowed stiffly, spun on his heels, and stalked from the room.

****

Pamela's and Elizabeth's bedchamber doors opened at same time.

'Did you sleep well Miss Chetwode?'

Stepping onto the landing Elizabeth nodded. 'Yes thank-you Miss Wybrow. Did you?'

They fell into step beside each other.

It was not a lie exactly, for Elizabeth had slept well until a bad dream woke her. She could not remember what it was about, but the unfamiliar shapes around her made it worse.

Her room, although not large, was neat. There was a fairly comfortable leather covered banquette under the leaded window-door, and the columned veranda that encompassed the house immediately outside, gave her an attractive of view of green meadows beyond.

Pamela's blue-grey eyes shone. 'Yes, I did. It is wonderful knowing you are next door. We shall be able to creep into one another's bedroom to talk.' Her glossy gold-brown lashes fluttered. 'Just like real friends Miss Chetwode.'

Sadness tugged at Elizabeth's insides. Real friends? Did Pamela have no friends apart from a paid companion? At the same time, Elizabeth knew how it felt to be lonely. Before Mama passed, she had had good friends, but after being taken up by Lady Bucklow never saw them again.

Pamela linked her arm through Elizabeth's.

'I have never had a real friend before.'

Elizabeth had to gulp back her heartfelt compassion, and just said, 'Are there no suitable girls your age Miss Wybrow?'

'Not according to my parents.' Pamela steered them both to the top of the grey-carpeted stairwell. 'Mama does not want me mixing with common girls. Although I am not sure what she means by common. I think the rector's three girls are lovely. Samara is my favourite, but Hagar and Phinia are pleasant too. Mama however, will not hear of me being friends with them. She says they are beneath me.'

She squeezed herself on the stair next to Elizabeth. 'Mama considers the Snapes to be suitable, but the daughter, Jane Snape hates me. Once, when I was with there with Jane and her three friends in Jane's Garden, they all ran off saying horrible things about me. I wandered round on my own until tea time. When Mrs Snape asked whether we had all had a lovely afternoon, they pretended I was with them all the time. I did not want to tell tales, or say what really happened, so I kept quiet.'

Elizabeth's heart went out to Pamela. Is that why she was so bright and cheerful? Forcing a happiness, she did not feel, and adjusting her manner so no one knew how unhappy she was?

'Mrs Smith-Jacobsen at Hooby Lodge,' Pamela continued in lowered tones as they approached the top of the second leg of stairs, 'thinks I am not good enough for her daughter Rhoda.' She grinned. 'Mind you, I think I might be able to stand the daggered looks if Henry Smith-Jacobsen looked my way sometimes.' Her eyelids drooped. 'He is the most handsome man ever.' She sighed. 'We only go three times a year though. The first time is to join the other members of the Hooby Lodge mid-summer show committee, then to the show itself. The following Monday we all help clear up.'

Surprised by Pamela's apparent infatuation with Henry Smith-Jacobsen, all Elizabeth could manage was, 'Oh.'

Voicing an opinion might cause embarrassment or hostility. A young girl's heart shattered so easily.

Not hers though. No. Elizabeth had promised herself a long time ago that she was never going to be at the mercy of any man. She was never going to fall in love and end up like Mama. She was never going to be abused until death's blessed release. She had learned from Mama's mistakes. Poor innocents like her mother made such dire errors, that only the observing foolish made the same ones too. And she, Elizabeth Chetwode, once known as Mary-Beth Westernbury, was no fool.

Her thoughts turned immediately to Jemmy. Suddenly, shiny velvet butterflies, began skimming along her spine. The earl had had such a startling effect on her, but she must be strong and resist. Her self-preservation demanded it.

They reached the bottom stair.

Without warning Pamela's arm tightened under hers. 'Miss Chetwode,' Pamela whispered excitedly, 'now you are here and are a friend to Lord Bauval, I am sure we shall receive invitations to all sorts of soirées.' The velvet butterflies continued skimming traitorously along Elizabeth's spine, then right to every nerve ending.

'Although,' Pamela tacked on, 'Papa is sure his lordship will not keep his word.'

The butterflies skidded to a halt. 'Mrs Wybrow, doubted it most, surely?'

Pamela shook her head. 'No. Papa said Mama was a fool for believing the earl.'

The butterflies began fluttering again. She felt alive, vibrant, and euphoric.

'Papa seems most put out by the whole thing.'

Before Elizabeth had time to assimilate her opposing feelings, Pamela sharply inhaled and whipped her hand from Elizabeth's arm. She clapped a hand across her mouth.

'I have said too much.'

'There you are Pamela,' Mrs Wybrow bustling from the breakfast parlour prevented Elizabeth from raising her brow in query. 'Good morning, Miss Chetwode.' Luckily, she did not notice Pamela's dismayed expression.

Her eyes darted instead to Elizabeth's *Grenadine* day-dress. 'You look rather fine this morning.' She glanced at the suddenly composed Pamela. 'I think we may pop into Thistleton dearest. I believe Madame Abbe will accommodate us.' She eyed Elizabeth's dress again. 'Did you choose that fabric Miss Chetwode, or was it recommended as the latest thing?'

There was something in Mrs Wybrow's voice that irked Elizabeth.

'Grenadine is recommended as suitable for town or country wear, and is extremely comfortable. Feel it.' She thrust her skirts forward hoping her employer would not see the angry flush on her cheeks.

Mrs Wybrow grasped the material. 'Yes, I think one or two fashioned in this will be perfect for you Pamela.'

Fresh from the shores of allied Spain, dark-pink Grenadine was the latest thing.   Elizabeth curbed her annoyance.

It started to rain just as they set out for Thistleton in the double-hooded 'sociable' that Mrs Wybrow referred to somewhat grandly as a Barouche.

Elizabeth was wearing her light-tan cashmere spencer and matching silk bonnet. She had changed into her oatmeal brocade dress as it was more suitable for town wear. Pamela looked stunning in a periwinkle blue spencer over a pale-grey silk frock. Her silk bonnet trimmed with pale-grey ribbons, and her black patent leather boots completed her outfit.

The silk fruit on Mrs Wybrow's claret hat wobbled as she inclined her head to Elizabeth. 'You look charming Miss Chetwode,' she declared with veiled censure. 'However, I am not sure those light colours are quite suitable for these parts. The roads here are so dusty.'

'But Mama,' Pamela said, 'do you not recall saying I should have something in light-tan?'

Mrs Wybrow's eyes narrowed. 'That was earlier in the year Pamela, well, before summer.'

'It was only last evening,' Pamela countered innocently as she skipped from the shelter of the columnar veranda onto the path.

Close-up, the veranda looked like an elaborate afterthought, maybe a recent addition for an otherwise plain grey-stone house. It did not look quite right. One of the gabled windows, in the room above, and slightly to one side rather than directly above hers, seemed to extend right over it. There was a column directly below that which made her think of escape routes. Maybe that was due to the window in the gable being much larger than she imagined a gable window to be? She gave herself a mental shake. She was being ridiculous.

Pamela, either unaware of, or choosing to ignore, her mother's disapproval blithely chattered throughout the short ride to town.

James tipped his hat to those he knew but did not stop to pass the time of day. He had no time to waste. He wanted to return home before his mother started her day-to-day routine.

His abrupt attitude and swift exit the previous evening was out of character for him. He would make it up to her somehow. A visit to London perhaps, where she could do some shopping and visit her old friends?

As the rain hit his cape, the earl thanked providence and nature that the last of the crop was harvested the previous day.

And what a day that turned out to be!

The afternoon that changed his life. He met the woman of his dreams. The other half of his inner self. His destiny.

All he could think of, was Miss Elizabeth Chetwode.

Her intoxicating desirability thrilled him. Her bewitching, yet contrary character exhilarated and excited him. His legs almost turned to dough each time he recalled her expression and the tone of voice when she scolded him. Moreover, she had a revealed purity of heart he had not expected. It was the way she peeked at him under glossy lashes with those beautiful chrysolite eyes flickering shyly when she realised her initial mistake

Now *that* was immensely intriguing. Just who did she imagined he was? Who was the 'someone' she mysteriously referred to? What promises had he made and failed to keep?

In the dark of the previous night, that part of their conversation had gone over in his head so many times, that it tormented him. The thought of the 'someone' being a beau, was torture. As he thought it through, however, he recalled her total innocence when he nearly kissed her.

She had never been kissed.

If he was wrong, it would not matter in the least as long as she loved him.

His heart thumped and his knees nearly buckled. What if she loved another? His heart gave a thump. That did not bear thinking about!

He tipped his hat again as he strode by the chocolate house and smiled at the three young ladies he knew quite well, entering it.

They were the rector's delightful daughters. He paused as Samara Newsome; his favourite stopped and beamed up at him.

Light brown lashes flitted onto her rain polished cheeks and up again.

'Good morning, Lord Bauval,' she said sweetly. 'A little different from yesterday I think.'

Not really wanting to chat, but not wanting to give offence to such agreeable girls, he inclined his head in salute and smiled. 'Indeed Miss Newsome. Although we must be grateful the harvesting is now finished.'

'Yes,' she replied before giving her younger sisters a surreptitious nudge.

The two blushing girls blinked shyly up at him.

'Good day Lord Bauval,' they chorused.

His heart lifted a little. The Newsome girls were a breath of fresh air. Not just in looks, but in attitude too. Most young women were either grumbling about the rain, and rushing to get out of it, or already safely under cover somewhere. These three however had obviously walked across the square without a murmur, despite the sudden downpour. Their glowing cheeks and bright smiles said more about them than they knew. He beamed down at them. 'Good-day Miss Hagar. Good-day Miss Phinia.'

He tipped his hat once more, and strode on.

He was still grinning as he crossed the square dodging street vendors, carts, carriages, stray animals, and unruly children.

Suddenly a figure materialised before him.

'Good-morning Lord Bauval.'

The woman with the expansive body and equally expansive voice stopped directly in front of him.

He halted to peer down into the face of a woman whose claret over-fruited hat wobbled precariously on a scraped back hairline. Grey eyes darted up at him as she wobbled a curtsey. The girl beside her curtsied with contrasting grace.

'Lord Bauval,' the woman gushed without preamble. 'May I present my daughter Pamela?'

Bauval's blue-black brows snapped together. Did these two complete strangers know him? Good manners prevented him from side-stepping neatly away, and just as he tipped the brim of his hat, he saw *her*.

His heart flipped before pummelling madly against his ribcage. His lungs let out air, but refused to let any back in. The blood began to pulse through him as his temperature started to rise. She was here. His siren.

His petite Boadicea, the enchanting Miss Chetwode dressed in the colours of fresh air and coffee-cream was hurrying towards them. His heart directly lurched back into place; air swept back into his lungs as he quickly remembered who the woman blocking his path was.

Making a valiant attempt to muster his absconding wits, he bowed.

'Miss Wybrow,' he marshalled smoothly, trying to ignore the fact that his whole being now thrummed with exhilaration as Elizabeth Chetwode drew closer.

Taking Pamela's hand, he raised it to his lips. 'Delighted to make your acquaintance, my dear.'

He saw another flash of cream out of the corner of his eye as she advanced. His heart quickened again.

Hell fire! What was happening to him? He snapped his heels together in a futile endeavour to put himself to rights.

'Mrs Wybrow,' he saluted witlessly. 'You are well I hope?'

Elizabeth hurried after her employer with a sense of joy. It would not be nearly as difficult to get a letter off to Jamie as she originally supposed. All she needed to do was give her letters to the postmaster herself. That was no hardship at all. Lady Bucklow expected a weekly update, and on their way here Mrs Wybrow had agreed that Elizabeth ought to take each letter personally to the receiving office rather than handing it to the post coach. That meant she could also collect Jamie's replies without anyone knowing.

The earl, delighting in, but still endeavouring to control his irrational thoughts, inclined his head the moment she was close enough to hear him.

'Miss Chetwode,' he breathed, the intensity of his yearning making him weak all over, and leaving him devoid of coherence.

She looked stunning. Her face glistened with fresh rain. Moist caramel lashes flicked up at him.

His tongue twitched with a desire to graze it along their crystal tips.

Elizabeth came to a rapid standstill. 'Oh.'

She was so engaged in thought she did not notice the earl until he spoke. Seeing him there suddenly caused her foolish heart to leap with absurd joy. She was being ridiculous. She must not let him affect her. He was not in her life's plan whatsoever. Stepping beside Pamela she looked up, and instantly wished she had not. Intense onyx irises roving over her face sent the now familiar velvet butterflies pirouetting along her spine.

She was such a fool.

She instinctively dashed the raindrops from her cheeks with a gloved hand. James' tumultuous yearning made him weak and strong all over again. Her large chrysolite irises widened under the glistening crystal raindrops. He swallowed as strands of her golden hair that had escaped from under the cream bonnet strippled her damp pink cheeks.

She blinked up at him, 'I,' delicious full lips parted, 'did not see you, my lord.'

His enraptured fascination instantly diffused into wounded humour.

Elizabeth watched his black irises transform as tiny flecks of silver glinted out, and his whole face slanted to a grin.

'I am big enough surely?' he growled.

She blinked, wondering if she actually heard him correctly. Was he was teasing her? His grin said he was. Right in front of her employer too.

'Forgive me,' she murmured in dulcet tones to conceal her pique at being put to such a disadvantage. 'I shall be more careful in the future.'

Now she was angry with him. He had not meant to annoy her, but all the same, he watched in dazed fascination as her cheeks surged a deeper pink. His knees felt like dough again, yet his heart raced with excitement. His petite Boadicea controlling the urge to vent her battle cry on him fuelled his longing more than she could ever know. Certainly, more than he could have ever envisaged any woman doing so before yesterday. At the same, time her expression filled him with mischief. He wanted to haul her into his arms and kiss her properly.

For his own sanity he changed tact, and purposefully turned to Mrs Wybrow.

'I see the weather has not put you off showing Miss Chetwode around. Rain is quite a deterrent to some,' he babbled. 'The delightful Newsome girls braved the square and are enjoying the fare of the Chocolate House.' To conceal his acute yearning, he avoided looking at Miss Chetwode, yet he wanted to linger. 'If I was not at business I would be there now,' he fibbed. 'Such a pleasing trio of young ladies.'

He knew he was behaving like a garrulous nincompoop, but his need to remain near Elizabeth Chetwode overrode all else. 'I expect Samara will be making her debut next year will she not?' He managed a glance at Pamela. 'Two beautiful young ladies making their mark together, diamonds of the first water, and dashing every Mama's hopes that *their* daughter will be the rage of the Season.'

Stop, you garrulous fool!

'How fortunate for me having the supreme advantage of knowing both beforehand.'

The fruited hat wobbled. 'My daughter is not quite old enough for the coming Season, my lord.'

Bauval's eyes swept fleetingly to Elizabeth then back to Pamela. 'Miss Wybrow do please forgive me.'

'There is nothing to forgive.' Mrs Wybrow trilled. 'It is Pamela's supreme poise causes everyone to think of her in that light.' She turned directly to Elizabeth, 'Have you made the necessary arrangements to send your letters to your benefactor, Lady Bucklow?'

'Yes, Mrs Wybrow.' Elizabeth knew Mrs Wybrow mentioned Lady Bucklow only to impress the earl.

A welt of rain suddenly hit them.

At this point, the earl mustered up what little remained of his wits and bowed. 'It has been a pleasure, ladies.'

Elizabeth's spirits sank. In spite of her momentary pique, she wanted to see the glint of mischief in his face once more. She wanted him to acknowledge her with more than one sentence. Most of all, she foolishly wanted to believe that he truly intended to be her mentor.

He must have read her thoughts.

'I do hope my charge is all you hoped for Mrs Wybrow.'

The moment he turned to look at her, Elizabeth's insides frothed with butterflies. She felt alive, vibrant, and euphoric.

'Miss Chetwode.'

It was a farewell because with that, he tipped his hat and bowed.

'Good day to you all.'

As soon as he was out of earshot, Pamela clutched at Elizabeth. 'Miss Chetwode, you have brought us such luck.'

'Really Pamela,' Mrs Wybrow sniffed, 'luck has nothing to do with it. Lord Bauval recognises Quality. Miss Chetwode has merely brought that to his notice.' She suddenly smiled. 'I believe we have earned a dish of chocolate. Come along. If we hurry, we shall be able to pay our respects to those darling Newsome girls.'

The earl stepped out from the clerk's office with relief. His man of business now knew his exact requirements. All he had to do was throw out his own personal bait. After leaving Wybrow House the previous day, he had called on Felton; Felton always knew the latest rumours.

As a rule, James never listened to gossip, but he had to know more about Wybrow.

And what he discovered chilled his soul.

The last girl employed as Pamela's companion had left in disgrace. She too was an orphan. Felton had no idea what eventually happened to the girl. The most, shady part was the rumour that Walter Wybrow had something to do with it. Mrs Wybrow, however bandied it about that the companion had a lover, yet nobody saw the girl with anyone but the Wybrows.

Instinct caused James to take immediate action the moment he heard Miss Chetwode was going to Wybrow House.

Of course, nothing would change Wybrow's basic character, but a keen eye would prevent him from taking any unsavoury advantage of Miss Chetwode. Mama was always complaining that he did too much anyway, so a treasurer-clerk, cum-manager would please her.

Wybrow was sure to take the bait. A promise to double his current wages, a rent-free refurbished home on the estate, a carriage and horses from the Bauval stables, free fuel from his share of the northern mines and produce from the farms.

Just to protect Miss Chetwode.

****

Although the sky had cleared and the air was still damp, Lady Levana greeted Betty warmly. 'I am so glad you braved the weather, dearest.' Observing the pinched expression on Elizabeth-Ann's face, she carefully concealed her alarm. 'Betty, you look somewhat pale, come and sit near the fire.' She guided her oldest and dearest friend towards the hearth.

Lady Interton smiled weakly. 'I am alright. Truly I am.' Lady Interton eased herself down on the edge of a wing chair and shivered.

Lady Levana drew another wing chair beside Betty's. 'You do not look alright. Do you want to talk about it?'

Two ashen lips clamped together. Pale blue irises rimmed with smoky grey, rolled slightly. Sparse once golden lashes fluttered. She shook her head.

'No,' she whispered, 'it is only my foolish imagination.' Her slender arm, encased in fine embossed black silk, slid from the cape and waved ineffectually at the hood of her cloak.

'Here,' Lady Levana bent forward. 'Let me.'

With a gentle nudge the hood fell from the white, but still elegantly wavy hair. The only covering now was an exquisite black lace cap perched on a crown of coiled waves.

'No wonder you are chilled, you are not wearing your bonnet.'

Lady Interton's mouth pursed. 'You know I cannot abide the restriction of a bonnet *and* hood.'

Lady Levana smiled briefly. 'I know.' She paused to assess the situation. 'We shall eat luncheon in here my love, as it is so cosy.'

Lady Interton pulled a thin face. 'It cannot be lunch time already?'

'It is dearest. I do hope you have not been neglecting yourself.' *Again.*

'I have not. I eat as and when I please.'

'You are still too frail.'

Lady Interton rallied. 'I cannot help not being hungry, Levy.'

Lady Levana put a soothing hand on Betty's black-clad arm. 'I know dearest, but you must try. I could not bear to,' she swallowed, 'for you to be ill.'

Betty sighed. 'I am over all that Levy.' She shuddered.

Levana's hand tightened. 'What is it dearest?'

Betty shook her head. 'No,' she said on a whisper, 'I cannot say.' She eased her arm from Levana's and folded her slim white hands into a knot. 'If I told you, you would think me mad. No, I have to work through this myself, besides I do not believe in ghosts any more than you do.' She took a deep breath. 'I have to face my demons alone, or I shall never overcome them.'

Lady Levana stilled. This was far more serious than she initially thought. Betty was at breaking point. Never during the last four and a half years had she talked of ghosts and of being mad. There was something dreadfully wrong.

What would it take to rid Betty of the torment of her past and to eradicate the consuming pain and relentless guilt of something that happened long ago?

Betty had worn the hair coat of repentance next to her skin for far too long. It was time to remove it; time to forgive herself.

'Betty,' Lady Levana declared brightly, 'I feel we have been immersed in the country for an age. We would both benefit from a change. I need a new wardrobe and you have the knack of knowing exactly what suits me. Come with me to London?'

'No!' Betty shot out. 'I have to stay here. You know that.'

'I do, my love,' Levy soothed, 'but it will not be for long.'

Betty shook her head. 'I have to know the instant I am truly forgiven.'

Lady Levana sighed. 'Even if the grave was cleared and planted, and you came across it and discovered it full of flowers, would you really believe that Fate, the Gods, Time-' or Mary-Jane? her mind silently added, 'have really forgiven you?'

Grey-rimmed blue irises misted. 'Yes,' was the soft conviction. 'When my Mary-Beth's grave is nurtured and in full bloom, then, and only then, shall I know dear Mary-Jane has completely forgiven my dreadful betrayal.'

Levana pursed her lips. This had gone on far too long. There was only one way to solve it. To do that, meant going against Betty's express wishes.

Chapter Four

Again, Elizabeth attempted to dismiss her shock and confusion, and ordered her stomach to stop churning. It was mere coincidence, nothing more, that a woman dressed all in black, peering from a carriage window, looked just like Mama, only older. Just a coincidence! Yet, as the elegant carriage rumbled by, their eyes instantly locked.

For a second: for an eternity!

And again, the hair on Elizabeth's spine rose, her nerves-endings jangled, and her stomach still churned.

Pamela's voice broke into her disordered thoughts.

'This one, Miss Chetwode,' Pamela whisked the gown from the tissue on her bed, 'will always be my favourite, even when the others arrive.'

They were in Pamela's bedchamber inspecting Pamela's new clothes that Madame Abbe said were just the thing for a young girl with Pamela's colouring.

Pushing away from Pamela's bedpost Elizabeth, stared abstractedly at the gown. It was a beautiful pastel green dotted with tiny yellow rose buds.

She gave herself a mental shake. 'Yes, it is lovely, as the others will be.'

'Miss Chetwode,' Pamela frowned, dipping her head to one side so the chestnut-gold streaks in her dark hair caught the light, 'do you mind that I will have so many new things and you do not?'

Elizabeth composed herself. 'Not at all. I have more than enough, more than I really need. More than a normal chaperone.'

Interest rippled across Pamela's face. 'Yes, Mama is very curious. Did Lady Bucklow allow you to buy anything you wanted? Mama thinks she did and that you took advantage, but I do not believe it. I believe Lady Bucklow wanted the best for you.'

Stunned, Elizabeth leaned back against the bedpost and gawped at Pamela.

Took advantage?

What did they think she was? An adventuress out to fleece the gullible? Completely forgetting about the woman in black, Elizabeth felt the colour flood into her face.

Had she hoodwinked a generous woman of means into taking her in? The colour instantly drained at her unintentional deception.

Pamela hugged the dress to her.

'Oh no.' Pamela's wounded tone made Elizabeth feel worse. 'Please, tell me you did not take advantage of Lady Bee?'

Elizabeth slowly shook her head. Whatever she said would not be the full truth. Honesty was as separate from dishonesty as black from white.

'No,' the half-truth came out as a whisper, 'I promise that I did not.'

'Thank goodness.' Pamela threw the gown onto the bed and flung over to Elizabeth. 'Oh, dearest Miss Chetwode, I knew it was not true.'

Elizabeth found herself locked in a tight, slender armed embrace.

'You are such a wonderful person. I cannot believe how lucky I am to get you.' Pamela pulled back slightly. 'You could have gone anywhere, been a companion to a duchess, a princess, any titled lady, yet Lady Bee let *us* have you.'

Elizabeth returned the hug before gently easing Pamela away from her.

She did not deserve such praise, and felt something wrench inside her at the thought of disappointing the sweet and lonely Pamela.

'Miss Chetwode, I know it is proper for us to use surnames, but we should not have to be so formal when there is just the two of us. May I call you Eliza, as a code of friendship between us?'

Elizabeth shook her head. 'Your mama would not approve.'

'Mama never needs to know. You can call me,' her eyes danced, 'Ella?'

Despite her misgivings, Elizabeth chucked.

Pamela chuckled, 'Eliza and Ella?'

Elizabeth's stomach jolted as she flicked her eyes to the window and muttered a swift apology to the sky.

'No,' she breathed wondering if she was jumping backwards into the bleakness of her past, or forwards into a perdition. 'If you really want us to be less formal,' she faltered, remembering, that it was dear Mama's wish for her to be known as Elizabeth Chetwode rather than Mary-Beth Westernbury. 'I think Mary-Beth would be rather nice.' She suppressed a peculiar shudder. 'Only when we are alone though. Do you promise?'

'Mary-Beth? How perfect. Yes, I promise. Only when we are alone,' Pamela whispered, 'and you can call me Ella.'

Pamela's simple pleasure brought a lump to Elizabeth's throat, but for Miss Wybrow's sake, she forced a smile. 'But, in private only, your parents would not approve, if they knew.' She hesitated. 'Also, you must promise not to tell anyone our private names.'

Tissue paper rustled as Pamela drew out a pair of long, white satin gloves. She looked up quickly, her face bright with joy. 'Of course, I promise Mary-Beth. It is our special secret.'

Sadness slipped through Elizabeth. She too had known loneliness, and although Pamela had a mother determined to do the right thing by her and a father who supposedly doted on her, she lived an isolated existence.

Rather like Elizabeth's own life after Mama died.

Yes, Lady Bucklow had given her a somewhat gilded life style. She was in demand as a pianist and singer by Lady

Bucklow's family and friends. She loved teaching children all sorts of things when they came to Bucklow Place, or if she accompanied Lady Bucklow somewhere where there were little ones. She tutored the older siblings too. She took dogs for walks, which was how she communicated with Jamie, wheeled matrons about in rickety bath chairs, and ran errands for just about anyone and everyone. She was friendly with girls of her own age, both above and below stairs, yet was neither. Her own sense of aloneness was different from Pamela's though. An undercurrent of fear governed Pamela's. Her own was governed by deceit.

Her heart skipped a beat. A deceit Jemmy would eventually find out about.

Pamela's eagerness to have a true friend was touching and pitiful. Elizabeth's heart sank, because she too would soon be abandoning the lonely Pamela.

After a light lunch, Mrs Wybrow said that shopping exhausted her and she needed a nap. The girls could decide whether they wanted to stay in and read quietly, or go for a walk into the village.

Elizabeth would have welcomed the chance to read, but Pamela wanted the village, and as the skies had cleared, she could hardly refuse.

It was not a large village, and not as busy as Thistleton. A few tiny shops arced the lane of the bow-end of an otherwise long green. Alongside them, was a stone-walled inn with a well-thatched roof. Next was a clinking forge. Then there were several sets of tiny terraced stone houses snuggling together, and on the far side, along the straight edge of the green, were sturdy individual houses with enough turning room at the front for horses and carriages. Apart from a muddy road leading out of the other side of the tiny houses, the whole village was surrounded by meadowland.

Elizabeth chuckled with delight. 'How lovely,' she breathed as they walked in from the opposite side of the green.

Pamela was surprised. 'You like it?'

Elizabeth smiled. 'You do not?'

'It is so provincial.' Pamela sighed as they strolled toward the shops. 'I can't wait until my debut so I can go to London, meet new people and attend wonderful balls.' She frowned. 'Why do I have to be eighteen and a half before I am allowed to do anything?'

'London is not all good,' Elizabeth began, 'there are parts-'

'Look,' Pamela froze. 'There is Henry Smith-Jacobsen.' She waved in the general direction of the shops. 'Mr. Smith-Jacobsen!'

There were quite a few people about.

Two bowed older woman carrying baskets hobbled across the green. Men in white smocks sitting on a tree-bark bench outside the inn chatting and smoking pipes, and a man holding a bay Clydesdale, waiting for the blacksmith. The only other person was a rather ordinary looking gentleman dressed in a brown frock-coat and black breeches, who having been diverted by Pamela's call, changed direction and strode towards them.

As soon as he reached them, he touched his somewhat worn *chapeaux claque* hat and bowed. 'How are you, Miss Wybrow?' He took her gloved hand and placed it briefly to his lips.

His drab country clothes did not do his slender build, fine elegant features and fair hair justice, Elizabeth thought. He would look much better dressed in the height of fashion. Goodness. Since when had she started judging people?

She of all people, had no right to judge anyone.

The instant he turned to her however, his flawless cheeks marbled pink. His fair brows arched as his face registered shock. Intense blue eyes scoured her face. 'And you Miss?'

Alarm fizzed through Elizabeth. Had he read her uncharitable thoughts? Worse, did her recognise her from somewhere?

'I am so sorry,' Pamela flushed. 'Mr. Smith-Jacobsen this is Miss Elizabeth Chetwode,' she said rapidly. 'Mary-Beth,' the name she promised only to use in private slipped out. 'This is Mr. Henry Smith-Jacobsen.'

Elizabeth's stomach churned as Henry Smith-Jacobsen impaled her with his astonished gaze for a split second more. Then a muscle in his cheek twitched breaking whatever spell it was, and his demeanour instantly changed.

'Miss Elizabeth, Mary-Beth Chetwode,' he enunciated while reaching for her hand and drawing it slowly to his lips.

The kiss was light and brief, but Elizabeth felt his lips quiver as his hand went into a brief spasm, and although like his gaze, the twitch only lasted a split second, she felt the pressure of his fingers on hers.

'I am pleased to meet you,' she mustered, withdrawing her arm.

He drew a shuddering breath. 'You are new to these parts Miss Chetwode?'

'Yes, she is,' Pamela cut in. 'She is my companion, and she is perfect.'

Elizabeth, still floundering from the impact of his recognition, if that's what it was, felt Pamela's arm link hers and squeeze. The simple gesture was reassuring.

His brow momentarily creased as he looked from Pamela to her, then back to Pamela again. 'We have not seen you at Hooby Lodge recently. Mr. and Mrs Wybrow are well I trust?'

Pamela's turquoise bonnet glistened as she angled her head. 'Yes, thank you.'

His eyes flicked to Elizabeth then back to Pamela. 'Rhoda has been wondering how you are. I know she will want me to pass on her regards.' He paused, 'May she call on you?'

Pamela's arm tightened in Elizabeth's. Her blue-grey eyes danced. 'Of course.'

His face reflected delight. 'Now,' he stepped back and bowed, 'I must not keep you any longer. Please give my regards to your parents, Miss Wybrow.' He flicked a glance at Elizabeth, 'Miss Chetwode.'

They said good-bye and murmured their thanks as he stepped aside.

Still arm-linked, Pamela practically bolted them across the green.

'He is divine is he not?' she breathed as they reached the far end. 'And to think Rhoda has asked after me.

'Mama will be so pleased if she calls. I hope they invite us to Hooby Lodge.' She pulled Elizabeth along the damp narrow pavement. 'They hold regular soirées,' her eyes were still dancing. 'Perhaps we will be invited to their next one.' She squeaked with excitement. 'I can wear one of my new gowns. Mary-Beth, you have brought us such luck. Papa cannot help but be pleased now. Come,' she motioned to one of the shops, 'I have a farthing in my reticule.' She lowered her eyes sheepishly. 'It is change from an errand I ran last week. Mama never asked for it back. I can buy some bon-bons to celebrate.'

They left the shop sucking the sweets that Elizabeth paid for.

'I cannot think what happened to my money,' Pamela moaned as they started walking. 'I am sure it was there yesterday.'

An icy shard crept up Elizabeth's back. Losing the money did not mean too much. It was the thought of it being taken from Pamela that upset her. Taken by her parents perhaps? She gave herself a mental shake. She was being ridiculous. Why would they take the money, when all they had to do was ask for it? It was not as if they were drunkards, like her father. The coin must have fallen out of Pamela's reticule without her knowing.

Their evening meal was as grim as the previous one. However, Mrs Wybrow had changed into a vermillion satin gown and Elizabeth wondered if this was a special occasion.

As the four of them went into dinner, Mrs Wybrow eyed Pamela.

'I am so glad you decided to dress for dinner Pamela.' She then turned to Elizabeth. 'You are a good influence, Miss Chetwode.'

Mr. Wybrow muttered something disapproving, but inaudible under his breath.

As they sat down, Mrs Wybrow mentioned their meeting the earl in town that morning.

'His lordship seems quite genuine. I believe he really does feel an obligation to Miss Chetwode. Mind you, Pamela behaved so prettily, I suspect she quite bewitched him. I would not be surprised if he calls just to see her.'

'Oh Mama!' Pamela squealed excitedly. 'Do you really think he might be interested in me?' She darted a look at Elizabeth. 'He is exceptionally handsome is he not?'

Before Elizabeth had time to respond, Pamela had already thought of something else.

'Rhoda wants to call and see me mama. We met Mr. Smith-Jacobsen this afternoon, and he asked why we had not been to Hooby Lodge recently. Oh, Mama, do you think we will be invited to their next soirée? Mr. Smith-Jacobsen was so exquisitely civil was he not Miss Chetwode?'

Elizabeth waited for Mrs Wybrow to reply first.

'It would be indeed agreeable to be invited to Hooby Lodge,' Mrs Wybrow threw her husband a smile. 'You see what it means to have a beautiful daughter on the threshold of womanhood?' Her hand swathed through the flickering oil-light. 'Everyone wants us.'

Mr. Wybrow's tiny metallic eyes flicked momentarily to Elizabeth, then his wife. 'Indeed,' he replied smoothly, 'our lovely Pamela will be hailed everywhere she goes.'

'And Miss Chetwode,' Pamela piped up happily, 'will be in such demand.' Her eyes shone against the gloom of the room. 'I believe Mr. Smith-Jacobsen was rather taken with her.'

Mrs Wybrow jumped as if something startled her.

'Really Pamela, Miss Chetwode is your companion and it will do you well to remember that. She is not here to be addressed by Society, nor is she here to intrude in our circle of friends. When we are invited anywhere, she will remain in the background with the other duennas.' She paused, 'if she does accompany us that is.'

'Mama it need not be so. She is meant to be my friend. A friend should be allowed to join me whenever I wish.'

'My dear, a paid companion is quite different from a cherished friend.' Mr. Wybrow flicked his metallic glance between them. 'Miss Chetwode is aware of her position. She will not let us down.' He arched his brow at Elizabeth, 'Will you Miss Chetwode?'

Elizabeth swallowed her slowly rising fury. How dare they talk about her like that. Of course, she knew she was only servant. Less if her growing instincts were right. A slave even, because she would not put it past the unpleasant Mr. Wybrow to find some excuse to not pay her when the time came.

Not that the money meant that much. Being a paid companion was the means to an end. Now, regardless of the pittance offered, it counted as a matter of principle.

'I will not let you down.' Her jaw ached with self-control.

Half an hour later she almost pounded her bed in rage. She could not stand another moment of it! She would write and tell Jamie that she was quitting the ghastly Wybrows' immediately. She did not want their lofty friendship, their grudging good will or even their paltry wage. They could keep it all. She had Mama's money, so had no need to be anyone's servant.

Thrusting her hand into the bottom of her portmanteau she snatched out her writing box, and pushing the wash-jug and bowl aside, set the contents out beside it and plonked herself onto the bamboo chair. She quickly opened the phial of ink, dipped her pen in and poised it over the smooth vellum.

Then paused.

How should she start? How could she express her dissatisfaction?

Her insides lurched as she realised that she was not exactly unhappy. Furious, and upset perhaps, but not really unhappy.

Then there was Pamela. Could she leave poor Pamela in the lurch? The earl had described Miss Wybrow as flighty.

Yet although somewhat too spontaneous at times, she was good-hearted and discerning.

For some reason, Mrs Wybrow treated Pamela like a twittering child, and for some reason, Pamela behaved that way in front of her mother. Besides, how could she admit defeat when she so zealously discouraged Jamie from leaving Longton's? How could she give the feeble excuse that she did not like the way the Wybrows' looked down on her?

She sighed. They were right. She was not *crème de la crème*. She was not entitled to join in as one of them. The problem was the way they made it so plain.

Perhaps Lady Bucklow's liberal attitude led her to believe she could fit into Society anywhere as she had managed to fit in somewhat while there. She sighed again. No, she would not leave, she would write to Lady Bucklow now, and Jamie in the morning.

Having finished her letter to Lady Bucklow, Elizabeth put the writing box away and took a deep breath. Lady Bucklow would be very satisfied with her praise of the Wybrows. It would be another success under her philanthropic belt and one more fib for Elizabeth to add to the seemingly ever-growing list.

Elizabeth thought about going to bed. However, although the light had faded it was still far too early, and having noticed a dusty leather-bound book under the bed earlier when putting on her boots, she decided to read for a while.

Rising from the bamboo chair, she walked over to the small bed and pulled the large dull looking, dog-eared reference type book out from underneath. Then sitting on the floor, she began turning the pages.

It was filled with engravings and printed pictures some kind. Each picture was covered with a film of tissue set in the binding, facing a page of what she assumed was the subject matter. Taking great care not to tear or crease the tissue, she uncovered the first picture plate.

And gasped!

The nudity on the page was not so bad, but the indecency of the female's pose was sickening and degrading to all women. She instinctively closed her eyes and turned over a handful of pages at once only to be confronted with equally disagreeable pictures. Hoping there was something of interest somewhere in the book, she flipped some more pages and peeled back more tissue, glanced at the prints and gulped. What had she expected after seeing the first few prints? An anatomical explanation? Having cast her eyes over the explicit text, she snapped the book shut. The dull linen cover was not empty after all. The gold outline of a naked woman writhing in dance flickered in the candlelight.

Hastily pushing the book back under the bed, she blew out her candle and staggered over to the banquette beneath the leaded window and falling against the upholstery turned her attention to the dark-green meadows beyond the oblong lawns.

The sky was slowly darkening into an opaque grey.

The meadow grass at the front of the house was beginning to look like two oblong lakes of treacle, separated by a dusky sunken sparsely gravelled path that was pitted with ruts and grooves. The word precarious came to mind, because any person fleeing would have to know each rut and groove before reaching the perimeter wall.

Fleeing? Whatever was she thinking about?

A shaky moment later, Elizabeth had drawn the thick curtains across the window and settled herself back on to the banquette immediately behind them. Out of sight and as far away from the dreadful book as possible.

****

James Bauval reclined in an armchair, his long fawn cashmere-clad legs stretched out in front of the now ebbing hearth, and *café noire* velvet elbows resting on each arm. His head rested on the back of the chair. A cream cravat fell in folds over his teal waistcoat. Three oil-lamps blinked incompatibly around him, making the half-drunk glass of brandy on the table beside him, glisten with colour. The soft mumble of Lady Levana and her cousin Elizabeth-Ann coming from the small gallery, hardly reaching his engrossed mind.

What a twist his life had taken. First was the appearance of Miss Chetwode who managed to turn his life upside down within seconds of their meeting. Then his introduction to the Wybrows. And now the decision to take on Walter Wybrow as a treasurer and clerk-manager for the estate, something he never thought to do before yesterday. After all that, his mother was presently contriving to get her cousin to visit town for a few weeks, which was a fool's errand, because for the last four and a half years the grieving Lady Interton had flatly refused to leave Rutland under any circumstances.

His heart broke for Betty, who had never stopped, and probably would never stop, grieving the loss of her only child four and a half years ago. Of course, none of them would forget sweet Mary-Beth, with her plaintive face and thin wasting body. The poor child knew she was not going to make it. Huge faded blue eyes over gaunt cheekbones told him she knew. When he heard, he came post haste from town, and although at seventeen, she was far too young, he promptly proposed. That was what they expected of him. His chest shuddered as tears of pain, regret and grief rimmed his eyes. He loved her from the moment, that as a shy five-year-old, he held the beautiful new-born Mary-Beth in his arms.

When had it started to go wrong? At what moment did he know that as much as he adored her, it would never work? How could he hold her as a babe in arms one minute, and hold her in passion the next? For that is how it seemed. For him, she would always be like a baby sister to love and protect. Yet, he would have given everything to save her. He would have conceded to them all and married her, just to stop her pain; just to give her life.

When she refused him, he was filled with guilt that he could not save her. Now, he quivered as he recalled, that full of tender brotherly love, he had hugged her until she gasped for breath.

'I am not well enough to be anybody's wife,' she had rasped when he finally let go.

He had unthinkingly replied, 'I can wait.'

The next three months were the worst of their lives.

Witnessing her deterioration from consumption, hearing her breathless with coughing and choking on the bloody fluids that filled her lungs was something he never wanted to see or hear again. He began to tremble at that memory.

To know she was dying and there was nothing any of them could do about it, had distressed them all almost beyond endurance.

To see her once glossy light gold hair slowly dull and watch her already sallow skin turn a yellowish brown, filled them all with unimaginable grief.

To know she would never cause a stir at her first ball, that no man would ever take her in his arms and love her the way she deserved, hurt him most of all. To know that she would never be loved the way a man in love, loves, and is loved in return. There would be no husband and children for her.

Yes, he adored her, but as a sister only.

An aching guilt gnawed his shuddering insides. Guilt that his love was not enough. Guilt that she expected to be his wife one day.

A soft rustle brought his mind up sharp.

'My dear,' Lady Levana began with gentle reproach, 'it is quite past the hour to join us. Dear Betty has retired to her guest chambers, and I have come to bid you goodnight.'

He was up and out of his chair in a second.

'Mama, I am so sorry,' he held out his arms. 'Please give my apologies to cousin Betty.'

Lady Levana allowed his embrace, then drew back with a frown. 'You look rather pink, my love. Did you fall asleep? However, I will forgive you, if,' she gave a deep sigh, 'you help me.'

His brow creased. When had he ever refused to help his mother so that she had to address him so solemnly and with such formality?

'Of course, I will help you, Mama.'

She stared up at him. 'It is a rather delicate matter,' she began earnestly. 'Delicate as in lacking in credibility.' She took a deep breath. 'What I want you to do is beyond common sense.'

The earl looked down into his mother's face and saw real anxiety ingrained in each furrowed line. He drew her to sit in the chair he had just risen from then gently knelt down beside her. 'I am listening.'

Several minutes later, with a thumping heart, he sat back on his haunches, and gazed up at her with shocked grief.

'You want me to oversee the clearing-up of Mary-Beth's grave? I had no idea it was not tended already Mama. Surely, our Sexton ensures all the graveyard is attended to?'

He swallowed his guilty, aching disquiet. He had never visited Mary-Beth's grave since her burial. Not once had he laid flowers there or wandered by just to see it. Not through selfishness, or lack of care, but with the thought, that down under the ground was a coffin of nothing but dust.

Dear sweet, gentle Mary-Beth's dust.

Guilt and pain gnawed through him again. There were so many times he promised himself he would go, but had never made it. Something else always came up that required immediate attention. Lame excuses. Besides, he assumed Betty and Mama did it, which on reflection was ridiculous.

The day after Mary-Beth's burial, Mama tearfully announced that, to spare her more distress, Betty never wanted her daughter's name mentioned again. Engrossed in his own grief and guilt he never questioned it.

'Oh Jemmy,' Lady Levana sighed, 'you must have known Betty absolutely refused to have it cared for?'

'No,' he muttered, trying to ignore the ache of culpability. 'I did not.'

She twisted long slender fingers together. 'I thought you knew.'

He bowed his head at the sadness in her voice. 'Know what?' he whispered. 'Is there a reason why she refuses to mention my second cousin? Is there an explanation why her grave is so badly neglected?'

The expression on her face changed.

He shuddered down his anguish. 'You can tell me surely?'

The dying fire silhouetted Lady Levana's soft features.

'Dear Jemmy,' she groaned. 'That is just it. I cannot tell you. I have given Betty my word.'

She glanced at his immense outline cutting through the gloom. Her son, whom she loved above all others, must never know the dreadful secret that dragged Elizabeth-Ann into the depths of despair. He must never know of the scandalous act that caused her cousin to lose someone so close and so dear, that it almost cost her sanity and that Betty believed her Mary-Beth's death was recompense for the life she ruined so long ago.

The misery in his voice shocked Lady Levana.

'Mama, I do understand why she will never stop grieving, but refusing to have the grave looked after is overwhelmingly distressing. And although I do not understand why it will be good for her to know the grave is in full bloom after all this time, naturally, I will do as you ask.'

His gut knotted with grief. Of course, he would make sure it was tended, whether Betty liked it or not. He owed it to Mary-Beth's memory to tidy and care for her last resting place.

'I shall begin first thing in the morning.'

Lady Levana shook her head. 'No, she must not find out. I have persuaded her to visit London for a few days; you may begin then. We travel the day after tomorrow.'

The gas lamps winked and blinked, sending shadows bouncing off the walls. Reflections from the past.

Forgive me darling Mary-Beth, he pleaded silently.

The soft click of a door jerked Elizabeth awake, which was a surprise because she had not realised that she had fallen asleep on the banquette. She was cold and stiff from the draught of the window.

She listened, kept very still and waited.

Silence. No creaking floorboards, no padding footfall. No controlled breathing. She must have dreamt it. Silently easing herself from the banquette, she cautiously parted the curtains. The room was much darker beyond the little space she occupied by the now moonlit window, so her eyes had to adjust before she really believed the room was empty.

She shivered as she remembered why she took sanctuary there. She ought to go straight to bed and try to forget about the sickening book, but her stomach churned at the thought of having to lie above it. The only thing to do, was to move it.

Her tulle dress rustled as she knelt down and felt about under the bed, sweeping her hand back and forth.

It had gone.

An icy shiver skidded down her spine as she remembered what woke her. It was not a dream. Someone *had* been in her room.

The icy shivers spread outwards freezing her hands and toes. It took all her strength of mind to remain calm and resist the urge to run to the gable window, hoist it open, and flee over the veranda into the night.

Chapter Five

The sharp freshness of the morning air, and the sound of the church clock striking six woke Elizabeth earlier than usual.

Pulling the bed-covers up over her head, Elizabeth snuggled right down into the comforting warmth of bed. Six was too early to be facing the day.

Then she remembered. This house was different to Lady Bucklow's home and Lady Bucklow's system. Even though, she was not part of the family, Lady Bucklow had treated her with the upmost respect.

Here she was just a hired companion. Here she was being paid to follow the rules.

Then she remembered the other letter she planned to write this morning.

With sigh of acceptance, she eased into sitting position shuddering at the chill, and thankful that at least, the bed was comfortable. The room too, really. The room although not nearly as elaborate as her room at Lady Bucklow's home, had the basics. There was a small walnut dressing table with a tiny mirror on a stand on top and a drawer underneath. There was the bamboo chair, and on the same side near the window, was a floor to ceiling alcove with a high rail attached along it for her clothing. The pull-across curtain was made of the same material as the curtains at the window.

Not looking forward to the chilly water in the wash-jug she had bought up the previous evening, Elizabeth, eased herself from the covers, and stood up, mentally preparing herself for the shock of cold on her skin.

Blasts of fresh cold air hit her as she sidled from the bed to the washstand. Puzzled she looked at the drawn curtains and frowned. They were moving slightly, so slipping over to them, she drew them apart, her jaw instantly dropping in shock. One of the windows, the left one nearest the clothing alcove was wide open, and was latched back on a hook on the outside wall outside.

As Elizabeth stared, a compelling fear forced her knees onto banquette where she craned forward and peered out of the open window. There, she saw that the veranda floor was much lower down from the window than she first thought. The drop, at least three foot was certainly not for the faint hearted.

Had someone, somehow climbed up to the veranda, opened the window from the outside, and latched it back? Why? Why would anyone do that?

Drawing some deep breaths, Elizabeth gulped down her fear. Whoever it was, would not get the chance again. Stretching right out over the ledge, she grappled with the latch attached to the wall hook, and after some effort pulled the window in, and silently closed it.

There had to be an explanation. Had she got up in the night, opened it, climbed out onto the veranda and latched the window back before climbing back in again while asleep? Surely not? Was there a way of securing it from the inside so that even if she was sleep-walking, she could not open it again? Some ribbon knotted around the metal handle in such a way that it would take a while to undo perhaps? Common-sense though, told her that ribbon could be undone too easily.

Turning to face her bedchamber door Elizabeth stared at it, wondering if someone had crept in, crossed the floor, opened the window, climbed onto the veranda, latched the window open, climbed back in and then crept across the bedroom again. Crept past her bed. Seen her sleeping. Stood over her perhaps? It was an alarming thought.

Was there a way of securing the door too? She had previously noticed that there was a lock under the brass handle, but no key.

She thought of the vile book. Someone must have entered because whoever had crept into her room and taken it, must have entered again to open the window.

Shards of ice spiked through her, twisting her stomach into freezing knots with every new thought.

Supposing whoever came in for the book knew she was on the banquette and did not come back into the room, but climbed onto the veranda and opened the window from the outside, expecting to find her still there? Supposing that same someone had entered through the door, expecting to find her on the banquette and thought to attack her in some way?

Maybe she ought to quit while she still had her wits?

An image of James Bauval, tall, steady, and strong, flowed into her mind, and with a jolt, she realised she could or would not leave without speaking to him first.

Heaving in a breath, she went to the water jug, poured water into the bowl, and dipped in her hands, and shivered.

Everything felt chilled. Her under garments, her stockings, shoes, and dresses hanging up in the alcove behind the curtain were cold.

Elizabeth chose the dress farthest away from the window because it was not quite as cold as the others. It was a high waisted leaf-green embossed tulle, with long sleeves. The bodice and skirt were plain enough, but the inserted neckline was layered with ivory organza lined with leaf-green chiffon that covered her skin.

Then she reached for her writing box, and opening the curtains wide, so the room was a little lighter, she started writing what became a long and much thought-out letter to Jamie.

A while later, after tidying her room, and readjusting her clothes, she then concentrated on brushing her hair into a coil and pinning it up. She then pulled several feathery strands around her face. Next, she slicked her brows upward into a refined arch, dampened her eyelashes with wet fingers and drew them to the outer corners of each eye. She then sucked at her lips to add a little colour to them, and pinched her cheeks to add colour to those to. These were just some of the little tricks Lady Bucklow taught her to make the best of herself.

At the time she wondered why she needed to bother, because who was going to see her? Yet another part of her knew it did not matter whether anyone noticed or not. Lady Bucklow said it was all about feeling confident about oneself. Right now, Elizabeth was determined to walk into the breakfast room with confidence, not fear.

Elizabeth had already put the letter to James and the letter to Lady Bucklow into her reticule ready for posting later. Maybe Mrs Wybrow would allow her and Pamela to ride into Thistleton this morning? The thought cheered her somewhat.

Pamela met her just outside the bedroom door again, and as they walked down to the breakfast room chatting, Elizabeth's spirits rose.

However, to Elizabeth's consternation, it was Mr. Wybrow who greeted them as they approached the breakfast parlour.

His metallic eyes flicked momentarily over Elizabeth before he greeted Pamela. 'Good morning my dear.'

He pecked his daughter's cheek then inclined his head.

'Miss Chetwode,' he gave a watery smile. 'I should like to see you in my study as soon as you have broken your fast.' He swished a hand in the air. 'Nothing to worry about. Just a small business matter.'

He took a gilt fob-watch from his waist-coat. 'Shall we say half an hour?'

That icy feeling slithered down Elizabeth's spine again. 'Of course, Mr. Wybrow.'

Was it about the conversation from the previous evening regarding the difference between being a simple deunna or a treasured friend?

If Pamela thought anything of it, it did not show. She still chatted cheerfully during their breakfast of hot chocolate and buttered toast.

Were they still friends? Perhaps Pamela now realised that a mere companion could never be more than an acquaintance after all. Pushing all thoughts of to one side, and determined to forget about the book, the open window and all other suspicions, Elizabeth concentrated on being an amiable companion.

Exactly half an hour later she was outside the dark oak door, drawing her shoulders back, and aiming for a confidence she did not feel. Then, taking one deep breath, she knocked, and at his command, pushed it open and masking her real feelings, walked serenely through.

He stood up as she entered. 'Miss Chetwode,' his rich tone always at odds with his manner still managed to amaze her. 'Come,' he waved her to the chair in front of his desk, 'pray do sit down.' His mouth moved to a reedy smile. 'There is something I missed at our first meeting.' He waited until she sat down, before seating himself.

His effortless courtesy so at odds with the rest of his manner, might have charmed her if she was not already so wary of him.

She still remembered her manners though. 'Thank-you, Mr. Wybrow.'

His chair scraped as he drew it to the desk. Then he gave something between a chortle and a snuffle as he brought his arms to rest on the desk-top in front of him and leaned forward.

'You are in looks today, Miss Chetwode.'

In looks?

He smiled at her perplexed expression. 'No need to be shy Miss Chetwode. An older man such as myself has no qualms in complimenting a young girl.' The left side of his mouth rose higher than the other. 'As you are in my employ, I see no reason to balk in expressing my great admiration for you.' His arms moved so that his clasped hands were just a little nearer to her. 'You have made an excellent start. Pamela adores you, and Mrs Wybrow is very satisfied with your conduct.'

A *frisson* of alarm crackled through Elizabeth as his hands unclasped and his fingers inched nearer. Thankfully, he could not actually touch her because of the size of the desk. All the same, she found herself pulling inwards and backwards just in case.

His metallic eyes stilled as he suddenly came to the point. 'We failed to discuss money.' He did not give her any time to respond. 'Your day to day living expenses will be met by us of course. Then there is the ten shillings every ten weeks as agreed in writing. However, due to your exceptional beginning, I am prepared to increase that to fifteen. Now,' he continued with a flourish. 'I believe you bought some *bon-bons* for Pamela yesterday?'

'Yes.'

'No need to apologise Miss Chetwode,' he swished his hand at her, 'but we cannot have you spending your money on our daughter.' He shook his head. 'Although what she does with her allowance is beyond me. Here,' he withdrew his hands to open a drawer in front of him. 'I think this will cover immediate, and future incidentals.' With that he pushed several coins over to her.

Five shillings? Just for a few *bon-bons*?

'No, Mr. Wybrow, there is no need. Please,' she reached out and quickly pushed the money back. Too late, she realised what a mistake that simple movement was as a clammy hand moved the coins back towards her, then quickly covered that clammy hand over hers and squeezed.

'Miss Chetwode,' he murmured, his voice now silky. 'I beg you not to be too hasty. There is always a little extra room for generosity.' His tongue slaked across his lips. 'Mine,' he swallowed. 'And yours.'

This time it was not just ice that slithered down her back. Every inch of her flesh felt as if tiny, invisible insects were nipping her skin. 'I-I,' she floundered. 'Do not need any extra, generosity.'

His metallic eyes roved down slowly from her face and lingered over the bodice of the green dress.

'How refreshing Miss Chetwode. I see there is more to you than meets the eye. An orphan not in need of largess is rare indeed.'

Suddenly the vision of the vile book under the bed reared before her. She scraped her thoughts together as she fought to keep the panic from her voice. 'That is not what I meant.'

As his eyes flicked from her bodice to her lips, his hand tightened, the skin on the top of his head creased. His brow shone. His breathing quickened.

'Is it not?' he murmured with a sickening pleasure.

She used his momentary lack of concentration to her advantage and swiftly withdrew her hand. Resisting the urge to wipe it on her skirts, she merely folded both hands demurely on her lap. 'I think we are at cross purposes,' she looked at him quickly, regretted it immediately, and looked away. 'I only meant, that-,' *Meant what?* That she was an heiress and did not need charity from anyone? Yes. That was exactly what she meant.

She met his gaze with conviction. 'I only meant that the agreed wage is sufficient for my present needs, Mr. Wybrow. The little money I have was left over from my journey.'

His demeanour instantly changed from sly charm to cutting dominance.

He raised a sarcastic brow. 'Lady Bucklow's benevolence I presume?' he sneered. 'Or,' he tacked on, 'Lord Bauval's.'

Elizabeth stared at him, speechless due to anger combined with an odd excitement sweeping through her. Wybrow's guile had not worked, so he instantly turned to subtle intimidation, but his mention of James Bauval made her perversely animated.

Mr. Wybrow raised a querying brow.

He expected an answer, but the thought of his vile book, his crêpe hands on her skin, and his metallic eyes roving her body nauseated her.

She made an instant decision. She would leave Wybrow House immediately.

A knock startled them both.

Dabbs entered.

'Lord Bauval to see sir. Shall I send him in?'

Two chairs scraped back in a flurry.

'You may go,' Mr. Wybrow said in clipped tones.

Flustered, Elizabeth made unseeingly for the door.

'Goodness!' Lord Bauval's rich, wry tone brought her to a rapid halt on the threshold. 'You *are* in a hurry to see me.'

As she looked up into his face, her chrysolite irises were bright with something more than surprise. Mutiny? Curbing his immense pleasure at seeing her, James glanced to the desk where Mr. Wybrow stood poised to greet him. Metallic beady eyes glittered and quickly darted away from Miss Chetwode's back.

Bauval's immense pleasure changed to alarm, but he managed a deep calming breath as Miss Chetwode muttered her apologies, brushed past him, and fled.

Out in the corridor after the study door closed and once Dabbs disappeared in the direction of the kitchen for refreshment, Elizabeth paused. What was she going to do now? Even if she took the back entrance of the house, the earl would see her on his way home. And as he had taken it into his head to look after her, she would not get very far without being caught and questioned to the hilt. What could she say? If it came down to it, Mr. Wybrow had not actually said or done anything improper. Distraught and confused, she hurried to her room.

James Bauval cantered his liver-chestnut thoroughbred up and over the hogback with a satisfied air. Wybrow appeared delighted at the idea of working for him. He even offered to start right away by working in the evenings until he finished with Chalmers Brothers. As the terms included a house on the estate, Bauval had already started the necessary repairs on Nimbus Folly, the disused rectory.

The towered house set just beyond the estate's small burial ground and dilapidated chapel, had not been used for years. After the old rector died, Reverend Newson tactfully declined the place, saying it was too large for his needs. It had a large tiled ball-room hall, two withdrawing-rooms, a huge library, two studies, a large and small parlour, an enormous kitchen and other rooms Bauval could not remember about. There were several spacious bed-chambers. The upkeep was probably too costly for a man with three daughters to launch.

Wybrow though, obviously had no such concerns. His status on the estate more than made up for the expense. Besides, he only had Pamela to bring out.

The earl paused at the top of the hill to look at the estate surrounding Bauval Park that was his since great grandfather Jemmy Bauval, the third Earl of Alstoe died ten years earlier. There were no other males in the line, so the old earl had had it written into his two daughters', and later his two grand-daughters' marriage bonds, that all future children were to have the name Bauval as given names. He smiled to himself. What if he had only girls? Would he decree all his progeny had to carry a name down the line? Chetwode, for instance? That had quite a ring to it.

Progeny? Chetwode?

What the devil was his brain about now? He needed progeny like he needed a hole in the head! He turned the liver-chestnut mare down the hill and galloped for home.

Elizabeth pushed the near-empty portmanteau back under her rail of dresses with a sigh. During the last hour or so, she changed her mind about going, several times. She was; she was not. She had to go. She could not go. It was only the sound of Bauval leaving the house that finally brought her to her senses. She could not possibly go without having to explain herself to someone. Besides, the portmanteau was too heavy for her to manage all the way to the highway by herself. Then there was the question of the coach. Although she arrived without a chaperone, Jamie had at least seen her safely onto the first one and had even given two respectable looking matrons a shilling each to keep an eye on her. Boarding a coach alone could be asking for trouble. No, she just had to hope Mr. Wybrow meant her no harm and that she had imagined it all.

The knock at her door made her jump.

'Miss Chetwode,' Pamela burst in without waiting for a reply. 'What do you think?' she exclaimed. 'The earl has asked Papa to be his man of business on the estate. Is that not wonderful?' She hardly drew breath before adding, 'We are to live in a large house in the Bauval Park estate with its own gardens and ornamental lake. We may select plants and flowers from the estate nurseries anytime we like. We can have full use of the stables and grounds, and Mama can have any number of servants she wants.' Her voice dropped. 'Oh Mary-Beth,' she whispered. 'You have brought us such luck.'

The use of her old name hardly registered with Elizabeth. All she could think about was living in the grounds of Bauval Park, closer to James, *Jemmy* Bauval.

'Just think,' Pamela rushed on, 'we can go anywhere we like. We shall be accepted everywhere now we have his patronage.'

She clapped her hands together.

'We shall be able to entertain almost anyone. Maybe the earl will introduce us to his set, not as employees, but as personal friends. Imagine,' she continued breathlessly, 'friends to an earl.' She tossed her head. 'Oh, Mary-Beth, we have fallen on our feet at last.'

Elizabeth was baffled. 'Fallen on your feet, at last? Whatever do you mean?'

Pamela's hand flew to her mouth. 'Oh no!' Her pretty dove-grey day dress rustled as she plopped onto the corner of the bed right opposite the bamboo chair where Elizabeth sat. 'I have said far too much. Please forget I said it.'

That icy sensation crept along Elizabeth's spine.

Whatever it was that lay beneath the surface of this family, unnerved not only her, but Pamela and Mrs Wybrow too.

She swept a concerned gaze over Pamela. 'I will,' she promised, 'forget that is, but,' she reached over and gently took Pamela's hand in hers, 'dearest Pamela, if you ever need to tell me anything in confidence, you can trust me, I promise.' Even as she spoke, the icy feeling spread outwards but for Pamela's sake she suppressed a shudder. Instead, she drew a ragged breath, forced a smile and squeezed Pamela's limp hand. 'However, you are right about Mr. Wybrow's new position. It is indeed, wonderful news.'

Pamela rallied. 'Oh Mary-Beth,' she whispered returning the squeeze. 'Our luck *has* changed since you came.' Her hair auburn bobbed with gold high-lights as she tilted her head up. 'Promise you will always be my friend?'

'I promise.'

'Thank-goodness,' Pamela murmured. 'Only sometimes things can go so dreadfully wrong. I mean without anyone being actually to blame. I could not bear it, if,' she faltered. 'If you refused to be my friend.'

Elizabeth suddenly felt very grown up. 'Pamela, I would never refuse to be your friend. Whatever happened.'

Pamela brightened. 'Thank-you,' she whispered. Then, 'Come Miss Chetwode, Papa is waiting for us in the parlour.'

Mr. Wybrow flicked his metallic stare over Elizabeth as they entered the small salon Lord Bauval had escorted her into the day she arrived.

Shifting away from the dresser wedged between the two wall mirrors, he swung a tiny glass to his lips.

'A small toast my dears,' he took a sip. 'Too early I know,' he was addressing Pamela. 'Deplorable, imbibing at this hour, however,' he turned to Elizabeth. 'Our good news, however merits a small celebration does it not?'

'Indeed Mr. Wybrow.'

'Indeed Miss Chetwode,' he echoed, the sneer so slight in his rich voice, she wondered if it was merely the taste of the port on his tongue that caused the inflection or something more menacing.

'After just over three years of making our home here, Bauval has chosen me to be his chief man of business. A most singular honour. Naturally,' he made his way along the room, motioning for them to sit on the sofa before dropping into Queen Ann chair. 'It is still somewhat beneath me,' he said grandly. 'However, unlike Chalmers, I shall be the helmsman, rather than merely managing accounts. I shall have far more free time,' his eyes narrowed, roved over Elizabeth's neckline, then flicked back to his glass. 'We are to leave Wybrow House quite soon though.' He gave an exaggerated sigh. 'His lordship has insisted on us taking up residence in the old but rather impressive rectory.'

Pamela squealed. 'But Papa, it is rumoured to be haunted.'

'Rumoured?' Mr. Wybrow scoffed. 'Overlooking the Bauval burial ground does not mean the dead will rise up and join us. While, I agree the outside may not seem impressive, once the refurbishments are complete your Mama will be able to entertain as she wishes.'

He stood up.

'I have to go now, but I believe Mrs Wybrow has plans for you to accompany her into Thistleton where she will be choosing,' he waved his hand noncommittally. 'Whatever is needed for our new home. We are to move in within the month.'

Pamela squealed with delight. She jumped up and threw her arms round his neck and kissed him. 'Oh Papa, you are so kind.'

The next two weeks flew by. Elizabeth managed to send off her letters each week. She accompanied Pamela and Mrs Wybrow into town, and they visited Nimbus Folly every afternoon so Mrs Wybrow could see how the refurbishments were coming along.

Pamela had chosen a bed-chamber with a separate dressing room that did not overlook the burial ground, and Elizabeth had the one next to it that did. She did not mind, because the mullioned windows were not above a veranda and were unopenable from the outside. Her room did not have a separate dressing-room like Pamela's. However, there was a suite of fine Queen Anne furniture in there that included a wardrobe large enough for her frocks, a chest of drawers, and a *vis-à-vis* dressing-table mirror. The dresser for her jug and bowl matched the escritoire. Moreover, her chair was brocade, not bamboo.

Mrs Wybrow hinted that Pamela might be able to have her very own parlour decorated in whatever colours she chose.

One clear afternoon, as they left Nimbus Folly to take a short walk round the enclosed garden, before heading back to Wybrow House, Pamela linked her arm through Elizabeth's.

'It will be so exciting once we actually live here in the grounds of Bauval Park.'

Elizabeth chuckled. 'My room overlooks the graves of the late Bauvals' remember?'

'Oh,' gesturing beyond the path, Pamela drew them away from the neat lawn, 'Look at the cemetery. It is not scary at all.'

Elizabeth smiled. 'No, it is not. In truth, it looks rather peaceful.'

Pamela's arm squeezed hers. 'Let us go there now.' The auburn-gold curls, sprang from beneath a plain beige bonnet and bounced over her *fuchsine* cape as she turned.

Something in Elizabeth's insides knotted. She had not visited a cemetery since Mama was buried all those years ago. All those years ago? Suddenly what seemed like a life time ago, materialised into a mere four and a half years.

'Miss Chetwode, are you alright? Only you look quite pale? Is it the thought of going into the grave-yard? We do not have to go.'

Elizabeth stared blindly at Pamela for a moment. Then as the knot dissipated, she nodded. 'Yes, of course we may go.'

Forging a smile, she drew Pamela towards the little cemetery gate.

'It is beautifully kept.' Pamela whispered as they threaded their way round the tombs. 'Look at this one.' She read the inscription and the date from a clean smooth stone. 'It looks so recent, yet it is over fifty years old. And oh,' she caught sight of a small flat stone set into the neatly trimmed grass and hurried to inspect it. 'This must be a child.' She lowered her voice, 'Poor thing.'

'How very sad,' Elizabeth agreed.

Pamela crossed a small, wild-looking overgrown, unkempt rectangle of ground to a inspect large tomb beyond and was studying it closely.

'Mary-Beth,' Pamela chuckled beckoning to Elizabeth. 'You are wool-gathering. Come and look at the previous earl's grave. Do you think he was as handsome as our earl?'

Whipping up the earl in her mind sent the unwanted, but now familiar rainbow butterflies, skittering through Elizabeth which caused her to rush over toward Pamela. Her haste caused her to stumble through the wild unkempt patch.

'Ouch,' Elizabeth let out a yelp as her foot hit something hard under the matted undergrowth. Bending to inspect what it was, her hand brushed against an unseen obstacle.

Curious, Elizabeth tugged at the grass and weeds with her hands. Whatever it was, was dangerous lying there, invisible to all.

She pulled back a little, and stared. For there in the depths of the miniature wilderness was a tiny stone cross.

This was a grave?

She was standing on a grave! Stepping back, she impulsively bent and parted the foliage to read the moss encrusted words on a flat ground level stone slab. She could only just about make them out.

'*Mary-Beth 1792 to 1812*'.

Elizabeth's heart missed a beat; her legs turned to jelly. It could not be. Scrabbling furiously at the moss lower down she just about managed to make out the miniature words. '*May the sin of the parent be forgiven*'.

She re-read the whole inscription again, then looked about her. This one single grave lay forgotten and uncared for, yet the others were neat and lovingly remembered. Was it an oversight? How could anyone forget their child?

What did it mean, 'the sin of the parent'? Her heart bounced as the dreadful possibility hit her. Was this Mary-Beth a baseborn child? a concealed nonentity, cast into the ground and left to rot?

Elizabeth pursed her lips. Well not any longer. From now on, this girl's grave, her namesake, Mary-Beth would be as cared for as the rest of the graves.

She would buy plants, and make it bloom in a blaze of colour.

'Pamela, Miss Chetwode!' The demand shrilled through the otherwise peaceful air. 'Whatever are you doing?'

Two faces looked up to see an irritated Mrs Wybrow by the iron gate.

'Come out of there at once.'

Two pairs of feet instantly obeyed, skimming the turf as they hurried towards her.

'What a morbid occupation for two young women to be indulging in,' Mrs Wybrow chided.

She addressed Elizabeth.

'Really Miss Chetwode, fancy allowing Pamela into such a place.'

Mrs Wybrow tutted, before saying, 'Mrs Smith-Jacobsen has invited us to a small soirée she is holding at the end of the week, and just supposing one of them personally delivered the invitation. How would that look? Two young girls promenading a cemetery as if on a pleasure trip?'

With a rustle of taffeta, she swivelled round and stalked off.

Elizabeth, ready to offer comfort, cast a sympathetic glance at Pamela.

Pamela however, instead of frowning, was giggling.

'The Smith-Jacobsens'.' Her eyelashes fluttered. 'Just imagine if Henry had delivered our invitation personally?' She began following her mother. 'He might have thought we were ghosts.'

Elizabeth's senses prickled. Ghosts? Was the young dead Mary-Beth a ghost sitting on her shoulder, or merely a figment of her foolish imagination? She had to find a way of going into the little cemetery on a regular basis to find out.

She forced a light-hearted chuckle. 'I doubt it.'

****

James Bauval threw in his hand with a sigh. Having accompanied his mother and Betty to London, he then sought out his old friends. Not long ago, an evening of good-natured banter, and a game of cards, would lift his spirits. For some reason, however, he just could not concentrate. His desire to be back home and nearer to Miss Elizabeth Chetwode seemed to consume him. Wherever he was, whatever he was doing, his thoughts unaccountably turned to her. The way she looked at him the first time he saw her. The way raindrops glistened on her golden lashes, and her school-marm tone. Especially that school-marm tone!

His heart skipped a beat.

'I am done.' He rocked back in his chair. 'I am leaving for home early in the morning.'

One of their group, Viscount Around chortled. 'If I did not know you better, I would suspect you had a fast-piece hidden away.'

'Very fast,' quipped Lawrence, laying his cards on the table and drawing a pile of notes towards him. 'Been here for two days and this is the first time he has played.'

'And lost,' a third laughed. 'Who is she? Spill Bauval.'

'There is no fast piece on the go.' Bauval addressed the new Lord Rawsthorne, 'I have been out and about with my mother and her cousin Betty.' How Mama had managed to persuade Betty to come to town, he would never know. His head shifted to the third member of the group. 'So, there is nothing to spill, Theo.'

Theo Kenelly narrowed shrewd eyes at Bauval. They had been through the war together. He knew a smooth evasion when he saw it. But he also knew not to press it further. Bauval was pretty tight-lipped about his paramours. Even before Mary-Beth.

Mary-Beth. Whatever made him think of her after all this time? A shadow must have crossed his face.

Lawrence chortled. 'Someone walked over your grave Theo?'

Theo glowered. 'I hope not, but if they had, I will thank you not to find it quite so amusing.'

Bauval rose, 'Goodnight gentleman.' He bowed stiffly.

A fast piece indeed.

Chapter Six

Betty Interton sighed as Jemmy's curricle disappeared from view.

'He seems rather preoccupied, and in a great hurry to get home.'

'Come in, dearest,' Lady Levana who was standing beside her countered tenderly. 'We have not discussed our itinerary for the next three weeks.'

'Three weeks?'

'Dearest,' Levana guided Betty back into the hallway of the fashionable London town-house, then gently but firmly ushered her into the Chinese salon. Gesturing her cousin into a comfortable high-backed chair before sitting down on another, beside her, she said, 'I have already received several invitations.'

'Then you must decline or go alone.' Betty's tone rose, 'You know I cannot bear to attend social events now.'

'Betty,' Levana remained gently firm, 'We can hardly ignore old friends. Dear Veronica Bucklow left her card yesterday, and would like us to let her know when we can take tea with her.'

Betty groaned. 'Veronica asks too many questions.'

Levana ignored the protest, concentrating instead on the colours of the room. The figures of the East engraved on wood. The pastel lanterns had been removed, but the curtains of cream slub-silk were drawn neatly back from the full-length leaded windows. She suppressed a sigh. The immense house, built by their grandfather and now owned by Jemmy, held many memories for them both. Echoes of soirées, card parties, luncheons, and balls. Especially the balls. Lavish crushes that became a highlight of every Season.

How quiet it all seemed now.

'Hetty Raunce, too,' Levana added lightly.

Against all expectations, Lady Interton chuckled. 'Is she still the card queen?'

Levana's spirits lifted at Betty's sudden animation.

'I believe so,' Levana replied, encouraging Betty's humour.

'Ha,' Betty chuckled, 'she never got the better of me.'

Levana's spirits soared even more at Betty's sudden enthusiasm.

'It would be good to see Hetty again,' Betty mused.

Levana acted quickly. 'And Veronica Bucklow. May I accept, for us both?'

Betty reflected for a moment. 'Afternoon tea only?'

'Yes.' In spite of her joy, Levana just gave a nod. It was a wonderful and unexpected start, and it would not do to press anything more onto her cousin, yet.

Betty's fragile frame relaxed a little. 'Then we shall accept both invitations.'

Levana concealed her delight.

Betty drew a breath. 'We had such wonderful times back then. Hetty and Veronica were such fun back then. Then at some point, Veronica started taking in all kinds of waifs and strays, and things changed. Do you remember?'

'I am not sure I do.' Wanting to keep Betty buoyant about their old friends, Levana quickly changed the subject. 'Should we have some refreshment before our shopping trip?'

Betty shrugged, then in a faraway voice murmured, 'Hetty and Veronica, such dear, dear friends.'

Levana rang the for the maid.

Lord Bauval arrived home late the following evening to find a pink edged invitation from Mrs Smith-Jacobsen in his post.

He tossed it to one side. He did not want upset her, but was far too busy to attend soirées at this time of year. He would send his apologies along with a small token to signify his regret and hope she would not take it too badly.

He had made excellent time on his journey back and was in a light mood.

Vance, his valet tapped lightly on his study door and came through with a supper tray.

'Is all well in town milord?' He set the food down in front of Bauval.

'It is Vance,' Bauval replied pleasantly. 'How about here? Everything gone smoothly during my absence?'

What he really wanted to know was how *his* little plan was going.

'As far as I understand my lord.'

His heart bounced whenever he thought of his plan.

'How is,' he took a breath. He must try to get Miss Chetwode out of his thoughts now and again. 'Nimbus Folly coming along?'

Vance's expression never altered, but his head inclined slightly.

'Very well my lord.'

Bauval raised a brow. 'But?'

A trace smile hovered on Vance's lips. 'Well,' he began, trying to be solemn. 'Mrs Wybrow *en famile* have taken it into their heads to visit the place every afternoon. I am sure you have no objection my lord, however I believe Dawkins & Co. are a little-'

'-Harassed?'

'Exactly so my lord.'

Bauval leaned back in the leather chair, steepling his fingers under his chin. 'Tricky one Vance. I told Wybrows to do whatever they wanted.' He chuckled ruefully. 'I should have seen it coming. Maybe I can divert their attention to other exertions.'

Exertions? His mind buzzed as the delightful image of Miss Chetwode blazed unbidden through his mind, yet again. The way she set upon him. Her look of astonishment when confronted. Large chrysolite irises widening under flickering caramel lashes. Raspberries and cream skin. Hair, rosy-beige under a dipping sun.

Her scolding.

And that nearly-kiss.

Exertions? Oh yes.

'An excellent plan my lord.'

James blinked up at Vance.

'To divert them my lord?'

Bridling the visions, Bauval dragged himself back to reality. 'Yes, yes of course, thank-you Vance. That will be all.'

Elizabeth woke with a start, and immediately wondered if the large stick wedged against the door was still strong enough to prevent anyone entering her room. Not that anything untoward had occurred since the open-window incident. Thankfully, they all seemed to be too busy with the forthcoming move. Mr. Wybrow was out most of the day, presumably completing all his assignments at Chalmer's, and had not appeared since his interview with Jemmy. Mrs Wybrow crooned that he went to Bauval Park each evening, in spite of his lordship not being there.

'He works so hard that I sometimes fear for his health. Mind you, it is somewhat unseemly for a Gentleman of his status having to stoop so low. If only-.'

She had stopped abruptly then hustled off to oversee their housekeeper. Again, Elizabeth was left wondering what it was Mrs Wybrow meant.

As the village church clock struck four, the lonely, eerie sound reminded her of churchyards, and of graves and tombs.

Mama's grave.

Mary-Beth's grave.

Not wanting to think about either, she burrowed under the bedcovers. What was it about this place in the dark that made her brain quiver and her flesh creep? She never felt like this at any of Lady Bucklow's homes, or at her own home all those years ago.

A lifetime ago.

She had just reached that peaceful place of being almost asleep, when suddenly her mind crowded with amazing colours. Pinks, purples, yellows and white. The rosy-pink of autumn lilies. The deep purple of violas and autumn crocus. And lemon-mist. All Mama's favourite-coloured flowers seemed to dance in her head.

The uneasy feeling vanished instantly and she had her answer. She would fill Mary-Beth's grave with those. Then, when she arrived back in London, she would do the same for Mama's grave.

With that, she drifted into a peaceful sleep.

Mrs Wybrow waved a letter in front of them. They had had breakfast and were in the parlour planning their day. Not that there was much to plan these days, as most of the time they went to Nimbus Folly.

'Pamela,' Mrs Wybrow's lace cap fluttered. 'Please do not make any plans for today. His lordship has invited us to ride out with him in his carriage this afternoon.'

Elizabeth's insides immediately rose and fell in waves. The thought of seeing him filled her with excitement. An excitement she did not want, but could not help feeling.

Mrs Wybrow drew a pained breath. 'Of course, that means we cannot go to our new home today.'

She looked very pointedly at Elizabeth. 'By the way, Mr. Wybrow feels it is only proper to give you an occasional afternoon off, so you need not come with us.'

Elizabeth's whole being plummeted. Every part of her despaired. Not see Jemmy? Not accompany them in his carriage? In her turmoil, she completely missed Mrs Wybrow's odd tone.

'However, I require you make a brief visit to Nimbus Folly, just to ensure my orders are being carried out. Please take the curtain samples with you.'

Elizabeth drew a silent breath. It was for the best. James Bauval had too much of an unsettling effect on her.

She did not want a man.

She did not want to fall in love.

Her heart skipped a beat.

Fall in love?

Of course, she was not in love with James Bauval.

Was she?

Mrs Wybrow babbled on, 'A walk in the fresh air over the fields will do you good. The rest of the time is then yours to do with as you please. Pamela,' she tacked on decisively, 'it is you, his lordship is really interested in. Wear your pale green silk bonnet, the *crème de menthe* carriage outfit and your ivory half-boots.'

She turned Elizabeth. 'You may leave immediately after luncheon.'

'Mama,' Pamela protested. 'Miss Chetwode ought not to go out alone.' She looked to the window. 'What if it rains?'

'There is too much wind for rain, besides, this is Papa's decision-.' Mrs Wybrow stopped abruptly, softened her voice then added regally, 'I am sure Miss Chetwode is grateful for such kind consideration.' She looked at Elizabeth. 'Are you not Miss Chetwode?'

Still trying to control her chaotic thoughts, Elizabeth merely nodded.

Suddenly, however, a brilliant idea struck her. She could start on Mary-Beth's grave this very afternoon.

The wind had not prevented the overhead dark, thunderous clouds, so the canopy was drawn up over the magnificent Bauval carriage.

To James' surprise, only Mother and daughter met him at their door.

'Good afternoon, Lord Bauval,' Mrs Wybrow beamed, steadying the fruited hat as she eyed the carriage. 'I see you have prepared for the worst. Most considerate my lord.'

James acknowledged her with a slight bow and a smile before stepping deftly aside to let them by, then dropping into pace beside them. His mind however was on the whereabouts of Miss Chetwode.

'Good afternoon, Miss Wybrow. How pretty you look this afternoon.'

As they made their way to his carriage, his concern mounted.

'Is Miss Chetwode not to accompany us?'

Mrs Wybrow turned as his driver helped her up.

'No, my lord.' She averted her eyes. 'Mr. Wybrow feels that she should have the afternoon off.'

Alarm coursed through James and he found himself involuntarily scanning the windows of Wybrow House.

Mrs Wybrow noticed. 'She is on an errand my lord.'

Bauval relaxed a little. He was just being foolish. Naturally she needed time off.

But where was she?

The carriage began bouncing over the gravel.

He thought quickly. 'I thought we could drive round some of the estate first.'

That might give him an idea of Miss Chetwode's whereabouts. 'Then take tea at Bauval Park.'

'How delightful,' Mrs Wybrow gushed, 'Pamela will be thrilled,' she turned on a rustle of mustard and brown, 'will you not my dear?'

Pamela nodded prettily, yet the sweet smile did not quite reach her eyes.

James looked at Pamela Wybrow. She was fashionably pretty, although a mite too slim for his taste. A little filling out here and there and she might take the *ton* by storm when her time came. Reverend Newson had implied she was air-headed and flighty, yet, although she laughed easily there was an underlying tension behind those blue-grey eyes. Her gloved hands, placed so demurely on her lap were not quite relaxed. And every so often one finger jumped as if suddenly released from a spring. She glanced out of the carriage, looked up at the sky and sighed heavily.

'Pamela really.'

Pamela turned to her mother. 'But, Mama, it has started to rain.'

Mrs Wybrow tutted slightly. 'Surely you are not worried about a little rain?'

'What about Miss Chetwode?' Pamela faltered.

Mrs Wybrow's demeanour instantly changed.

'Goodness child,' she forced with brittle gaiety. 'What a worrier you are. Miss Chetwode can look after herself.'

Pamela swallowed.

'Mama, what if she gets caught in a storm? You, hate being out in storms.'

James watched a flicker of unease cross Mrs Wybrow's face, then swiftly change to nonchalance.

'She will not be out for long. Besides she set off eagerly enough.'

Apprehension squirmed through James. The woman obviously did not care about Miss Chetwode being caught in a storm.

Her biting tone jarred through him.

'Her errand is simple enough dearest.'

She turned to James. 'Please excuse my daughter.' She reached out and patted Pamela's *crème de menthe*-coloured lap. 'My darling Pamela has everybody's welfare at heart.'

Pamela's milk-white cheeks tinged to light pink. 'But Mama-'

'-Pamela, I am sure Lord Bauval does not want to talk about a hired companion. Please let us change the subject.'

Bauval's apprehension grew. The woman was just a little too brisk in her dismissal of the hired help, and her forced indifference did not ring true to her underlying unease.

Had she forgotten that he had made himself Miss Chetwode's champion?

His senses thrummed with alarm. Yet, like a cat on a cautious prowl, he maintained absolute self-control.

'Of course,' he marshalled smoothly. 'Tell me Mrs Wybrow, how is Mr. Wybrow?'

Obviously relieved at the diversion, Mrs Wybrow wafted her hand through the air. 'Extremely well my lord,' she beamed.

'He seems most eager to start on my estates. He is not working too hard I trust?'

Mrs Wybrow's mouth opened, but he did not give her time to reply, 'He spends some of his evenings at Nimbus Folly I believe. Most commendable.' He swiftly inhaled. 'However, it would not do for him to over tax himself. I need him to be in top form when he starts working for the estate properly. A wearied man is of little use.'

'Pray do not think it! Why, he is spending this very afternoon at home.' Mrs Wybrow's sickly smile nearly made him turn the carriage round and hurtle back to Wybrow House.

Every muscle in his body contracted but he forced himself to remain outwardly calm. Mr. Wybrow at home? The image of Wybrow lying in wait for Miss Chetwode sickened him. He quickly checked himself. No, he was allowing his imagination, his silly, foolish imagination run riot. Surely Mr. Wybrow would not stoop that low? Besides his wife would not possibly agree to, or turn her back on, such liberties.

'An afternoon at home?' he raised a brow. 'What a pity I did not know sooner. He could have joined us.' He reached inside his cashmere coat and pulled out a gold watch. 'Why,' he smiled, 'It is not too late to turn back.'

'Oh no, my lord!' Mrs Wybrow spluttered quickly. 'Please do not inconvenience yourself. Dear Pamela will be most unhappy to have to return so soon.'

She turned swiftly to her daughter. 'Will you not dearest?'

Pamela blinked. 'I-'

'-There,' Mrs Wybrow declared crisply. 'Unhappiness all over her face. Really, Pamela, you should not be quite so transparent. His lordship will be most offended.'

A glacial chill rippled along every nerve of his lordship's body. Something was wrong. Miss Chetwode was alone on an errand somewhere, Pamela was on-edge, and Wybrow was at home. Moreover, Mrs Wybrow was behaving as if - the icy chill exploded into heat. His stomach lurched.

No. The idea was just too ridiculous. A wife might turn a blind eye to her husband's infidelity, but actively encourage it? Never. He was out of his mind to even think it. A wave of nausea gripped him as questions raced through his mind. What if Miss Chetwode was party to the whole thing?

What if she was not?

How long ago did she leave the house? When was she expected back?

Marshalling his thoughts once more, he took up the conversation again. 'Not at all,' he addressed them both and controlling his rising alarm, affected a smile. 'I admire Miss Wybrow's honesty.' That part was true. 'It is a rare quality to speak without guile.'

'Oh, Pamela is extremely honest my lord.'

'I can see that,' James leaned forward. 'Miss Wybrow, your concern for Miss Chetwode does you great credit. It looks as though a storm *is* brewing, and while I am sure your Mama is perfectly correct in thinking Miss Chetwode cannot possibly come to any harm, I cannot have my guests worrying, can I? I insist on putting matters right. Where did she go on her errand?'

Two voices spoke at once.

'The village.'

'Nimbus Folly.'

James looked at Mrs Wybrow. 'The village?'

'Yes, my lord.'

Pamela's reaction was instant. 'No Mama. You sent her to the Folly with fabric samples.'

Mrs Wybrow shot Pamela a quelling look. 'I did no such thing. I sent her to the village to *get* fabric samples.'

'No Mama-'

'-Pamela,' Mrs Wybrow hissed. 'Please do not contradict me. I should know where I sent her.'

Bauval' insides knotted. Hell fire! One of them was lying, and he had a pretty good idea which one.

Glancing up at the gathering clouds, Elizabeth stood up and rubbed her aching back, but pleased that she had managed to snip the grass down to the soil with some scissors she had had in her portmanteau. The now damp piece of linen for her knees, was still on the ground, and rain-drops were now skimming the rim of her bonnet. It was too bad, because she had hoped to clear all the grass and dig over a little of the soil on Mary-Beth's grave on this visit in preparation for planting. She sighed and closed her eyes.

'Miss Chetwode?'

Elizabeth spun round.

'Mr. Smith-Jacobsen?'

How long had he been there?

As he inclined his head and doffed a shining steeple hat, she realised he was dressed in the height of fashion rather than the country clothes she saw him in before. A pale blue cravat frothed from the neck of an exquisitely-cut grey thigh-length coat. His grey and yellow dog-tooth check breeches tapered neatly into glossy brown boots.

'Forgive me for startling you,' he said glancing down to the grave, 'may I be of assistance?'

Elizabeth blinked up into his intense blue eyes. He was doing it again. Spearing her with his gaze as if he knew her.

'No, I have just finished for today, but I thank you.' As he arched questioning brows she added hastily, 'I can see everything from what will be my window. This,' she explained, drawing his attention to the scissor-cut grass, 'looked like a wild patch, from above.'

The fair skin on his brow creased. 'From above?'

Elizabeth realised he did not know of their imminent move.

'We are moving into Nimbus Folly.' She indicated the house beyond the low stone cemetery walls.

He swivelled round, drew a breath and swivelled back to her.

'That place is derelict. It is totally unfit to live in.'

He noticed her surprise and the flawless skin above his fair brows creased. 'Forgive me for being so direct Miss Chetwode but to my mind that place needs tearing down.'

He bent down to retrieve the small piece of linen she had kneeled on. As his hand brushed the little stone cross, Elizabeth saw him flinch.

'Mary-Beth?' He sounded mildly dazed.

Rising with concentrated grace, he then studied her for a few moments. His fair cheeks had marbled pink. Intense blue eyes scanned her face.

'Miss Elizabeth Chetwode,' he enunciated slowly, 'does this tomb mean anything to you?'

Puzzled, Elizabeth stared at him. 'No. It is just that I noticed it was unkempt and decided to,' her voice trailed, what right had she to interfere? At the same time, a peculiarly intense compassion laced through her. Nobody, irrespective of birth, crime, or anything, deserved cutting off so completely. No person deserved such shoddy treatment as to have their grave ignored while all the others were so cared for. Drawing in a deep sighing breath, she said, 'To tidy it up a little. The others are neat; why should this one be any different?'

He blinked down at her. 'Why indeed?' he replied softly. 'However, I do not think it fitting that you should do it, Miss Chetwode.'

Something she did not understand flared within her. 'I can assure you that it is most fitting Mr. Smith-Jacobsen.'

She noticed an admiring smile cut through his astonishment at her tone. 'I see you have compassion as well as spirit Miss Chetwode.'

He gently took her bare, somewhat grimy hands in his, raised them and pressed his lips to her fingers.

'Commendable qualities,' he murmured, 'rare and commendable qualities,' he added in a strange faraway tone. 'However, surely you have done enough for today?' He glanced upwards. 'There is a storm gathering and Miss Wybrow may be wondering where you are.'

The relief at not being pressed further, caused her return blithely, 'Oh, there is no need for me to return yet, Mr. Smith-Jacobsen. Lord Bauval has taken Mrs and Miss Wybrow out in his carriage and I may to return to Wybrow House at my leisure.'

He frowned. 'You are completely alone?'

She nodded. 'Yes.'

Why was he looking at her like that?

'Then I shall accompany you.' A sudden streak of lightening wrenched through the air. 'Quickly!' He spun her round and without waiting for any assent, hurried her out of the cemetery as the rain began pelting them. Wheeling towards her, he unbuttoned his coat and dragged her under it.

Elizabeth struggled. This was most unseemly.

'No,' she managed before he enveloped her completely. 'There is a tree on the other side of the path.'

Her feet barely skimmed the ground as he wrapped one arm securely round her waist.

'A tree? Surely your studies taught that you must never shelter under a tree in a storm?'

Her studies? How did he know about her studies? Did he know about her Mama, and her father too? Did he know how Min, Mama's closest friend and their larger than life, next-door neighbour who had managed to stop her father from attacking her and trying to force the envelope Mama had told her to keep safe, from her secret pocket? Did he know about Mama's very last words as she looked at the painting of the two identical little girls above the fireplace, and whispered, 'Forgive, Mary-Beth, please, I beg you; *forgive.*'

No. Of course, he did not. She was being foolish. He could not possibly know about her past.

'Here,' Henry whisked her off the path and round some shrubs onto an overgrown track. Seconds later she was bustled through an out-of-the-way rickety door into an immediate but rather dreary refuge.

He let her go. 'The Belvedere, my dear,' he smiled at his pun. 'Not perfect, but it will keep us safe and dry until the worst is over.'

Elizabeth blinked trying to see through the gloom. They were in a summer house of sorts.

A sudden burst of thunder made her jump, and in the same instant Mr. Smith-Jacobsen flung his arms round her waist.

'Mr. Smith- Jacobsen,' she gasped. 'Please let go.'

He did.

'Forgive me Miss Chetwode, but most young ladies are afraid of thunder. I only thought-,'

As lightening skittered above them, the whole area flashed with brilliant silver light, exposing a fabulous silhouetted mural on the wall in front of her.

'I had no idea Mrs Wybrow ordered this to be refurbished too.' Elizabeth exclaimed, with awed shock as she moved towards the bright colours. 'It is-,'

There was another thunderclap as she made her way to a gilt bench in front of the mural.

'I wonder who painted these beautiful flowers and birds?' She wheeled round to Mr. Smith Jacobson.

Mr. Smith Jacobson was completely motionless. Rigid, and tense as if frozen. His expression was taut and troubled.

'Have I done something wrong Mr. Smith-Jacobsen?'

She shuddered. Had someone just walked over her grave? She thought of the tomb of the other Mary-Beth.

Suddenly, his demeanour changed and he appeared to relax as he gave a wry chuckle. 'Miss Chetwode, please continue with your observation. You started by saying, 'It is.'

Not wanting to upset him further, Elizabeth drew a breath.

'Forgive me, I was tactless.'

'Not at all," Smith Jacobson drawled, 'I am interested in your opinion.'

'You brought me here to give an opinion on the mural?'

The wooden floor creaked slightly as he shifted. 'Indeed not. I brought you in here to protect you from the inclement weather.'

All sorts of questions ran through her mind at once. How did he know about this place? What was he doing on Bauval land? Why was he in the cemetery?

He tilted slightly forward, removed his hat and put it gently down on a curved-legged gilt table she hadn't noticed until then.

He stepped towards her. 'Miss Chetwode, I believe I have confused, or even frightened you. Pray forgive me. Although I should like to hear your views on the mural, my only intention was to protect you.' He took her hands in his and smiled down at her.

Another man offering to be her champion? 'Protect me from what?'

He drew her onto the gilt bench and sat beside her. 'From the storm Miss Chetwode.'

James felt an anguished apprehension at the barrage of rain following the lightening. Not that he was afraid of storms, but his Boadicea was out there, helpless against the elements. If she knew the area, she could take refuge. But where? She knew only him and the Wybrows. His heart seemed to skid to a halt, before bouncing frantically into action again. What if she had returned to Wybrow House? Worry and concern for her welfare caused bile to rise into his throat which he swallowed back. She might encounter something far worse than a storm.

His mind fought for a solution. They had not quite reached the fork in the road that led to the village, so they still had a chance to turn back. But if she was at Nimbus Folly, she would have to make her way back through open fields, or go the long way, all the way around the outskirts of Bauval Park. Either way she risked a thorough soaking.

Then arrive home to what? A licentious welcome from her employer? He mustered his flustered thoughts.

Pamela squealed as a thunder-clap crashed above them.

'Three,' she squeaked as it grumbled away.

'Nonsense,' Mrs Wybrow snapped, 'I counted fifteen.'

Another fork of lightening streaked into the carriage.

'Two,' Pamela squealed at the ensuing thunder-clap.

James made up his mind. Tapping smartly on the hatch, he called. 'Round the estate and though Rector's Gate if you please Mills.'

'A slight change of plan,' he then announced pleasantly concealing all alarm. 'Imposed on us by the weather.' With luck Miss Chetwode might be at Nimbus Folly, rather than on her way home, so he could invite her to join them.

Mrs Wybrow appeared to reel a little. 'There is no need to inconvenience yourself. We are more than content to go around the village.' She glanced at Pamela. 'Are we not Pamela?'

Pamela blanched. 'But Mama, what about Miss Chetwode?'

Mrs Wybrow leaned over to the window, 'I believe it is easing off already. Look over there, the sky is quite clear.'

'That may be,' James agreed smoothly. 'However, we cannot be too careful. Although the horses are sturdy, I should not like to test them beyond their endurance.' His smile was amiable. His insides however were dancing like jigging skeleton bones.

Pamela visibly relaxed. Mrs Wybrow, though, was trying valiantly to hide her dismay.

Elizabeth felt foolish. Whatever had got into her? Mr. Smith-Jacobsen must think her a ninny. Of course, he only brought her into the summerhouse to protect her from the storm. Why did she question him?

He was now sitting beside her, staring intently at the mural.

He turned to her, 'Do you paint?' he asked pleasantly.

'A little.'

His mouth slanted upwards. 'Then perhaps,' he motioned back to the wall, 'you could add something to the scene sometime?'

'How could possibly add to such exquisite beauty?' she gasped. 'I will spoil it.'

He sighed heavily. 'Then it will remain unfinished until it decays all together.'

'Surely it can be renovated?'

As he shook his head, his fair hair glinted as it caught the tiny shafts of light, reminding

Elizabeth where she was, and why. She glanced round at the grime-covered windows, 'It is clearing up, I had better be on my way.'

'Miss Chetwode,' he took her hands in his and held them so close to his chest that she felt his heart beating. 'Miss Elizabeth Chetwode, a rose with such a name that smells as sweet-'

'-Any other name Mr. Smith-Jacobsen, and *would* smell as sweet.'

He gave a slow smile. 'Of course, Miss Chetwode, but there are exceptions to very rule, are there not?'

As she frowned up at him his gaiety faded, his face darkened and he whispered so softly she only just caught it.

'Oh Mary-Beth my sweet delicate angel.'

Although Elizabeth's stomach lurched, a greater strength forced her to remain calm. He knew her as Mary-Beth? She fought hard to recall a Henry Smith-Jacobsen and winced as the memories of childhood washed over her again. He must have seen her with Lady Bucklow at some time. Had he been introduced to her? How and when did she become his angel? She must not panic. Gathering her fleeing senses, she took a breath and hoped for the best.

'I do not understand Mr. Smith-Jacobsen.'

The intense blue eyes blinked as if he just remembered where he was. His brows arced. He ran an elegantly gloved hand through his blonde hair.

'Forgive me,' he murmured, 'I did not mean to alarm you. Come,' he suddenly rose and pulled her gently up. 'Let me tell you about the mural.'

Without letting go of her hand he moved the bench and drew her behind it so that they were close to the mural.

Tracing a finger over the painting, he sighed, 'See this peacock?'

'Yes. He is very beautiful.'

'And proud.' Smith-Jacobsen's elegant finger trailed downwards to a pair of harmless grey doves nestling together. 'Too proud to notice these two little lovebirds snuggling together.' His voice dropped lower. 'Little lovebirds who loved each other, yet were doomed from the beginning.'

Chapter Seven

Fear caused James to silently curse. Now stationary, they were directly outside the iron and wood Rector's Gate, and Mills was taking a devil of a long time tinkering with the lock.

The coach door opened.

'Milord, the gates are locked from the inside. We will have to go all the way round.'

No. Miss Chetwode might have left by then.

With a swift apology to the Mrs and Miss Wybrow, James sprang from the squabs, and jumped down onto the overgrown track.

'If you give me a leg up Mills, I can climb over, unlock it from the other side and open them.'

Mills, muttered something incomprehensible, but cupped his arms so James could haul himself through.

The women heard scraping and then a laboured heave from the coachman, then a soft thump.

'What a lot of fuss about nothing,' Mrs Wybrow sniffed. 'To think that a mere companion merits this ruckus. I am sure she will already be on her way back to Wybrow House now.'

Several squeaks and grinds later, the hinges of the huge gates groaned open.

James then sprang back inside the coach and settled on the squabs.

'Success,' he beamed. 'I was not sure I would be able manage to do it.'

The carriage wobbled as Mills climbed up behind the ditching-board and took up the reins.

James tapped his hand on the side of the carriage behind him and they moved off. 'I am relieved, because it is so much quicker this way.'

As the coach rumbled through the entrance, Pamela leaned out the coach window.

'Look through the trees. Our soon-to-be home!' She drew back inside again.

'Indeed Miss Wybrow,' James smiled, still happy that they had managed to open Rector's Gate. 'This is the gate nearest to it. We have made it in good time I think.' He threw Mrs Wybrow a glance.

Her cheeks coloured in response.

'Mama,' Pamela turned to her mother, 'we have our own entrance. How wonderful.'

Mrs Wybrow forced a smile, then shuddered.

James frowned. 'Are you quite well Mrs Wybrow?'

'I, I am thinking of-of Miss Chetwode,' she stuttered, 'maybe she took shelter in-instead of going straight back.'

Her remark curbed his happiness, and his terse, 'I certainly hope so, Mrs Wybrow,' silenced her.

Elizabeth looked over and out of the grimy windows. 'I think the storm has eased.' She turned to Mr. Smith-Jacobsen who was still gazing at the wall. 'I really should be on my way.'

Engrossed in the mural, he remained silent. His shadowed face roving slowly over it then eventually resting on the two grey doves. A gloved finger traced each one over and over again.

Continuing the caressing motion, he sighed. 'Do you believe there is only one true mate for every person Miss Chetwode?'

'I have never ever thought about it, Mr. Smith-Jacobsen.'

He brought his head round and down so that his face looked directly into hers. 'One true love for each man and each woman?'

Elizabeth blinked up at him. 'I am not sure.'

The intensity of his gaze puzzled her. 'I believe in love,' she added more firmly than she intended. 'However, whether there is only one true love for each one of us,' she gave an elegant shrug. 'I cannot say.'

Suddenly and quite unexpectedly, the immense figure of James Bauval came to mind.

Her one true love.

She stifled an uncertain chuckle. Had the storm addled her wits?

Quickly collecting her scattering senses, she forced a smile.

'I really must be going Mr. Smith-Jacobsen.' She stooped to pick up her reticule from the bench. 'Thank-you for bringing me in here and out of the storm.' She paused, 'The mural is exquisite. I do hope Mrs Wybrow will let us use this summerhouse.'

He wheeled to her. 'Us, Miss Chetwode?'

She stared up at him for a split second. 'Miss Wybrow and I.'

He gave a forced brittle laugh. 'Of course. Forgive me Miss Chetwode. The past,' he threw his arms apart, 'comes back to haunt us does it not?'

Elizabeth's stomach lurched. Quickly placing the ribbon handles of her bag over her arm and reaching for the gloves, she pivoted to the entrance. She could not let him see her face. One look would tell him just how her past haunted her.

Without waiting for any more help, she pulled the ramshackle door open.

'Thank-you again Mr. Smith-Jacobsen,' she muttered before slipping out into the overgrown garden. 'You have been most kind.' Without waiting for a response, she closed the door, and keeping her eyes down on the overgrown path, hurried off. With a deft thrust, she side-stepped the rickety gate, skirted the glistening shrubs and slammed straight into a man.

'Miss Chetwode,' James, so relieved to see her, instantly wrapped his arms round her. 'Thank-goodness you are safe.'

The richness of his voice sent warmth cascading through her.

Even so, she was not going to make the same mistake with him as she did with Mr. Smith-Jacobsen.

Her chin shot back and up to meet his concerned gaze. 'Safe? I am not afraid of storms.'

Her raspberries and cream skin glowed. Her chrysolite irises sparked fire. Her deliciously full lips parted ready for a quick-fire retort to anything he might say. But James never gave her the chance. He used that second to put his mouth gently over hers.

His lips sent fluttering velvety butterflies sashaying through her body, leaving a silky heat in their wake.

As she returned his kiss, his insides flamed. As the flame spread, nothing else mattered. The desire to draw her closer overrode everything else.

Elizabeth was floating. She was heavy, yet weightless. Letting her reticule and gloves fall to the ground, her hands began to slide up over his broad shoulders, and to his face without her knowledge.

It was her fingers feathering his skin that finally bought him round to what he was doing. He dragged his mouth away.

Elizabeth, still dazed because of the effect his kiss had and was still having on her, could only gaze up at him. His taut skin seemed to be at odds with the gentleness in his eyes and the tender swell of his lips.

Slowly moving her hand, she delicately traced the outline of his bottom lip with her fingers.

In spite of nearly sagging with pleasure at that simple innocent touch, James concentrated on her face. Her chrysolite irises, no longer blazing with fury, had pooled to velvet softness. Her sleek caramel lashes fluttered and flickered against her flawless skin.

Suddenly as if coming out of a trance, her eyes widened and her lips parted sending wisps of warm breath through his white cravat.

'No.'

The whispered plea and racked expression brought him rapidly to his senses.

She now pushed weakly at his burgundy jacket.

'Let me go.'

The kiss that had fired them both was forgotten as his eyes roved her face, a chilling disquiet crept through him, and he inwardly shivered. How could she sometimes, look so like his late second cousin, yet be so different in character?

His heart lurched and writhed with pain.

Was she a wraith, a ghost come back to torment him?

Without warning she rapidly withdrew; her arms snapped to her sides as she fixed him with the school marm stare he found so enchanting the day they met.

'Lord Bauval,' she scolded, 'that was ungentlemanly!'

Every part of him soared with elated delight. There was nothing ethereal or wraith-like about Miss Elizabeth Chetwode now. Her ire made her human, vibrant, and alive. It thrilled, beguiled, and bewitched him.

It lit his soul and brightened his heart.

Elizabeth immediately noticed his somewhat amused expression.

Her whole being had turned to weightless floating silk, and now he was laughing at her! She was such a fool to allow herself to get so carried away by his games.

Moreover, she must not let him see the effect he had on her.

She took a swift governing breath.

'You may be lord and master of the village, but that does not give you the right to take liberties with me.' She thrust her chin round. 'I have to go. Now if you will excuse me.' In spite of her fury, the silky weightless feeling still glided through her. She did not seem to be able to control it. Her head reeled and her skin still tingled.

Bending to retrieve her reticule and gloves, she then stood upright, moved aside and brushed past him.

The wavy 'm' of his top lip stretched into a lazy smile. 'And if I do not excuse you?' he drawled.

The quizzical arc of one blue-black brow added fuel to her accelerating blaze. He was not taking this seriously. Being lord and landowner did nothing for his sense of propriety. Instead of respecting his position as a gentleman, he obviously used it for his own ends.

Lady Bucklow had warned her of such men. Philanderers who abused their position in society to prey on innocent women. Never in a million years did she expect to be the recipient of such behaviour.

Men like that usually exploited women for their own ends. Fabulously wealthy heiresses for instance, or simple employees who could not disobey.

The floating silk twisted into knots.

And that was all she was to him. A simple employee to amuse himself with.

'Then you are nothing but a philanderer sir.'

A philanderer? Heat pulsated through him as her eyes sparked prisms of gold fury. Did she know how lovely and utterly irresistible she was?

Her scowling brought out the rascal in him and with it a desire to keep their lively *tete a tete* going.

'A philanderer? Such harsh judgement Miss Chetwode, and,' his lower lip rounded to a sensuous curve, 'so undeserved.'

His rich yet soft voice tempered her anger. Perhaps she was being too hard on him, especially after all his help.

She peered up into onyx eyes flecked with a silver.

'Forgive me,' she murmured.

He had expected a spirited school marm set-down, not a back-down. Suddenly she looked vulnerable and fragile again and he was filled with the overwhelming need to protect and nurture this audacious, delightful, woman.

For the rest of his life.

The thought jolted him into remembering his manners.

'No,' he mouthed softly. 'Forgive me.' He gave a rueful smile. 'Not doing too well as a champion, am I? Come,' he placed his arm gently through hers. 'Miss Wybrow and her mama are waiting in my carriage for us.'

They had already rounded the tower before Elizabeth had a chance to take stock of the situation.

'I have completed my errand, so I am to go back to Wybrow House.'

James tensed. 'Miss Wybrow is extremely worried about you being out in the storm.' He noticed then, that despite the downpour, she was hardly wet at all. He cast his head backwards. 'The summerhouse, very resourceful. I suspect you found shelter there,' he smiled.

There was no hint of query in his voice, even so, Elizabeth could not look up at him.

As they reached the carriage Mrs Wybrow's furious face swung from the carriage window. 'Miss Chetwode, I thought you were to go straight back to Wybrow House!'

Elizabeth's jaw dropped. She had not been ordered to go straight back. Mrs Wybrow had told her to return at her leisure.

Already somewhat overset, Elizabeth's voice vibrated. 'I thought I was to return at leisure?'

'Certainly not. Mr. Wybrow is expecting you. Whatever will he do-?' Mrs Wybrow stopped short, 'think? He will be beside himself,' she gulped. 'With worry.'

James glanced at Mrs Wybrow then at Elizabeth.

The confusion on Elizabeth's face told him that she was bewildered by the anger. Her flittering stilled. James watched with alert concern as her face paled. Her elegant hands knotted. Golden lashes, diamond studded with minute specks of rain, fluttered as she blinked. 'Mr. Wybrow? But,' Elizabeth's voice trailed.

In that instant, James saw more than confusion. He saw aversion and fear. The need to protect her triumphed over his anger at Mrs Wybrow.

'I suspect,' he grated, surprising himself at his composure while feeling extremely discomposed, 'the storm caused Miss Chetwode to take shelter.' He inhaled with relief, 'A sensible decision.' He drew a firm breath. 'Thankfully we met just as she started back home.'

As he turned a bland face to hers, Elizabeth wondered if James understood her suspicions? Mrs Wybrow had not mentioned that Mr. Wybrow was going to be home. The familiar chill crept down her spine and seeped into her limbs. Mr. Wybrow at home in the middle of the afternoon? Alone? Why? She darted a look at Mrs Wybrow and her insides plummeted. Her head swam. No, it was not possible. She was being ridiculous. With a concerted effort she pulled herself together. Mrs Wybrow could not have any idea of her husband's vile inclinations. If she had, she surely would not be encouraging them?

Gathering her scattered thoughts, she managed to nod.

'Yes,' she agreed, ignoring the churning in the stomach, 'I encountered Lord Bauval just as I started my walk back.'

Pamela's face pushed alongside her mother's, at the carriage window. 'Miss Chetwode, thank goodness you are safe.'

The fruited hat on Mrs Wybrow's head wobbled.

'Pamela,' she hissed, 'mind your manners.'

James took immediate advantage of the diversion by swiftly taking Miss Chetwode's arm and hurrying her round the back of the carriage.

'My housekeeper will be wondering where we are.'

Elizabeth attempted to pull her arm free. 'I am not invited.'

His abrupt halt caused her to swing to face him. 'Not invited?' Black irises sparked fury. 'Whatever gave you that idea?' Tiny lines under his eyes darkened. 'You think I would ask Miss Wybrow and her mother and not include you?'

He was miffed. The wavy 'm' of his top lip planed. The strong muscles of his arm hardened over the softness of hers.

He gave a faint humourless laugh.

'Miss Chetwode, I was extremely disappointed to discover you were not accompanying us.' His heart skipped a beat. While it was true that he had organised the outing to keep Mrs Wybrow from disturbing the workforce at Nimbus Folly, it was a way of keeping his eye on Miss Chetwode too.

As ironic humour crept into his voice, and Elizabeth watched, fascinated as a smile played across his mouth, slanting his whole face into a grin.

'Extremely disappointed,' he finished on a husky, evocative note.

Her chrysolite irises dilated. Her mouth pursed. A heat engulfed him. Marshalling his thoughts, he firmly reminded himself why he brought her round this way. He let go of her arm and turned her round to face him. 'If you ever need me,' he whispered urgently, 'come to the house. Whatever the time, whatever the circumstances. You will be moving into The Folly soon, and I shall tell my staff to admit you at any time from now on.'

He saw Mills attending to the steps to the open door of the carriage. 'Thank-you, Mills. Miss Chetwode will be accompanying us.'

****

James paced his shadowed study floor in apprehension. He had made up his mind after observing his three guests earlier, as they ate cakes and drank tea.

Mrs Wybrow obvious agitation had caused her to be caustic to Pamela and Miss Chetwode throughout. Miss Chetwode had maintained an air of calm, but behind those chrysolite irises, he detected anxiety.

Pamela however kept a cheerful patter going for them all to respond to.

It was Pamela who mentioned them all being invited to the Smith-Jacobsen's soirée that was being held in a few days. Mrs Wybrow disdainfully informed her daughter that it was only the Wybrow family who were invited and that mere companions were not included.

Pamela's protest was met with a scathing put-down.

Mrs Wybrow's hands had fluttered about, and every so often she sighed, made a murmured reference to poor Mr. Wybrow, shook her head, then made an effort to involve herself in conversation.

It was then that the idea came to him.

James, who initially had had no intention whatsoever of going to the Smith-Jacobsens', politely excused himself, sought out Vance and gave him two very specific instructions. Once that was done, he returned to his guests with apologies for his brief absence.

Vance appeared an hour to later to say that one particular message, the most important one, was received and promptly accepted.

So, where the devil was Wybrow?

When James escorted the trio home, he expected Wybrow to be there, ready and waiting for him as instructed, but Wybrow was not at home, and nobody knew where he was and what time he left Wybrow House.

Had Wybrow ignored the instructions on purpose? The breath stuck in Bauval's throat at the thought of Wybrow going anywhere near Miss Chetwode. He had a mind to ride back over there immediately, and carry her off.

The glow of an oil-lamp flickered as he paced the floor.

A fierce wind threw lashing rain against the dark study window. For although the storm abated hours ago, the rain had continued all afternoon and into the evening.

The knock at his study door brought his shoulders up with a jolt. At last.

Vance entered. 'Are you ready to dine my lord?'

James veered to him. 'No, Vance. Are you sure Wybrow understood my message?'

Vance remained unruffled. 'Yes, milord.'

'Then where the devil is, he?'

Ignoring the inquiry in his butler's face James pressed on, 'Very well, I shall go and look for him. I will ride my hunter. I shall not waste time changing. All I need is my old oil skin cape and sturdy boots.'

'Very good milord.'

Once at the stables, and refusing Mills offer of company, he set off with the wind and rain against him.

The open fields were not viable in this weather, and the front of the house too long a way round, so James settled for Rector's Gate instead. The oddity of having not used the old gate for an age, to going through it a third time in one day, crossed his mind.

Was it some kind of omen? He shook his head at his foolishness, and set off.

****

Walter Wybrow slumped drunkenly back into a dust-blanketed armchair causing his single flickering candle to send eerie shadows onto the newly papered walls of Nimbus Folly. It was freezing. The least the lord of the estate could have done was to have a fire ready, even if he was not here to greet him. Annoyed, Wybrow had gone down to the cellar where he knew a dusty collection of flagons full of old wine were stored. Having sampled them all he returned to where he now sat, swinging one nearly-empty flagon loosely in his hand over the side of the chair.

He was sozzled, but then he deserved some recompense for the acute disappointment he endured this afternoon.

Miss Chetwode had evaded him. If he did not get his way with her soon, he would go crazy. And where would they all be then? Him in the asylum, and his wife and daughter fending for themselves? He gave a disgruntled snarl. It was his right. She was only a hireling like the other. His for taking.

James bowed his head against the elements and passing Nimbus Folly saw an unusual glimmer of light through a slightly open door. Curious, he reined to a halt, slipped off his mount, placed the reins over a post and hurried across the threshold towards the glimmer.

Hearing a moan coming from somewhere inside, James swung his cape behind him and thrust through the first interior door he saw.

He hated this place. Always had, ever since Mary-Beth's death.

What a horribly untimely thought.

Quickly marshalling his senses, he strained into the darkness, realised the first room was empty so barrelled out.

The moaning changed to a slurred monologue and James suddenly found himself in the doorway of a dimly lit room, staring at the deeply intoxicated, maudlin Walter Wybrow lolling dazedly in a covered armchair. The sight of him disgusted James. His first thought was to leave. The thought of Wybrow coming round enough to make his inebriated way back home, however stopped him. Judging from the state Wybrow was in, it appeared he had been waiting at Nimbus Folly all this time, and had made himself cosy in the meantime.

The problem was what to do now. His proposition would go right over Wybrow's head.

Despite Bauval's sudden appearance, Wybrow's drunken monologue continued, and James wondered if his guest had even noticed him. Moving silently, he settled himself into a covered chair opposite. He could sit it out all night if he had to. Wybrow would come out of his inebriated state some time and James, intended being there when he did.

'She was a nobody,' Walter suddenly slurred.

James rocked forward.

Walter Wybrow jerked one eye-lid up to stare foggily at the cape-outlined shadow opposite.

'Have a drink.' He brought the flagon up and with a wavering arm offered it to James.

James recoiled.

Wybrow, although drunk recognised the gesture. 'Suit yourself watchman.' Raising the flagon to his mouth, he drank. The opened eye closed as he then slung it, empty, onto the floor. His head flopped over the chair back. 'His new wife got the lot. I went to law. Futile. Watertight Will.' His head rolled forward; his tiny eyes blinked open. 'Dish-inherited by a twenty-year old stepmother.' Wybrow's head swayed. 'The gold-digging witch.'

Under normal circumstances, boozed maudlin ramblings did not interest James, but in this one did. He inclined his head and Wybrow continued.

'Told Mrs Wybrow I would leave her.' He hiccupped, and rolled his eyes. 'She could not do without me. Promish-ed everything. Pamela's inheritance and dowry. Her brother's annuity.'

He guffawed.

'Anything.'

His mouth slewed to derision. 'No questions ash-ked.'

Wybrow then managed to lean forward to look James directly eye. 'To have all the perks ash-ociated with a gentleman of means.'

His mouth slid into a lewd grin. 'Chetwode's only the hired help, and I mean to get my money's worth.' He tapped his nose. 'If you-sh take my meaning?'

Wybrow's head began to nod and roll back. Spittle glittered disgustingly round his lips. Any minute now he would be out cold.

With heroic self-control James resisted the urge to leap up and throttle him.

Instead, he calmly rose, hoisted Wybrow to his feet, hauled him effortlessly through the house and out into the biting rain.

At the sudden rush of cold air Wybrow tried to wriggle free, but his body clumsily drunk, prevented him from being really difficult. James easily pulled him over to the thoroughbred, pitched him across the saddle, secured his feet into the stirrups, and set off for Bauval Park. The thoroughbred, unused to such inferior horsemanship skittered slightly and James was further annoyed at Wybrow for upsetting such a fine animal.

Once back at the stables, Mills held the lantern up to get better view of the man slumped over his master's finest horse while James gave him lengthy instructions.

'Aye, milord.'

Letting go of Wybrow, James handed over the reins. 'I know you will carry out my orders completely.' He drew a breath. 'Not my usual style but, in this instance, I must follow my intuition.'

'Doubt if 'e'll be any the wiser come mornin' milord.'

Curbing his distaste, a droll smile crossed James's mouth. 'No, but Theo will.'

With that, he left Mills temporarily in charge and hurried off to the house to do his part.

He had two letters to write. One to Theo, and one informing Mrs Wybrow that her husband would be away on Bauval business for a few days. Both letters were brief. His note to Theo Kenelley merely asked that Wybrow be a guest in his home for a while.

An hour later and with great satisfaction, James watched the late coach disappear from Stranton Corner into the night towards London. With the satisfaction of a job well done, he turned his mount homeward.

****

Elizabeth had no idea which way to go next. The thick inky darkness covering the ground and sky meant she could not tell where one ended and the other began.

All she knew was that the main road was to one the side of the village, and that the hazards of being outside were preferable to the abhorrent Mr. Wybrow's intentions.

Before today she had managed to quell her silly imaginings. Now though, she knew what Mr. Wybrow planned. The worst of it was, that his wife seemed to condone his actions.

She shuddered and hugged the carpet-bag closer, before making the decision to turn right.

Having reached a sodden path, she now inched one foot forward and felt an absurd gratitude that she was on soft mud rather than wet grass. Mud meant she was on the track that would take her past the village to the main road. Once there, she would find somewhere to hide until the morning coach arrived.

Her brother Jamie would raise his brows. However, once he knew the circumstances, he would agree that she had done the right thing, and would insist on travelling to Wybrow House to retrieve her portmanteau.

Her insides churned, being a lone female, especially at night was dangerous. This ordeal, however, would only last until the morning coach stopped at Stranton Corner. Once on the coach, although travelling alone, she had the security of others around her.

Slipping and sliding over the track she tried to recall how long it had taken when she came this way with Pamela on their way to the village. Not this long surely?

The rain whipped so hard against her that the hood of her cape kept blowing off and had soaked her bonnet. Her skirt hems were drenched, and her boots were soused with mud. Yet nothing would deter her. The rigours of the midnight road seemed nothing in comparison to the vile expectations of Mr. Wybrow.

She was never going back. Nothing could make her change her mind. Nothing.

Lonely Pamela would have to come to terms with the defection she so dreaded. Elizabeth was heartsick. Poor Pamela.

Then there was Bauval.

A champion indeed? Go to him for help? Make him believe Mr. Wybrow was intent on evil? He was employing the man was he not? Mr. Wybrow had gained James Bauval's trust had he not? No, there was no justice to be had there.

Suddenly, she stopped dead. Her stomach began churning and her knees began wobbling. Her head spun. There was the other Mary-Beth's grave to consider.

Oh, was she mad? Had she lost her sanity? What was a simple name-sake to her? She was being too sensitive, too emotionally involved with someone who was nothing to her. Swallowing, she steadied herself and willed herself to move.

Nothing happened.

This was ridiculous. She was ridiculous. The inability to move was merely the result of her foolish frantic thoughts. All she needed to do was move one foot. She tried to pull her knee up but nothing happened.

Exasperation flexed through her.

Her reward for her moment of hesitation, was being entrenched in mud.

James squeezed the thoroughbred's ribs. A careful pace under the dire circumstances was one thing, but a skittish to-ing and fro-ing quite another. What he needed was a hot bath followed by a late supper, and a good brandy. Currently, all he had was an uncooperative mount, and a rain-drenched cloak.

Urging the horse on with a squeeze of his heels caused it to jump forward a fraction.

With silent frustration James dismounted and slowly led the beast forward. Thoroughbreds, a new breed, were highly-strung. There was probably a hedgehog on the path.

A piqued wail immediately changed his mind however, as a shadow materialised directly in front of him. He stared as the shadow struggled to move, and instantly knew who it was.

'Miss Chetwode?'

Elizabeth's eyes head swam with dizzying confusion.

It could not be him, could it?

A moment later, he was looming over her like a black, calamitous apparition.

She must not admit to being stuck in the mud. Yet, a tiny part of her was relieved.

'Go away,' she rasped. 'Leave me alone.'

His humourless chuckle sent chills cresting down her spine. She would not allow him to help her. Nor would she allow him to prevent her from leaving.

'Go away? How can I possibly go anywhere with you standing right in my way?'

Elizabeth might have stamped her foot, if she could. This was too bad. First the dreadful Mr. Wybrow, and now him.

'I am not doing nothing,' she informed him stiffly. 'I am trying to move.'

James, bit back a retort, because in spite of the spark of fire in her voice, she was obviously weary and heartsick. He also suspected she had a bag of belongings underneath her cape.

Then without warning, his mind changed tact. Had Wybrow had got to her after all?

Perhaps that was what the drunken ramblings were all about? Justification for his actions? Holding back his alarm, he modified his tone. 'Trying to move?' he echoed gently. 'Trying to move where?'

'Away from this horrid place,' Elizabeth spat out.

Every part of him surged with compassion.

'Away,' he asked softly, 'why?'

His tone filled her with a tenderness she could not explain, and she choked back a sob.

'You are leaving after all I have said Miss Chetwode? Did I not tell you to come to the house if in difficulty? This very afternoon to be exact?'

Her tiny sniff drew warm air away from him.

'Go away,' she repeated raggedly, 'you are nothing to me.' It was true. He was nothing to her, nor she to him. Their only connection as far as she was concerned was his astonishing similarity to her brother.

James Bauval, fourth earl of Alstoe's insides plummeted. 'Nothing to you?' he echoed. 'I hoped,' he continued softly, 'that you cared for me a little.' The rain wetted his lips as his throat dried.

'You see,' he breathed. "I want you to be my wife.'

Chapter Eight

His towering shadow created a barely visible outline, yet he felt potently immense. Her spine shivered with sparklets of light. How could he have this effect on her? She was so weak!

He smelled of fresh rain and night air, and something indefinable.

His wife?

Her whole being soared!

And instantly plummeted.

'How can I be your wife; you know nothing about me?' *I want to teach little ones. I want to watch them learn and grow. I cannot do that if I am a wife.*

Mud squelched as he moved closer. He felt the warmth of her breath on his cheek as he slowly lowered his face.

'I know enough to want to do this.'

Her arms still hugged the overnight bag under the cape and her feet still refused to move. However, his warmth and his nearness, only caused the sparklets of light to sparkle even more. They overrode all thoughts of remonstration.

She heard his soft low growl and almost dissolved at his solid strength as his arms slid round her. Instead of kissing her, as she thought he was about to do, he smoothly lifted her from the mud.

'You are perished, my darling,' he murmured, placing her gently on the grassy edge of the track. 'Why did you not come to me before,' he paused, 'this?'

Elizabeth, incensed that he was strong enough to free her, while she incapable of doing so, eradicated all the glittering feelings. Having to be rescued galled her beyond reason. His proposal, and his endearment slipped from her mind as she tipped her head up to stare at the shadowed outline of his face.

'What I choose to do is none of your concern, now please step aside so I may continue.'

His low amused laugh only added to her irrational anger and he immediately regretted it.

His hands still rested on her waist. 'Forgive me, I did not mean to upset you, but, I do not understand why you are here, under such circumstances.'

A dreadful thought struck him and he drew back in shock. 'You were not thrown out surely?'

Elizabeth's anger drained to bafflement. 'Thrown out?'

He used her moment of perplexity to quickly whisk her into his arms and onto the waiting animal behind him. Ignoring her breathless protest, he deftly mounted behind her and locking one arm round her waist under the cloth bag, clicked the horse into motion.

Elizabeth could not believe she had allowed this to happen, and her objections came out loud and clear. 'Leave me alone you brute!'

This time he did not regret the rumble of amusement rolling through him. She was impossible, stubborn to the core, but she had grit and mettle. How many females would take off in the night, and on such an awful one too, to face goodness-knows-what then declare their rescuer a brute? Where did she think she could go at this hour?

He curbed his humour enough to appeal to her common-sense.

'Miss Chetwode, I cannot possibly leave you out here alone to face the rigours of the night. You are cold and wet. What sort of a man would I be if I left you to your own devices? Anyhow,' he reasoned smoothly, 'you could not go anywhere without some help.'

He paused, waiting for an irate response. When none came, he resumed mildly, 'Trapped in mud is hardly progress is it?'

Elizabeth scowled. She hated his moderate tone and she hated that he was right. Furthermore, she hated at how safe she felt being close to him.

Even so, irrespective of anything he said, she could not go back to Wybrow House.

'Just how long were you stuck for, Miss Chetwode?'

His insides knotted as a thought came to him. 'Moreover, how did you think to escape the predicament?' His stomach lurched. Supposing he had taken the road instead of the track? Supposing, she had fallen and hurt herself too badly to move? What if she stumbled into the spinney beside the track? When would she have been found? Her rash behaviour scared him again as the worst scenario scorched through him.

What if he lost her too?

Masking his inward terror and with absolute self-control, he just about managed to calmly ask, 'Does anyone know you are out? Did you confide in Miss Wybrow for instance?'

'No,' came the side-on defiant reply.

Still quashing the terror, he took a deep breath, 'You took off completely unseen?'

Her profile never wavered. 'Yes.'

'How?'

The sure-footed Thorough glided through the inkiness, taking them by instinct over the lesser used paths toward Bauval Park.

'Over the veranda.'

James tightened his grip on her. 'What?'

Elizabeth winced. 'I had little choice my lord.'

He slackened his hold and resisting the urge to chuckle at the audacity of her tone, concentrated on his objections.

'You could have been severely hurt, killed even.'

When she remained silent, James wondered if she was mulling it over after all.

'How would Miss Wybrow feel if you were severely injured?' He answered the question himself. 'Beside herself with grief. Did you think of that Miss Chetwode?'

'I thought of everything and everyone.'

'Everyone?' he echoed. 'I doubt that Miss Chetwode, because if everyone came to mind then you would have remembered our conversation earlier in the day. Let me repeat what I said then.' He cleared his throat. 'If you ever need me, come to the house, whatever the hour, whatever the event.'

He felt her tense.

'Impossible,' she whispered.

'Why? Am I some kind of ogre?' Her elegant little shrug rattled him. 'I am not used to having my hospitality so completely overlooked Miss Chetwode.'

A tiny bandeau of moon appeared somewhere above them that sent filtering light to turn the raindrops dripping from her bonnet into winking diamonds. She needed warm dry clothes, a nourishing supper, and rest. 'You will catch your death,' he murmured into the rim of the rain-jewelled hat. 'Thank-goodness we are nearly home.'

Elizabeth's stomach roiled.

'I cannot go back there.'

She attempted to slide from the saddle, but the strength of his arm stopped her. 'My home Miss Chetwode, where,' he continued gently, 'you may have a hot supper and dry your clothes before we decide what to do next.'

'My reputation will be dashed if I stay.'

'But not dashed if you vanish into thin air?'

Elizabeth struggled to justify herself, 'I must leave immediately if I am to retain my honour.'

She could have kicked herself or bitten her tongue out. Now, he would demand an explanation, then, naturally brand her a liar.

A fury engulfed James.

So, the beast had approached her after all!

'You should have come to me,' he grated. 'Do you not trust me?'

This incensed her even more. What right had he to expect trust after his behaviour this very afternoon? What gave him the right to champion her cause then chasten her for non-compliance of the rules he made?

Her voiced dripped with loathing, 'You and Mr. Wybrow are as thick as thieves.'

Hell fires. He never gave his business dealings with her employer a thought beyond what it would do for her. Yet she saw it as a betrayal.

Elizabeth primed herself for his incredulity.

'I have sent him away on business. He has just boarded the nine-thirty coach. Our marriage will be announced before he returns. Then, as my fiancée he will have to show you considerable respect. In the meantime, we have to think of a way to explain your absence to Mrs Wybrow.'

Elizabeth missed the fiancée bit. Her mind was racing.

'Away?' She did not give him time to respond, 'I thought he was supposed to be your right-hand man on the estate? Your overseer, your accountant, your everything?'

'He is. However, I need him to conduct my affairs further afield from time to time. Right now, he is on his way to London.'

London?

She tensed. He sent the odious Mr. Wybrow to check up on her? How dare he pry into her life? How dare he assume the right of kin? She whisked her face round to challenge him.

The bandeau of molten moonlight lit one side of his body with a platinum glow. From the top of his hat to the visible part of his foot, he looked like a celestial ambassador.

A guardian angel.

Her guardian angel.

A cloud towed by the wind, suddenly blocked out the light again and the vision disappeared.

The instant change in her face from wrath to gentle sweetness took only a split second before being vanquished by the night. Yet that was all it took for his insides to start aching with tenderness, and more. Because, in that moment, he knew he loved her completely, and that the depth of his feeling had nothing to do with her likeness to his late second cousin. It had everything to do with her courage, her grit, and her character.

Instinctively, he drew her closer to him, and when she nestled with soft innocence against him, her unexpected soft compliance warmed his very soul. Soon her body relaxed and he knew she was asleep.

Elizabeth felt him ease her gently into his arms. A drowsy voice in the back of her mind niggled at her lack of decorum. Too worn-out to protest however, she let him carry her into the house without a murmur.

Vance immediately sent for a maid and by the time she arrived, James had removed Elizabeth's wet cape, the wool pelisse and drenched bonnet, had put the bag to one side, and was easing off her mud soused boots.

Elizabeth, now just awake enough to take in her surroundings, but not quite awake enough to do much about it, blinked. She felt absurd languishing on a chintz covered sofa with her various articles of clothing dripping over armchair-backs and her boots now being placed on a marbled hearth. She felt foolish that her escape ended in such an undignified way. At the same time relief seeped through her. What if he had not ridden along that track? Would she still be floundering in the mud? Even, if she had managed to extricate herself, what then? Would she have found shelter until morning? Would the post coach stop for a bedraggled woman at the side of the road? She felt foolish, yet for some reason, James was not behaving as if he thought her was foolish. Instead, he was treating her almost with veneration. Which was absurd in the circumstances.

Rising with easy grace, from the hearth where he had placed her boots, Lord Bauval addressed the maid.

'Miss Chetwode's clothes will have to be dried. She also needs something warm for supper. A bowl of broth perhaps?' He glanced at the dresser against the wall by the door. 'A little brandy would not come amiss either.'

Brandy?

The thought of touching alcohol reminded her of Westernbury and sent waves of revulsion through her. 'No!'

They both stared at her.

Elizabeth felt instantly ashamed at her vehement outburst. It was not as if anyone could force her to drink any brandy. A civil, 'no thank-you,' would have done. 'I do not like the taste.'

James quirked a brow. 'Warm chocolate then.'

The maid dipped a curtsey, gathered up all the wet clothing and hurried out.

The fire sparked orange, yellow, sending warmth over the room. Four oil sconces winked cheerily from the lavender walls.

Elizabeth noticed how the light made James' damp blue-black hair shine. His dark-grey, beautifully cut tail-coat sat perfectly over a pearl-coloured waistcoat. His trousers, a lighter grey than the coat, and, the latest in fashion tapered neatly into well-worn, but glistening boots. His cravat, not too flamboyantly tied, revealed a fine white silk shirt. His oilskin cape had protected him from the weather.

She sighed at all the luxury.

James looked down at her as her chrysolite eyes followed his every movement. He was relieved that she looked somewhat recovered. Her cape and wool pelisse had served their purpose well, because although the hem of her dress was moist, the rest appeared quite dry. All the same he decided not to risk being wrong. As soon as she had eaten, he would order her a hot bath and a complete set of dry clothes.

With smooth elegance he eased himself onto the sofa beside her. Then he gently took her clasped hands from her lap and enclosed them in his.

'It has been a difficult day for you, my love.' He squeezed slightly. 'I have not quite decided what to say to your employer, however,' his onyx irises flecked with silver, 'I shall have to think of something before I go and see her.' Elizabeth watched in fascination as the wavy 'm' on his top-lip planed to a conspiratorial smile. 'I could say you had a bad dream, walked over here in your sleep and that I found you, or,' his lips rounded to a sultry curve, 'I could tell her that we had an assignation.'

'Surely you do not need to mention anything at all? If Mr. Wybrow is not there, then I can return the same way I came.' She looked into his face and continued quickly, 'Tomorrow I can tell Mrs Wybrow that I have to leave.' She lowered her voice. 'Naturally I will not reveal my reason, but at least it will give me time to plan properly.'

James was disappointed that Elizabeth, obviously now thinking more rationally, completely missed the word 'assignation'. He wanted to see her eyes light with fire. He wanted to see that spark. He wanted a riposte. He wanted animation and vigour. He wanted proof that she was hale and hearty. This was not due to any perverse nature, it was because could not bear it she became ill. *Not like dear Mary-Beth. Please, not like dear Mary-Beth.*

His heart leapt as he moved closer.

His sudden shift in her direction was too swift for her to react to. She could only gasp as he rapidly let go of her hands before immediately pulling her against him.

'Have you not heard anything I said?' he grated huskily. 'You, my dear sweet Miss Chetwode do not need to go anywhere.'

One arm slipped behind her back pulling her tighter still. His free hand cupped her chin and drew it gently up.

A warm sensation washed over her as his onyx eyes turned to soft velvet. He made the softest of growls as his lower lip cushioned to a luxurious curve before lowering his chin to meet her mouth.

Her body tingled in anticipation of his touch. Every coherent thought vanished as her eyes fluttered closed and her mouth parted slightly.

Her faint sigh seemed to roar through him. He had never wanted anyone like this! None, of his paramours, or mistresses had this impact on him. Not ever.

Every primitive instinct called for free rein, yet stronger still, were the finer feelings that overruled all his body's demands. The need to cherish and protect her rose above all his own desires. One brief look into her upturned face told him of her sweet innocence. With extreme self-restraint, he allowed his mouth just to hover over the soft contours of her lips.

In spite of her warmth, she exuded a scent of fresh rain. He was tempted to glide the tip of his tongue under her top lip.

But, he did not.

Elizabeth felt utterly powerless to resist him.

She loved him.

The startling revelation sent waves of astonished shock through her. She had loved him from the moment he softened towards her, in the nearly harvested field, right in front of his workers. She had loved him from moment his expression changed from fury to gentleness, just before he prised, her stiff hands from her body then, asked her to forgive him for upsetting her.

A tremor ran the length of her spine.

She had done the very thing she vowed never to do.

She had fallen in love.

Her shiver strengthened him, and he drew back.

His rapid withdrawal made Elizabeth feel lost. Had she done something wrong? Had she let herself become so wantonly embroiled in his embrace that she now disgusted him? His onyx irises, that only a moment ago were velvet soft, now glittered down at her from underneath drawn brows. His lower lip, that only seconds ago was spellbindingly soft now clamped an upper lip that planed across his face in a flattened 'm'. The fingers on her chin loosened as he jerked his taut chin upwards.

He slid his arm away from her.

'You need to eat,' he growled.

Elizabeth's stomach immediately rumbled. She was starving, but over the last few weeks had become so accustomed to hunger again that it did not matter. The odd look on Bauval's face however, did.

'I must return to Wybrow House. No,' she raised her hand as he made to argue. 'I cannot stay here.' She glanced briefly up at him and wished she had not. His irises still glittered. 'It is not seemly.'

His raising of a sardonic brow made her insides flutter. 'Was it seemly to dash off into the night?'

Was she losing her mind? How had she managed to fall at the first fence of love? She was so weak.

'No,' she heard the tremor in her voice, 'but it was all I could think of in the circumstances.'

Suddenly her common-sense returned as rapidly as her mind had lost it. One moment, she was one her way up to her room next to Pamela's, and in the next, flinging herself over the veranda into the treacherous night.

So much had happened since then, and now it was time to return to reality.

'I am very grateful for your hospitality,' she ignored his ironic chuckle to continue, 'I can go back now Mr. Wybrow is away. However, I shall make arrangements to leave as soon as possible.'

'To become my wife.'

Her stomach churned at the injustice of having so foolishly fallen in love at all, never mind with an earl, and not be able to spend her life with him even though he seemed to want her. How could she tell him that her past, her circumstances, and, her capricious father, prevented any respectable union between them?

131

She looked up at him then, her face flickering with a mixture of emotion.

'I-I cannot marry you, Lord Bauval.'

Her caramel lashes fluttered, then flicked up. He saw her suppress a shiver. 'You know absolutely nothing about me.'

Then tell me, he wanted to ask, but her racked harrowed expression seared his soul and brought his memories flooding back.

'Oh, Mary-Beth,' his mind railed. 'What would you have me do?'

Elizabeth gave a yip of dismay. Her body tensed, her hair stood on end, and feeling she might vomit, she gulped.

Her shocked cry brought him back to the present.

'My love, what is it?' He attempted to move closer but she held her hands up to keep him away.

Elizabeth felt numb yet all her nerves shook.

'Miss Chetwode?'

She gulped again as a rush of nausea swept through her. Everything came and went in waves. Nothing seemed real.

Bile reached her throat, and coughing and spluttering, she swallowed it back, its bitterness searing her insides as it receded.

She dragged air into her lungs in great gulping breaths.

With a soft murmuring he drew her to him.

'There, there,' he crooned gently caressing her hair. 'It has been too much for you, my love. I shall not press you anymore tonight, but if it really means that much to you, I shall escort you to Wybrow House after you have eaten.'

Elizabeth breathed softly now, slowly coming to terms with the fact that he knew her childhood name. Her true name. His tortured *Mary-Beth, what would you have me do?* had momentarily startled her, now she must deal with it as calmly as she could.

She breathed a sigh of relief. How could he know of her past and be still willing to marry her?

No, she could not marry him. She vowed never to be at the mercy of any man. Never to be left for years, on end, scrimping to make ends meet, then have that same man, once handsome, honourable and sought after, to worm his way back and make such unreasonable demands that the rest of the family suffered too.

As they drank the soup at a small table Vance set up in the room they were already in, James smiled.

'This is known as the Pleasant room, as Mama says it is the most pleasant room in the house.'

Elizabeth looked at him. 'Your Mama lives here with you?'

'Indeed, she does, my love,' James seated directly opposite her, smiled. 'However, she is visiting London with her cousin Betty at present.'

Elizabeth felt the nearness of his calves tucked his under the table. The closeness both comforted and thrilled her. Yet, she must not think of marrying him. Besides the dowager countess would not like the idea of him marrying, a nobody.

'What is she like?' Elizabeth wondered aloud.

James looked up absently.

'She is a little faint hearted now and again, and given to fits megrims on occasions, but she is a survivor.' He chuckled lightly. 'If you call being woebegone, surviving that is?' He glanced up to see stark earnestness on her face. 'Oh, do not be alarmed, Betty has a heart of gold.'

Elizabeth frowned. 'You call your mother by her given name?'

James stopped eating for a moment. 'My mother? Goodness, no.'

Then it dawned on him.

'Ahh, Betty is not, my mother,' he continued, amused at his mistake and her confusion. 'My dear Mama is Levana. She and Betty are not only first cousins, they are inseparable friends too.'

He shook his head and chuckled softly.

It was obvious Lord Bauval cared for deeply for his mother, and his mother's cousin.

'Mama is certainly not a woebegone survivor. A more lion-hearted woman is impossible to find,' he paused a fraction, before adding enigmatically. 'Except for you.'

Elizabeth flushed. Was that a compliment? She decided it might be, after all he, spoke of the countess in such loving terms.

'And your Papa?' she pressed without stopping to think. 'Is he lion-hearted?'

James sighed, 'To tell the truth, I hardly remember my father. He died just before my third birthday.'

'I am so sorry.'

James sighed again. 'A sad business,' he continued ruefully, 'we have mining interests in the north; one day, he went down to inspect one of the shafts and the whole thing blew up.'

Elizabeth gaped at him, appalled. 'How dreadful. The countess must have been distraught.'

His onyx eyes flecked sliver. 'Yes, she was, but the tragedy drew us all so much closer.'

Elizabeth sighed inwardly. There was nothing she would love more than to have her dear Mama close.

'Lady Bauval sounds a truly wonderful woman,' she rallied despite that sudden inward sadness.

James smiled softly, not wanting to embarrass her.

'She is in fact, Lady Manse, but prefers Lady Levana. My father was a second son of an earl, but I inherited my title and all that goes with it, through my grandfather James Bauval, third earl of Alstoe.'

Not knowing what to say, Elizabeth nodded, and the conversation eventually turned how and when Elizabeth should return to Wybrow House.

Elizabeth was all for getting in over the veranda. James however, refused to consider it.

'We must think of something plausible,' he said gently. 'Staying here-.' Realising he was just about to break his silent promise not to mention marriage directly, he stopped. He did not want her almost fainting on him again. Goodness, she had given him a scare. Her stifled cry, her dilated pupils, the paling of her skin, and the sudden tensing of her body made him go hot and cold again just thinking about it.

He would go easy with her for the time being. She evidently needed some time to adjust to the idea of marrying him. That little fact irked him. Here he was, a man of considerable consequence, who by one means or another had dodged the snare of wedlock in spite of all the match-making done on his behalf, only to have this little Boadicea hedging.

What was the matter with her? She was completely alone and clearly had no means of support apart from that of being a drudge to a family of uncertain reputation. She had everything to gain from being his wife. Position, wealth, beautiful clothes, love. Love?

That was it. She expected *love*. He smiled to himself. Well, she had that all right. Now all he had to do was to prove to the delightfully upstanding Miss Chetwode that he loved her.

Elizabeth fixed him with an unblinking chrysolite gaze. 'There might be a way.'

Only complete self-control kept him from leaping up, grabbing her, and pulling her into his arms.

He arched a blue-black brow. 'There might?'

Her caramel lashes fluttered. 'Yes. I think I mentioned Lady Bucklow did I not?'

His forehead creased.

'On my way here for the very first time?'

A lazy smile slanted his cheeks. He hardly remembered what she said on that occasion, except that she came from London, that her Mama was dead and that she was going to the Wybrows. What he recalled in vivid detail, was the way she set on him. The colour of her hair in the dipping sunlight. The delectable swish of her chambray skirt. The way she fell on him.

'Lord Bauval?'

'Jemmy,' he reminded her huskily, and yes, I seem to recall

She shook her head to take her mind off the soft wavy 'm' of his top lip and the satin spellbinding mound of the bottom one. How could she have let her emotions get out of hand? How could she be so mindless as to have succumbed to this and to know if he took one move towards her, she would give herself whole-heartedly to him? She flipped her eyes closed to shut him out of sight, only to open them again the next instant.

'Lady Bucklow is my,' she paused and flushed under his fluid gaze.

'The first time we met,' he mouthed softly, 'we agreed on Jemmy.'

Elizabeth shivered inwardly as a deliciously peculiar feeling rolled down her spine. Molten heat, slowly gathering an unfamiliar momentum as it rolled. It gradually furled into her insides, and once there, seeped through every vein in her body.

She felt alive! She felt lost.

She dipped her chin so she did not have to look at him, yet good manners prevented her from shutting him out completely while she spoke. She raised only her lashes.

'Lady Bucklow,' she began, 'arranged for me to come to Rutland. She took me up,' she hurried on before his gaze melted her insides again. 'Taught me all I know.' Her whole body recoiled against the lie. 'No,' she suddenly threw out before she had time to think. Her head shot up to meet his eyes, 'That is not true I knew most of it already.'

Her chrysolite eyes looked directly into his face. Her hand slid to her mouth as if to silence some life-changing revelation. A wane of an oil lamp threw a golden halo over her hair sending the rest of her face into an austere shadow.

The next second James was engulfed in an emotion so fierce that every hair on his body stood up on end. Every nerve tingled. Blood pounded through his brain.

Because for that infinitesimal second, he saw not his lovely Boadicea, but Betty, his mother's cousin.

The lamp waxed bringing her back to full bloom and the image fragmented into tiny jigsaw pieces and vanished.

His look of complete bafflement gave Elizabeth courage.

'What I mean,' she rallied, 'is that Lady Bucklow educated me to the ways of Society.'

'I see,' he said mechanically, but all he saw in his head was something there, but invisible. Something imminent but obscure. Something he knew he should know, but did not.

An idea dredged up from somewhere in his subconscious surprised him. 'Then I have the perfect solution to get you back into Wybrow House tonight.

'I have yet to advise Mrs Wybrow that her husband is on his way to London. And there is also the matter of the Smith-Jacobsen's soirée.'

He watched the shadow cross her face on both counts and quelling a rising curiosity, forced himself into matter-of-fact tone. 'I will insist on escorting the three of you there myself.'

'But,'

He stopped her interruption with a slight of hand. 'Yes, I know what Mrs Wybrow said about you not going, but she can hardly refuse to let you be *my* guest.'

He had already refused the invitation to the soirée, but all he needed to do, was send a profuse apology saying his business had not taken as long as he expected and that he was delighted to be able to attend after all. A so-called abuse of his position, he knew, but only a minor one, and all for a good cause. 'Tonight,' he continued without urgency, 'I shall keep her talking,' he raised a brow, 'so, here's what I want you to do.'

Elizabeth slipped into the bedchamber, the room she thought never to set foot in again, still marvelling at Lord Bauval's daring plan.

They both knew that he would gain admittance to Wybrow House, and also knew that once in the withdrawing room, Mrs Wybrow would not leave until he did.

The next part that was a little more complicated. The part where Vance then knocked on the door to distract Dabbs away from the house long enough for Elizabeth to slip unseen into the house and creep upstairs.

Now, putting her things away, Elizabeth followed the rest of the instructions.

Ten minutes later, she was in bed staring sleepy-eyed at the sinuous shadows weaving mysterious patterns on the dull walls.

Chapter Nine

She heard her door creak. 'Mary-Beth.'

Elizabeth's eyes shot open.

'Mary-Beth wake up, Lord Bauval is downstairs and wishes to see you straight away.'

Elizabeth blinked against the flame of the candle Pamela held above her. 'Lord Bauval?' she echoed realising, that in spite of being determined not to do so, she had fallen asleep.

As Pamela moved closer, the flame whirled into a comet's tail then faded. 'He is downstairs in the small withdrawing-room.'

She spoke again without thinking, 'At this hour? What time is it?'

'It is only just past ten.' Pamela gave a soft tinkling laugh. 'You must have been asleep for hours. I do not know how you manage to fall asleep so early.'

Hours? Suddenly the whole thing, her flight and her evening with Jemmy, came back in a flash. Going downstairs was all part of the plan, but she really had drifted off.

James rose as his darling Miss Chetwode, and Pamela entered the candle-lit withdrawing-room. Only absolute self-control stopped him gawping at her. But his one outwardly cool glance was enough to set his senses thrumming.

Miss Chetwode, delightfully tousled and heavy-lidded, looked like a mythical goddess bathed in a halo of light. His heart lurched. *She really had fallen asleep*. His poor darling must be exhausted.

Excitement flared through him at the thought of her slumbering, beside him.

139

Where had that come from?

One or two golden waves feathered delicately pink cheeks, while the rest of her hair fell in sweet tumbles across the shoulders and down the back of her coral robe. Caramel lashes fluttered over large chrysolite irises fanning cheekbones and brows alternately. Her lips moistened by her tongue and delectably full from sleep rose and fell with innocent softness.

Perfect.

Her genuine drowsiness meant that there was nothing in her appearance or conduct to arouse suspicion about the true facts of the evening. Mrs Wybrow had no reason to suspect what Elizabeth had really been doing.

He inclined his head and smiled at Pamela.

'Thank-you Miss Wybrow.' He bowed again, 'Miss Chetwode,' he smiled, and resisting the urge to give her a secret wink, concentrated the plan instead. 'Please forgive this intrusion.'

Elizabeth managed a faint smile. How had she allowed herself to fall asleep? She must look a total mess. Her hair, although brushed just before she retired, would now look dishevelled. Her eye lids drooped every time she forced them upwards. Moreover, her lips, so recently wet with rain scraped every-time they came together.

'I came tonight for two reasons, Miss Chetwode.'

Two reasons?

'One,' he strolled to both their sides with sure lithe movements, to escort them gently to a sofa where all three of then sat, 'to inquire if I may escort the three of you to the Smith-Jacobsen soirée tomorrow afternoon. The second,' he glanced meaningfully at Mrs Wybrow before turning to address Elizabeth, 'was to ask your employer if I might speak to you privately.'

He turned back to Mrs Wybrow who waved her hand through the air as if overpowered by a much stronger force.

'I shall leave you now my lord.' Rising reluctantly from the Queen Anne chair she motioned to her daughter. 'Come

Pamela, my dear.' She sighed with an air of one suffering a great defeat. 'His lordship wishes to converse with Miss Chetwode alone.'

'She is not pleased,' James whispered softly as the door closed behind the two women.

'She knows that I ran away?'

Without thinking, he leaned towards her and gently brushed a stray wisp of hair from her cheek.

She smelled of an enchanting mix fresh rain and sleep at the same time.

'Not at all,' he murmured, with a slow smile. 'She assumes you have been in your room all evening.'

The warmth of his touch sent a tremor traitorous butterflies fluttering through her. She felt heavy, yet light at the same time. She felt delicate, yet powerful.

She felt weak, but wanted to feel strong. She did not want to be at the mercy of a man, yet here she was allowing herself to sink into an abyss of folly.

'It is my insistence that I escort the three of you to the Smith-Jacobsens' soirée,' he paused as a sly smile slipped across his face. 'The three of you,' he paused again to take another wisp of hair between his fingers, 'as equals, that has rather upset Mrs Wybrow.'

The ends of his hair blue-black hair glinted dark bronze in rhythm with the dancing fire. Shimmying shadows hovered across firm cheekbones and fine masculine features that accentuating the strength of his face. The cleft in his chin deepened, and her heart rocked.

Her chrysolite eyes widened with innocent surprise. What had he said or done to cause that reaction? Then slowly she moistened her lips with the tip of her tongue.

That pure and simple response caused that now familiar bud of tenderness to expand and grow within him. He wanted to crush her to him and never let go. He wanted her to be part of him forever. He wanted everything for her, yet she was all he needed

Then she frowned.

His warm breath gently fanned her face.

'I cannot possibly go as,' the money tucked away in Lombard Street came suddenly to mind. Several thousand pounds, for her come-out, and much more besides. Did money make her equal with the Wybrows? She could not be sure. Her mind raced; her spirits soared. Yes. She was their equal. Not better, but not their subordinate either. And it had nothing to do with money.

In her struggle to avoid falling in love with an earl, and in her efforts to evade Mr. Wybrow's licentiousness, she had briefly forgotten that she was an heiress. Why now, was she stalling? Her initial plan, well Mama's anyway, was to get to know, and be known by Society in some small way. Besides, she had four becoming dresses with matching slippers to choose from, two shawls Lady Bucklow gave her as a parting gift, one, intricately patterned fringed cashmere, the other, an ivory full-length wild silk. All, most suitable for mixing with the *ton*.

Was that what she wanted after all? It was all so confusing. She yearned to be with James Bauval, yet she did not want to be bound to him. Or did she? Could she give up all her initial desires and renounce her goals just for one man? A man of rank at that. A man who might expect her to be just an embellishment of finery rather than autonomous and independent?

James watched in fascination as the conflicting emotions darted over her face. First the uncertainty. Then analysis, and finally acceptance.

His whole being longed for her in every way. All he said was, 'So you will come?'

His onyx irises glimmered in the subdued light. His tanned skin planed over taut muscles in his face. His bottom lip curved to a bewitching sensuous mound. His top lip formed a wavy 'm'. His dark lashes swept down as he gently lowered his face.

I love you, a little voice whispered in her head, 'Yes,' she announced stoutly while wishing with all her heart that she did not have any such feelings at all.

She had planned never to fall in love. Never become an easy mark and be dependent on the good-will, or lack thereof, of a man.

Mama had told her so many times how handsome Papa had been. How she had loved him.

No, no, she had just made the wrong decision! She was never going to go through that. She was going to be strong. She had money.

Her mind swirled. Mama had sufficient money too. More than sufficient to move them far enough away from Papa's grasping hands. Elizabeth's mind swirled with sudden conflicting emotions. Why had Mama not done exactly that? Why?

Her sudden racked expression stopped James dead. Icy disquiet spread along his spine and right into his bones. What caused that look that was so etched in his memory? The look that he never wanted to see again. W*as* she a ghost come to mete out justice? As his heart thrummed in his ribcage, he marshalled his thoughts into line. How did she manage to cause so many emotions to vie within him? How could just one change in her expression make him feel like a rake and philander, when her previous one gave him, an over-whelming need to protect and nurture her?

'My love, what is it?' he mouthed into the softness of her cheek, 'what is it that troubles you so?'

Her head jerked back, 'Me?' she shot out, 'troubled?'

Her irises were now flashing prisms of yellow-gold fury. The soft light cast a rosy beige over her hair. In spite of her querying look, he saw conflict warring within her.

Swiftly recalling how evasive she was at their first meeting he wondered if she was afraid of something, and in some kind of perverse way hiding it by anger? Was that it; was anger a defence?

Elizabeth knew from the look on his face that her indignant outburst had set him wondering.

With an effort, she mustered some composure, 'I am not troubled,' she murmured on a softer note. The fluttering butterflies had receded, and now her stomach churned at the half lie. It was only a half lie because although she dreaded him finding out about her drunken father, she realised she did not mind him knowing about Mama.

Dear, dear Mama, cultured and refined, something she only became aware of during her stay with Lady Bucklow, was no-one to be ashamed of. Nor was, her brother Jamie and the secret inheritance.

Lord Bauval, however, did not know about those did he?

What would he say if he found out? That she had lied? That she disguised her real status to gain favour? Would he believe that she did not want status or favour?

Her stomach knotted. She could not tell him any of it. She loved him too much to see his face recoil in disgust. She loved him too much to watch him retract his offer of marriage. She loved him too much to spoil the memory it would become.

James drew his face level with hers, 'Forgive me my darling,' he whispered. 'You are brave, and extremely discerning. You are resourceful,' his fingers slipped into the loose strands of hair that fell round her cheeks, 'You are everything, I have ever wanted.'

His caress sent the now familiar feeling along her spine once more.

She blinked up at him willing him to take her in his arms. Wanting him, wanting to continue loving him, yet knowing the futility of her wish.

James, quelling his yearning to hold her, yet, not able to withdraw his fingers from the silkiness of her hair, abruptly changed tack. 'By the way,' he forced a grin to cover the way he felt, 'what exactly was *your* plan?'

The touch of his hand on her hair, and richness of his tone made her eyelids feel heavy so blinking slowly she looked mindlessly up at him. 'My plan?'

His smile planed the wavy 'm' to a smooth line. 'To prevent Mrs Wybrow knowing of your flight?'

'Oh,' Elizabeth shrugged. 'It is of no consequence now. All I meant to propose was that I stay at Bauval Park until early morning then go straight to the receiving office first thing and see if there was any post for me.' Her lashes fluttered innocently up at him. 'As Mrs Wybrow feels I should collect any letters sent by Lady Bucklow personally and promptly, she would presume I went out early for them.'

His heart slammed against his ribs at the thought of her delightful presence at Bauval Park. All night? He could kick himself. If only he had listened to her before putting his own idea forward.

'And your second reason?' she reminded him with sweet innocence.

His lazy smile revived the traitorous butterflies again.

'Ah yes,' he drawled, absently flicking a wisp of her hair gently between a thumb and forefinger. 'I realise you need a little time to adjust to our engagement, no,' he put a warm finger to her mouth the instant her lips parted in remonstration, 'please hear me out. The Smith-Jacobsens' are pillars of the community and the family is an old and respected one. George Smith-Jacobsen is a gentleman of substantial banking success and enjoys an excellent reputation, so,' he ran his finger along the soft mound of her bottom lip, 'I shall let it be known tomorrow, that we have an understanding. That way, it will give everyone time to get used to the idea.'

An understanding might not be so bad. It would protect her from Mr. Wybrow and could perhaps be rescinded later.

Perhaps? Regret coursed through her. Definitely.

****

Hooby Lodge was an impressive chalk-wash Queen Anne mansion.

145

The minute they stepped onto the top of the Italian mosaic steps, the door opened and they were ushered into an elegant marble-floored foyer.

'This way my lord,' the elegant green and gold liveried servant bowed before ushering them into a magnificent polished-wood oak-panelled hall, that was obviously a ballroom. As far as Elizabeth could make out, it ran the entire length of the house.

'Gill will help the ladies with the removal of their outerwear, my lord, and Manns will attend to you.'

Pamela's eyes shone. Her excitement at being invited to such a grand event had almost worn Elizabeth out.

'It is more, splendid than I remember,' she hissed to Elizabeth as another maid bobbed a curtsey before opening a burnished wooden door to announce them.

This next beautifully furnished room, several times larger than the long parlour at Wybrow House, was already buzzing with about twenty guests.

Elizabeth spotted the family that arrived just before them. A lean man, with his neatly proportioned wife and their daughters. She recognised the Newsome girls immediately.

'Lord Bauval.'

The tiny slender woman whisking towards them was not in the least bit how Elizabeth imagined Mrs Smith-Jacobsen to be. Some of her dark hair coiled and waved unfettered across a high forehead while the rest was pulled back into Grecian knot festooned with minute flowers at the crown.

'I am delighted you could make it after all.'

She gave the briefest of curtseys and held a silk gloved hand out for the earl to honour with his lips. Her delicate pastel-yellow gauze dress, shimmered over a light russet under-frock.

The earl took the offered hand and bowed. 'Your servant ma'am,' he purred.

'Thank you, my lord.'

She turned to Mrs Wybrow. 'My dear, Mrs Wybrow it has been far too long has it not?'

146

Her hazel eyes then flicked to Pamela.

'Miss Wybrow, how charming you look.'

She paused, then looking at Elizabeth, continued brightly.

'You must be Miss Chetwode?'

'Pamela's *duenna*,' Mrs Wybrow said.

Mrs Smith-Jacobsen ignored the interruption.

'One of the Cambridgeshire Chetwodes judging from the unique colour of your eyes my dear.' Her smile appeared somewhat misty as she touched Elizabeth's arm lightly. 'That amazing golden yellow with a dash of green.'

'Chrysolite,' James declared.

Mrs Smith-Jacobsen nodded with approval. 'Indeed, my lord. A most apt description. Now,' she cast around the room, 'do come and meet Rhoda.'

Miss Rhoda Smith-Jacobsen was as delicately boned as her mother, but not quite as pretty as her brother was handsome. Tonged ash-brown hair formed a ridge of curls round her pretty face down to her chin. The rest was pulled back to form two coils just above the nape of her neck. Her salmon pink *crepe de chine* frock was the latest high-waist London style.

'Rhoda,' Mrs Smith-Jacobsen drew her daughter away from a small group of young women, 'did I not tell you I had a surprise in store for you? Look,' she continued with a note of triumph, 'Lord Bauval has honoured us with his presence.'

Rhoda blushed as she peered up at the earl. Something about the flickering of her lashes and the puckering of her pink lips, annoyed Elizabeth.

Surely, she was too young to be presented to eligible gentlemen? Also, if they thought Rhoda was too grand to be friendly with the likes of Pamela, surely common sense told Mrs Smith-Jacobsen that the earl was too grand for them?

'I am sure you remember my daughter Rhoda, my lord? Rhoda, this is Lord Bauval.'

A *frisson* of irritation shot up Elizabeth's spine as Rhoda Smith-Jacobsen curtsied daintily in front of him. Her eyes followed his every movement as he took the blushing girl's hand and lifted it to his lips.

'Miss Smith-Jacobsen,' he inclined his head. 'Charmed. Once a lovely child; now an enchanting young woman.'

'Thank-you Lord Bauval,' Rhoda replied too flirtatiously for Elizabeth's liking.

Then it was Mrs Wybrow's and Pamela's turn.

Then hers, 'And this is Miss Chetwode.'

Rhoda still obviously flustered by the earl stared at Elizabeth in shock. 'Oh,' she shot out, 'I thought Henry was exagger-,'

'-Rhoda,' Mrs Smith-Jacobsen interrupted. 'Pray forgive her, Miss Chetwode,' she gave a wavering laugh. 'My son thinks it amusing to tease his younger sister.' She tutted. 'All it does, however, is put foolish ideas into her head. Talking of whom,' she tacked on before Rhoda could protest or apologise, 'Here he is now.'

To Elizabeth's relief, the greetings from Henry Smith-Jacobsen were made without any hint of the summerhouse, and they all moved on.

Elizabeth met Jane Snape. Then there were the Newson girls, Samara, Hagar and Phinia, who greeted them like old friends.

Later, some of the guests sang and played, and some gave narrations.

It was a well organised afternoon, decorous but not too fussy. After all, as Mrs Smith-Jacobsen observed, most of the girls were not yet out. Dancing and flirting were out of the question.

Apart from Rhoda, Elizabeth thought peevishly.

She quietly observed that Rhoda was introduced to all the gentlemen, and was thrust at the earl on the slightest pretext in a most unseemly manner.

At the same time Elizabeth watched out for when James Bauval took their hostess into his confidence. An understanding, she kept on reminding herself. Yet, although the earl had greeted them politely enough when he collected them from Wybrow House, he had said very little since.

The previous evening though, he took her in his arms, kissed her forehead, trailed his lips down her cheek before softly telling her to return to her room.

She glanced at him again, exquisite in a sliver-grey jacket, and dark grey neat fitting trousers. She watched as he strolled past a small gathering of young women whose chatter ceased as he went by, then, he ambled almost idly to where Henry Smith-Jacobsen lounged beside the pianoforte, sipping cordial and quietly looking at the guests. She saw James move up beside him then say something that drew Henry's eyes toward her.

She looked quickly away. This was it.

Her heart pounded.

'Miss Chetwode,' Jane Snape's voice brought her back to the others, 'I hear from Miss Wybrow that you play and sing rather beautifully.' She flipped a long dark curl from her ivory face. 'Mama has asked me to invite you both to our Michaelmas gathering next week. There will be an opportunity for you to show us all.'

A little bell tinkled.

'Ladies and gentlemen,' Mrs Smith-Jacobsen stood small but straight between her son and the earl, 'I have a most important and exciting announcement to make.' She looked quickly across at the earl.

The pounding in Elizabeth's ribcage increased. This was not what he promised. Not a public announcement. Not today. Not here.

'Lord Bauval-,'

Elizabeth's head swam as everything in the room became unreal. The silence of the guests made other tiny sounds seem like a blaring rabble. A rustle of a frock, an intake of breath, the squeak of a leather sole on the rug pummelled her head like the roar of wind and sea against rocks. Everything came and went in waves. Nearer, nearer, then away, away, receding into the shadows of the now late afternoon.

How could he?

'-So, after a five-year break, we shall be resuming the tradition of the Six-in-hand Point to Point at the post-Michaelmas fair.'

As a cheer went up Mrs Smith-Jacobsen waved her hand to quieten everyone. 'The gaming rules are exactly the same as previous years,' she proclaimed on a chuckle. 'But,' she continued cheerfully, 'the new chapel will be included, making four steeple points in all. This year there will be extra prizes as well as the usual flitch of ham.'

There was a ripple of applause. Henry slapped James heartily on the back before giving him a pumping handshake.

Mrs Snape hurried over. 'It is wonderful news is it not my dears? The Six-in-hand! Of course, we all thought it would be resumed last year to celebrate the French defeat.' She sighed then, 'But it was not to be.' She looked quickly at Pamela and Elizabeth. 'The steeple-point to steeple-point was re-started by the old earl in '02 to commemorate the Treaty of Amiens after many years of absence. It takes place a week before the first of November so that the winner may enjoy the ham on All Saints Day. But,' she continued on a warning note, 'If anyone but a Bauval wins,' she paused for impact, 'the village and surrounding areas will fall into enemy hands.'

'And so far,' a rich voice chipped in, 'I have won. I then present the ham to a deserving family, and the village is safe from a hostile foe.'

Elizabeth stared at him, his gross arrogance rattling her beyond reason. How could he possibly know he would win every time?

James watched as Elizabeth's eyes flashed prisms of yellow-gold fury. Now what had he done or said to overset her? It was he who had reason to be mad with anger, not her. She had made a fool of him. He clamped his jaw. It was better to say nothing for the moment. Later he would give her the two letters he collected from the receiving office earlier that morning.

One, bearing her sponsor, Lady Bucklow's seal.

The other?

He tensed.

The other, written in neat Legal style, was on professional paper, and, judging by the handwriting, was most definitely penned by a male.

Miss Chetwode had a lover, and judging by her wardrobe, a reasonably rich one at that. Part of him was angry that he was so deceived, yet a larger part of him was in agony at the thought of her loving another. The, initial 'my someone', flashed through his memory.

Elizabeth's mind still blazed with unreasonable fury. Her dear brother Jamie could put up a good show in a race.

Six-in-hand? Not with just animals that were used to him either. She had watched him whirl a vehicle and six with a sleight of hand, and just the tone of his voice spurring them on to triumph. There was no-one to touch him. Many had tried, but Jamie won every time. She quickly brushed the ridiculous thoughts aside. Jamie was no match for Lord Bauval. Besides she had no intention of informing her brother about the race. Even so, she still seethed. Lord Bauval had no right presuming the outcome.

Mrs Snape looked up at the earl. 'I do hope we will know all the details soon, my lord?'

James marshalled his thoughts, to reply levelly, 'Naturally, Mrs Snape.'

James waited until they reached Wybrow House before asking to see Elizabeth alone. Now as he faced her in the chilly parlour, pain filtered through him again.

Initially, the clerk was reluctant to hand the letters over. 'Miss Chetwode expressly asked me not to give them to anyone but her,' he said. But Bauval's status had overwhelmed him.

'I have something for you.'

Elizabeth was puzzled, 'Something for me?'

Caramel lashes flitted over chrysolite eyes. Her rosebud mouth curved to a delicious contour. A pulse in her slender neck fluttered as she swallowed. His eyes grazed the delicate cream skin below her throat and skimmed over the smooth white skin of her cleavage.

His pain intensified. She had deceived them all. So why did his heart skip a pained beat?

'Here,' valiantly toning down his anguish, he withdrew the two envelopes from the inside of his tail coat pocket and handed them to her. 'I took the liberty of collecting these from the receiving office this morning.'

'Oh,' Elizabeth looked at the two letters in her hand. The one with a seal was from Lady Bucklow, the other from Jamie.

Trying to hide his distress made him less than courteous. 'Oh?' he echoed tersely.

She looked up to see his imminently powerful body looming over her, looking every inch an avenging beast in stark outline against the flickering light. The lines of his face looked like silhouetted granite on rock. His mouth formed a thin line across his face. His eyes, dark and foreboding, loomed closer.

'Th-thank-you,' she stammered. 'However, there was no need to trouble yourself my lord. I had already made arrangements to fetch them myself.'

'Two letters?' he rasped. 'One, I assume is from Lady Bucklow?'

His querulous attitude permeating her insides, sent a chill through her.

'The other is from a lover perhaps?'

Elizabeth stared up at him in dazed confusion. A lover?

For a fleeting instant her face had that racked look, and he almost capitulated. Then the racked look vanished as rapidly as it came.

A lover? her frenzied mind repeated.

How dare he! Sweeping a breath into her lungs, she was just about to tell him about her own dear Jamie, just about to reveal a precious secret to someone she had slowly come to trust, but stalled.

Her champion indeed? Such empty promises.

Her mouth moved before her brain registered. 'It is none of your business my lord.'

'Oh, no? Have you forgotten I made you, my business? I gave you credibility where there was none? I took you under my wing.'

He suddenly leaned back shocked by his rising vehemence. Yes, he knew the Green God of Jealousy now perched on his shoulders, but did he have to be so barbaric? Did he have to give vent to his feelings in such a high-handed manner?

High handed? Of course, he had every right to be high handed. She was not yet of age. She needed his guardianship. That was it. As her guardian, self-appointed or not, he had every right to oversee this particular part of her life.

'Now,' he thrust out his hand, 'I suggest you give me the letter.'

She held onto the envelope. 'No.'

He knew he was being unreasonable. He knew he had no right to make such a demand of her. Yet, he needed to know. He needed honesty.

He kept his hand out.

Furious, Elizabeth tilted her chin up and fixed him with a school marm stare.

'Have you no idea how to behave Lord Bauval? Are you so wrapped up in your lordly position as to demean the rights of others?'

All thought of getting the letter went out of his head as her tone whipped through him.

'Intimidating females may be considered acceptable by men in general,' she declared decisively, 'As far as I am concerned, though, it is not. So please take your hand away.'

He was spellbound. Was this fiery creature who lectured him so soundly, a Godly envoy come to put him to rights? If so, she was a fine success.

His insides flamed. He had to make her forget about the lover that caused him to behave so irrationally. She must see that he had more to offer than anyone else. He was sure she was still an innocent, yet, and the thought pained once more, she obviously felt more than a passing affection for the person whose letter she held so protectively.

Never in his life had he met a woman of her spirit who needed such careful handling at the same time. Her courage and innocence filled him with tenderness.

However, his pride refused to let him concede with grace.

'As you wish.' He withdrew his hand. 'However, I mean to get to the bottom of this sooner or later.' He shifted his position so he could see her more clearly. 'As I am to travel to London tomorrow afternoon, I expect it to be sooner. I shall call on you in the morning and we may discuss it then.'

Elizabeth glared at him. He was dismissing her. Well, now that his true colours were revealed, she had no reason to stay.

Swallowing the lump that had risen in her throat, and mustering up her composure, she rose calmly from the chair, crisply wished him good-evening and left the room.

Now alone in her room, Elizabeth reread the letter.

Dearest Sis, I must see you on an urgent matter as soon as possible. I am on a case in Leicester, so I shall make a detour to visit you on my way. I cannot stay long, so if you can to meet me in Hooby village, by the blacksmith's, at eleven, on the twenty-ninth of September, it will save time. If you are not there, I will make my way to Wybrow House.

Elizabeth swallowed, the twenty-ninth was tomorrow, but Jamie must not come to Wybrow House. The Wybrows believed she was an orphan, so she had to think of a way to meet him secretly at eleven. It was wretched having to hide him away, as even Lady Bucklow never knew about him. Elizabeth had managed to keep him a secret, and when the family were in London, she used Lady Bucklow's spaniel as a cover to meet Jamie in a specific place along Bird Cage Walk, two roads away from Lady Bucklow's home.

What was so urgent?

There were no clues.

Tucking the letter in the bottom of her writing case, she got ready for bed.

Chapter Ten

'Good-day, Mrs Wybrow, and thank you.'

Turning away from Wybrow House, James rammed his shining silk steeple hat more tightly on his head than was comfortable, and set the Thoroughbred into a brisk trot.

It was bad enough that Miss Chetwode was not there, but having to endure Mrs Wybrow's gushing spiel about Pamela was worse. Now he had to go gadding round Hooby Village searching for Miss Chetwode, a long-winded activity for sure as there would be more folk wanting to pass the time of day with him than usual. His reinstating of the six-in-hand horse and carriage race would be the talking point for miles, and he would have to listen to the hearty congratulations, the simpering expectations, and the sorrows of the hard-done-by, who hoped to receive the flitch of ham at the end.

He now had it all planned. Elizabeth was young, and an orphan, so she needed a little time to sort herself out. After all she did not have to take the first man who offered for her. He would point out that she was not beholden to anyone just because they showed an interest in her first. He would woo her with love to make her forget the lothario in question.

And he planned to start that very morning.

****

Elizabeth watched Jamie flip the reins against two fine greys with perfect dexterity.

'Do you like the new equipage, Sis?'

Elizabeth managed a weak smile.

Her brother lengthened the ribbons in order to slide along the squabbed bench. He took her hands in his. 'Sis, it is no use feeling guilty about not seeing dear Min before she died.'

'Min did so much for us.' Elizabeth indicated the flat brown paper wrapped parcel on her lap. 'She must have rescued this precious picture of those two little girls especially for me.'

As she looked up, his top lip rose into a wavy 'm'.

'She also left me this.' He extracted a tiny locked silver box from his inside pocket. 'I have no idea what it contains except that it is *my* keepsake.' He swallowed. 'The Lombard Street bank has the key.' He withdrew a long, narrow, buff envelope from an inside pocket of his jacket. 'I have to present it along with this letter.'

Even from the far end of the green, Bauval recognised Miss Chetwode perched on the bench of a smart two wheeled phaeton. She had her back to him, and was so engrossed in the young man handling the vehicle, it defied decorum. He watched jealously as the man leaned toward her and took her hands in his.

Bauval's first impulse was to charge over and demand an explanation.

Pride and pain however, held him in check, and he watched in tight-lipped jealousy as she dropped a kiss on the man's cheek.

A kiss!

He closed his eyes to shut out the sight. Yet they were still there, in his mind. She, an angel in a fetching grey bonnet and pastel-blue pelisse, and the Don Juan with her, the fiend!

His eyes flipped open just in time to see his rival spring back onto the dash after helping her down, flick the ribbons, and set his horses at a perfect pace round the curve of the green.

Oh, but the insolent puppy was one Hell of a whip! The best Bauval had ever seen.

He gritted his teeth against the urge to gallop after him, knock him from the glossy squabs and call him out.

A penetrating pain, lancing his insides felt like a two-edged sword being thrust into him, again and again. To make matters worse, the mannerless brute had left Miss Chetwode standing at the side of the track gazing sadly after him.

'Mornin' milord.'

James Bauval whisked in a controlling breath. Now, he was well and truly cornered.

James Bauval stared unseeingly out of his study window. It was a damnable situation. He, who, with scant sympathy had watched his friends go through the rigours of unrequited love, was now racked with a deep agonising, pain, greater than anything else he had ever experienced. A terrible, all-consuming pain that left him battered and bruised all over.

Infatuation and passion, yes. But not this excruciating desolation now coursing through him.

Because, always there in the back-ground, was Mary-Beth.

Mary-Beth whom he loved too deeply to hurt, yet was never truly in love with. Mary-Beth, who expected to be his wife and the mother of his children.

Mary-Beth, who never knew what it meant to be held in the arms of a true lover.

The torment thrashed through him like iced swatches on the end of a frozen crop.

If only Mary-Beth had had a lover who took her in his arms and loved her the way she should be loved.

For if his Mary-Beth had loved another, he would have let her go. Her happiness meant more to him, than either his mother's, or Betty's longing for joint grandchildren.

He closed his eyes against the thought now hammering in his head. His jaw ached. His back hurt. His knees locked as grief caught at him again. How did anyone endure *this*? How did people bear the unbearable? Until now, the absurd expression 'unrequited love' meant nothing to him. Indeed, he had even secretly, and on rare occasions, openly, scoffed at such a concept. To him, it had always been simple, someone either loved someone, or did not. He had always felt people should move on in such clear-cut circumstances. Accept the not loving. Rise above it, gather their wits and keep going. How was he going to keep going? How was he supposed to carry on as if nothing had changed, as if his whole life was as seamless as it had been before Elizabeth?

He took a deep breath. He had to accept the unacceptable.

Miss Chetwode loved another. The pain of that knowledge leached the strength from his body so that it took all his willpower not to flop over his desk.

He had to let her go.

No human-being belonged to anybody, unless they mutually chose to belong to each other. He had no right to inflict himself onto her.

James reached for his writing paper and pen, and with a heavy heart, began writing the bleakest letter of his life.

The fourth Earl of Alstoe refused to look back. Vance had packed his case with the few necessities he needed. Few, because he had everything he required at his town-house in London. His mother and Betty would not mind that he had things to attend to before escorting them back to Alstoe House. They would mind about his mood though. However, he did not intend confiding in them and was relieved it happened while they were away.

With that thought, he flipped the reins, issued the command, and set the two well matched duns into an even trot.

****

'Mary-Beth?'

Pamela's voice reached her from some distant place.

'Whatever is the matter?'

Elizabeth wanted to run away and hide.

She wanted to be alone to wrap herself up in a black shroud of darkness and never see daylight again.

She wanted Mama.

She wanted everything.

She wanted nothing.

Yet, if it was all for the best as she told herself again and again, why did everything ache so unbearably? Why was she *not happy* the earl had written such a letter? Why had she allowed her heart to be broken? His letter about how he had overlooked her feelings and after much consideration was prepared to give up all claim on her, yet promising to still be at her side whenever she might need him. His letter ended, with him begging her to forgive him for causing her distress.

Distress?

To pretend to love her, and expect to be forgiven? How could he be so free with his feelings one minute and then just expect her to behave as if they never happened the next?

What a weak fool she was to be taken in by a liar who flimflammed her with soft words and gentle caresses and go against her own vow never to fall in love and end up doing just that.

He had obviously been amusing himself with someone too nit-witted to know better. Someone, who did not count in his own aristocratic world of wealth and privilege.

Wrapped up in her own torment, she hardly realised that Pamela was still beside her.

'Mary-Beth?'

Forcing a smile, Elizabeth looked up from the embroidery she was trying to concentrate on.

'I have a headache that is all.'

What a lie.

After having seen his horses safely into the stable yard, the earl strode into The Caldicot Inn. Two and a half hours was good going, even by his standards. With luck and clear roads, he could be at his town house in time for an early supper.

He ordered a pint of ale, and was making his way to an empty bench, when a commotion at the door he just came through, stopped him.

'Take your hands off me!'

There was a sudden hush everyone swivelled towards the brouhaha.

Foam from the ale splashed up as James snapped his mug down hard on the bar.

The Lothario!

'He's a horse thief!' was the cry. 'Send for the magistrate!'

'Thinks 'e can get away with it, just 'cos he's dressed like a gentleman.'

'I know his sort,' bellowed another ruffian manhandling the young man. 'he'll have an accomplice on his tail you mark my words.'

The Lothario's clear precise tones cut through the room.

'I have no such thing! You must have mistaken me for-,' His eyes suddenly met Bauval's.

Hell fire! The impudence of the sprig! The earl lunged forward, 'You dare to tar me with the same brush?'

The landlord appeared and suddenly jumped between them, 'No family feuds in here if you please.' He whipped round to the two men with their prisoner. 'What's up?'

The older one spoke, 'He's saying the greys are his, but, Ambert saw 'im come in with the two duns.'

'The duns are mine.' Bauval said swivelling to the landlord, 'And, we are certainly not family.'

Without any warning, his first meeting with Miss Chetwode darted into his mind. Her voice echoed through him. *You remind me of my - someone.*

She had called him Jemmy. Was this young man, *the* Jemmy? He had to admit, the youth standing before him bore some likeness to some of the Bauval portraits.

Sidestepping the landlord, he dipped his chin, and slanted his head. 'You must be Jemmy?'

The young man shrugged off his two captors, removed his hat, rubbed a large hand through cropped dark-bronze hair. Copper lashes flickered as looked steadily at the man in front of him.

'Nobody,' said the lothario with quiet deliberation, 'calls me Jemmy anymore.'

An icy disquiet crept along Bauval's spine.

He watched the young man gently tug the sleeve of his brown herringbone coat to just above the cuff of an ivory lawn shirt.

'Except,' the young man continued soberly, flickering gold honey-coloured eyes up to meet onyx ones, 'my older sister Elizabeth. Even then, it is only when she is discomposed and forgets herself.' His lips formed a wavy 'm' as a slow smile crossed his face. 'Which is not very often.'

Discomposed? Forgets herself?

The icy disquiet that had seeped into his spine only seconds ago, now cracked coldly through James' entire body. *Sister?* Miss Chetwode never mentioned a brother.

Brother? Hell fire! What had his letter done to her if this man truly was her brother?

James mustered his wits.

'Forgive me,' he extended a hand. 'I mistook you for someone else. I am the Earl of Alstoe, James Bauval.' He gave a wry smile. 'Jemmy, *still*, to my close family and friends.' The young man's dark-bronze brow arced, and the disquiet James had not managed to shake off, niggled his insides. 'It seems,' Bauval continued with absolute self-control, 'we bear a resemblance to one another. It is odd is it not?'

'Indeed,' the other agreed with a trace smile, 'I am James Westernbury.' He held out his hand.

Hell fire. He was no relation to Miss Chetwode after all. He decided to call the man's bluff. 'Is Miss Westernbury travelling with you sir?'

'Miss Westernbury?' Then his face cleared. 'Oh, my sister is Miss Chetwode, and no, she is not, Lord Bauval.'

The landlord stepped in. 'It is agreed then, is it? The duns belong to his lordship, and the greys to his likeness?'

There was a guffaw from the other patrons as he turned to James Westernbury. 'We owe you an apology, so, I hope a little extra service will put things right. Now sirs, may I suggest you both retire into the private parlour, to partake of my wife's first-class game pie. On the House.'

It was nearly midnight before Lord Bauval walked the horses into the stables at the back of his London town house.

What a night it turned out to be!

He and Westernbury drank more ale than was good for them. They had bantered like old friends and, although Bauval's mind brimmed with questions, neither mentioned Westenbury's sister again. Eventually, the conversation turned to horse-flesh. He could not recall which one of them suggested the race. But before he knew it, bets were flying around, and his duns and phaeton were poised alongside Westernbury's greys in the field behind the inn.

The news must have spread like wildfire, because men, women and children turned out to place their bets and watch the outcome.

The greys of course, were more rested than the duns, but the duns, still high from their recent gallop, fidgeted to race.

Now apologising to the groom for his late arrival, James quietly made his way to the shadowed London house.

Throughout his journey one sentence kept resounding in his head.

That Westernbury is one hell of an equestrian.

****

Elizabeth forced herself to ignore Mrs Wybrow irritability, who made her feelings plain when Pamela wanted to practice the duet for the Snapes' Michaelmas gathering.

'It is disgraceful inviting a *duenna* to sing with the daughter of Quality.'

Worst of all, Elizabeth could not get James Bauval out of her mind. Every second of every minute, he was there. Sometimes, she wished her heart would send him packing. Other times the longing to be near him, washed over her in great waves. But, whatever her thoughts, the dull ache remained.

The day of the Snapes' soirée arrived, and in spite of all her efforts to be strong, Elizabeth could not face it. Although ashamed, she pleaded a headache, and Mrs Wybrow, who had not wanted Elizabeth to accompany them anyway, readily agreed she should stay behind.

It was only after they left, that the idea about doing something about Mary-Beth's grave, came to her.

She was sure that the estate gardener would give her some late autumn plants, and with a luck, she would be able to see a little of the results of her efforts before she left for good.

That thought cheered her a little.

****

James took in the tasteful surroundings. Was he was doing the right thing coming to Bucklow House?

'Lord Bauval,' came the refined friendly voice. 'Whatever took you so long?'

The salon was cheerful and welcoming. The sofas and chairs dotting the room all faced each other, so that anyone sitting in them had clear view of everyone else.

The dainty woman addressing him was obviously a discerning and considerate host. Suddenly he felt much better about invading the home of a complete stranger.

He raised a brow.

She threw back her head and chuckled softly. 'My dear,' she beamed, 'you are the image of your grandfather.'

'Thank-you for agreeing to see me at such short notice, Lady Bucklow. However, it seems ma'am, you have the advantage.'

A maid came in and set a tea-tray on a small satin-wood table.

Lady Bucklow smiled enigmatically.

James remained silent as Lady Bucklow dismissed the maid and concentrated on pouring the tea.

'I understand, Lord Bauval.' She turned misting hazel eyes to him. 'Although I am not quite sure advantage is the correct word in this case.'

Her cheeriness vanished, as a pain, palpable to anyone with even the slightest sensitivity, filled her.

'Let me tell you about,' she swallowed, 'the two Mary-Beths.'

James cursed under his breath. His immediate reaction on leaving William Street two hours later was to go and confront Betty. Good breeding prevented him. His next thought was Theo's, but the idea of having to include Wybrow, or make excuses not to, deterred him.

He was sick at heart. How could his mother have kept something *so important* from him all this time? Did she think he had no rights on the matter? Did *family* not mean anything after all?

Family?

The word swirled in his head until he hardly knew what he was doing or where he was going. *They were family*! James Westernbury *Chetwode*, and his sister Elizabeth, were as much the legal lineage of the Bauvals as he was.

His carriage stopped, and his eyes turned to examine the gleaming brass sign in the middle of the polished oak door. 'Longton & Associates'.

Elizabeth would never have envisaged the satisfaction to be gained from putting a few plants in a desolate place. The gardener advised what flowers to use for the maximum autumn and winter colours she wanted. Violas, he explained, were hardy and flowered all the year round, and the late flowering Begonia with ornamental foliage, were handsome even when not in bloom. Alyssum, a pretty combination of pinks, mauves or white scattered among Stardust and Golden-moss daisies would make a pretty show, lastly, winter Aconite, with creamy-yellow petals, peeping out from the rest at the tail-end of winter. Then he showed her his stock of sturdy lovingly grown plants and picked out the best of each variety for her, with the advice of what to put where.

Now, she stepped back to survey her work. Most of the plants were still in bud but due to being moved, might take longer than otherwise to flower. Not that it mattered, because now the grave was awash with varying shades of green, she, as well as the other Mary-Beth, could feel at peace.

'Very pretty, congratulations Miss Chetwode.'

Elizabeth spun round to see Henry Smith-Jacobsen spearing her with his intense blue gaze.

He smiled softly.

'I seem to be making a habit of startling you.' He whisked off his steeple hat. 'Forgive me.'

'How can I forgive that which I did not curse in the first place Mr. Smith-Jacobsen?'

His pale face mottled slightly before rippling into laughter.

'Bravo, Miss Chetwode. I am delighted your headache has not discommoded you too much.' His blonde brows rose. 'It was a headache that kept you from the Snapes' soirée was it not?'

Had he come all this way just to seek her out? Her stomach clenched slightly.

'How did you know that?'

His eyes searched her face as he asked gently, 'Did it not occur to you that your absence would be noted, and inquiries made, Miss Chetwode?'

Elizabeth blinked up at him. 'I am merely Miss Wybrow's companion, Mr. Smith-Jacobsen.'

He took a deep sonorous breath.

'A very lovely companion; if I may say so?'

'Paid companions do not merit consideration.'

'Exquisitely lovely,' he added. 'Moreover,' he reached down and took her chin in his kid-gloved hand. 'Too interesting by far.'

She stood transfixed by his stare, strangely drawn to him by an overwhelming curiosity.

Why was he taking such an interest in her? Why were any of them taking such an interest in her? From what Mrs Wybrow said, they wanted Pamela, not her. Not Elizabeth Chetwode, the hired companion.

Why was he looking at her like that? 'Not enough consideration to be missed,' she babbled. 'It is Pamela they really invited.'

'Oh,' he breathed, 'you were missed all right. As for the Wybrows,' he shrugged, 'None of us really knows anything about them. They came from somewhere in America I believe.' He paused, 'About three years ago. The general opinion is that-,'

His blue gaze suddenly slid over her face to rest on her lips. 'Enough of the Wybrows',' he murmured softly.

The blue of his irises darkened. The intense expression on his face increased. His chin imperceptibly lowered.

'No!' Elizabeth gasped, instantly aware of his intent. Then twisting her face away from his grasp, she thrust herself away from him, took a frantic hasty step backward, before sitting unbecomingly on the edge of the prettiest blooms she had just carefully planted.

Fury and shame pitted inside her as she fought for a stinging rebuke.

'You-you,' She glanced around her. The sight of the crushed flowers broke her words as well as her heart.

Heart sore, and dispirited she threw back her head and groaned softly, 'Mary-Beth, I have failed you.'

She hardly saw the alarm of the blonde man hovering above her.

All she saw in her mind's eye was another empty colourless grave, as unkempt and as lifeless as the one she had just ruined.

Mama's grave.

Even Min's grave would be looked after by her family. Yet for all these years, she, Mary-Beth, the only daughter of her beloved mother, Mary-Jane, had failed to even visit her own mother's resting place, yet alone tend it.

'My dearest,' she groaned again. 'Forgive me.'

Elizabeth felt herself being lifted to her feet.

'Miss Chetwode?' There was a grey fear etched into the lines of his usually cheerful face. 'My dear Miss Chetwode, I had no idea.'

With hardly a notion of being present at all, she was scurried out of the cemetery, through the creaky gate, and into the gloomy sanctuary of the summer-house. Once there, she was guided over onto the bench by Henry Smith-Jacobsen.

'Please, I beg you, sit down Miss Chetwode.'

He sat close beside her and taking her somewhat grimy hand in his, held it gently in his until she caught her breath.

All the time, though, she heard him muttering, 'My dear Miss Chetwode, I had no idea, no idea at all.'

At last, she drew a soft shaky breath. 'It is ruined.'

She felt him squeeze her hand.

'No, dearest,' he mouthed softly. 'It is not. The gardener will do it for you if you but ask.'

'No, it has to be me.'

'Who is Mary-Beth to you, Miss Chetwode?'

Elizabeth remained silent for several seconds attempting but failing to dash away the memories of her past.

At last, she spoke.

'My mother's little girl,' she said in a far-away voice. 'You see,' she turned innocent chrysolite eyes up to him, 'my mama died at the same time as Mary-Beth. The same year,' a sob reached her throat, 'the same month, the same day.'

His blue eyes her searched face. 'That does not make her your mama's daughter.' He lowered his voice so as not to upset her further. 'I know for a fact that, that Mary-Beth's Mama is still very much alive.'

She turned away from his gaze. 'That is not what I meant.'

'Miss Chetwode,' he said kindly, 'I believe your headache and other events of the afternoon have overset you. My carriage is just outside Rector's Gate. Please, I beg you, let me escort you, home. Someone there will find something, a tisane perhaps to ease your,' he paused, obviously not quite sure just what her suffering came under. 'Pain,' he finished.

Elizabeth sat woodenly beside him, her brain stumbling over all she might have revealed. Had she told him her childhood name was Mary-Beth? Had she mentioned how Mama died? Or when?

'I am sure you know,' he continued gallantly, 'your sweet sister is up there somewhere,' he drew a breath and stroked her palm with gloved fingers. 'A loving child to an adoring mother.'

Deep down, Elizabeth knew his words were meant to be a comfort because he presumed her state of mind justified the simplicity, but Elizabeth knew he was soothing her with simple words.

She felt herself tense as he continued stroking her palm.

'I believe,' he continued in pacifying tones, 'that they needed to be together. Your Mama, and your dear sister, Mary-Beth.'

She turned to him, in confusion.

'I did not say I had a sister called Mary-Beth.'

His face darkened, then flushed pink. 'Miss Chetwode,' he said carefully. 'You most definitely mentioned that you had a sister called Mary-Beth.'

She opened her mouth on a denial, but his self-mocking chuckle stopped her.

'At first, I actually thought you knew the Mary-Beth out there, in that grave.' His voice trailed as the self-mockery subsided into a sigh. 'She died four and a half years ago of,' Elizabeth watched him fight for control, while he swallowed some huge emotion. 'Consumption.'

Elizabeth shuddered.

'Mama died of consumption too.' She gazed somewhere beyond him. 'None of us knew she had it until it was too late.'

She stared unseeingly into the distance remembering Mama's last words. *'Forgive, I beg you, forgive.'*

'I loved her,' Smith-Jacobsen continued on a whisper so soft that she hardly heard him. 'I loved her so much.' He smiled mistily down at Elizabeth, his eyes shining with repressed tears. 'We went through a sort of marriage service,' he said without shame. He shook his head. 'It was the only way we could be together. A service all of our own in that dilapidated chapel over there. Then,' his eyes brimmed with tears, 'we consummated our union right here in this room.' His eyes closed as his voice dropped to a languid contralto. 'More than once.'

Elizabeth drew back in surprise. 'You mean a real consummation?'

His eyes met hers full on.

'Yes,' he said with soft defiance. 'It was the only way we knew we could ever be together.' His eyes roved her face. 'And to think I thought you knew her. Had met her. Yet all the time you were only thinking of your own dear sister.'

Elizabeth's reasoning came full circle. 'No, that is just it, Mr. Smith-Jacobsen. I was not talking about a sister. I was talking about myself.'

His cheeks mottled again. 'Yourself, Miss Chetwode?'

Elizabeth noticed the changing emotions crossing his face. He obviously thought her fit for bedlam and that irked her.

'I was named Mary-Beth after,' she paused, because she knew Mary was her mother's name, but where did the Beth come from? 'Mary, after Mama. Although,' her voice trailed, 'I never knew where the Beth came from.'

His pink cheeks dulled to match the slowly dipping light from beyond the summerhouse.

'Strange,' he murmured. 'Because, *my* Mary-Beth was named Beth, after her mother, Betty. Only she never knew where the Mary came from.' His face twitched. 'Here,' he blinked into the gloom, 'it appears, is a case of two Mary-Beths. One named Mary after her mother, the other named Beth after *her* mother.'

He gazed into her face.

'Who by some strange quirk of fate, are so identical in looks they could be sisters. No,' he amended as his face searched hers. 'Twins.'

Something in Elizabeth's insides surged and knotted. Her words were stuck and would not leave her mouth. Her brain could not believe what it was telling her. Having already made herself look an idiot in front of him this afternoon was bad enough, she certainly did not want to go doing it again.

169

But this thought?

This thought, so ridiculous, so enormous in its implication that her tongue would not be stilled.

She and the other Mary-Beth were so alike that everywhere she went people looked at her as if she was someone they knew. Especially Mr. Smith-Jacobsen. The painting of the two little girls flashed through her mind. 'Or,' she burst out, unable to contain it any longer. 'Daughters of twins?'

He stared at her for several moments. Then as a muscle in his face twitched, he spoke. 'Come, Miss Chetwode, I believe we have talked enough for today. I declare you look quite worn out. I insist on taking you back home immediately.'

Leaning back on the chintz sofa Lady Levana smiled at her son. 'I am so glad to be back home Jemmy, and am thrilled you now have someone to manage the estate.'

James shifted in his chair. It was three days since Lady Bucklow's startling revelations, and only absolute self-control kept him from bursting out about his new-found information and demanding an explanation.

Although he realised that Betty's betrayal and ongoing deceit was too painful for her to discuss, Mama, an observer, was different. She should have told him long ago. Where had the deceit got them? Or more precisely, where had it got Mary-Jane Chetwode? And was it coincidence that *her* son discovered he too was a Cambridgeshire Chetwode the same day as himself; or fate?

Lady Levana chipped into his thoughts.

'You can take your seat in The House seriously and start thinking of marriage and having a family.'

It was the exact opening he needed. 'A wife, Mama?' His insides churned. 'You mean another find another Mary-Beth?'

'Another Mary-Beth? No.'

James inwardly winced at her shocked expression.

'Dearest, you need to be in love with your chosen companion not just carried along on the whims of others.

170

'This time it has to be real. I beg you, do not make any hasty decisions on what others might want for you. Forget the pain of the past. Look to the future.'

'Is that what cousin Betty did, Mama?' he asked with calm deliberation. 'Forget the pain of the past and look only to her future?' He drew a quick breath. 'At the cost to those she loved, or should I say, of the *twin* sister, she loved?'

Lady Levana stilled. 'You know? How?'

James felt her anguished dismay and knowing that her loyalty had caused her considerable distress, his heart went out to her. But he had to know. He had to be strong for all their sakes. He needed to hear every detail, whatever it took. Hopefully Mama's lion-heartedness would see her through.

Only after the expunging would come the healing balm and joy of meeting up with lost family.

A totally unconnected thought seared into his mind, *and Mary-Beth's grave will bloom.*

His voice dropped to a whisper, 'Mama,' he pressed gently, 'Have you ever thought that we have family out there?' He went and sat beside her. Closing a hand over hers, he added tenderly, 'Family that need us. Family that Betty has so desperately been pining for.'

Lady Levana lifted her chin to meet his eyes. 'Oh, Jemmy,' her voice came as a thready whisper on a breeze-blown cloud. 'I never thought of it like that. All these years my concern was for dear Betty.' She blinked. 'Although I have encouraged her to forgive herself, nobody else mattered.' Her gaze now shifted unseeingly ahead. 'I never thought,' her voice trailed. 'That there might be another Mary-Beth out there.'

Just the thought of his lovely Boadicea filled his insides with tenderness. 'Yes Mama,' he said, 'and she belongs *with* us.'

171

Chapter Eleven

More than another two weeks had dragged by, and Elizabeth had not left the Wybrow's employ after all. In some ways, a part of her could not bear to leave without at least saying an infuriated farewell to James Bauval, and giving him a piece of her mind. She had not seen him since his brusque departure after the Smith-Jacobsen's soirée, however. In other ways, she felt she had to make a stand by pretending he did not matter to her at all, and that his existence, wherever that was, was of no consequence to her, and that she had never believed in his promises anyway. At the same time, hardly a moment went by, without thinking of him, without remembering how she felt when he was close to her. Feeling that all over again gave her hope while contrarily, dashing that same hope. It was confusing, heartbreakingly painful and annoying all at once.

She had to be strong.

Another reason she had not left, was that Mrs Wybrow had seemed to value her presence since their move, and of course, Pamela relied on her.

Currently, although Mr. Wybrow only returned home at weekends, they were firmly established in Nimbus Folly.

Now, having just completed her morning routine, she stood in her bedchamber, staring once more at the painting of the twins on her bedroom wall. It was perfectly positioned as it was years ago, on the wall above the fireplace in her direct view every time she entered the room.

Mrs Wybrow had given her a *where did you get that from,* look when she had asked for it to be put up. However, her employer was really too busy organising everything to ask questions. By the time everything was in place, it had slipped her mind altogether.

Pamela had taken an instant liking to it, and she too, would often stand with Elizabeth just admiring it. Pamela had asked where it came from, and Elizabeth explained that someone she knew a long time ago, had given it to her. It was not a lie, and Pamela did not ask further.

Was one of the girls Mama? If so, where was the sister and why had Mama never mentioned her? Mr. Smith-Jacobsen said that the dead Mary-Beth's mama was still alive. Did she have an aunt somewhere out there? An aunt who looked just like Mama?

A memory of that day in Thistleton just as she boarded the Wybrow carriage for the journey home, shifted through her yet again.

She tingled all over remembering that her eyes had locked for one infinitesimal second on a pair of watery-grey irises peering from a passing carriage. Eyes that looked exactly like Mama's. She had spent hours wondering about it, only to dismiss the incident as her vivid imagination. A tingling sensation seemed to expand within her, whenever she thought of it. Never in her wildest dreams had she ever envisaged another Mama. No, not a Mama, an identical twin, just like the little girls in the picture.

Whatever had Mr. Smith-Jacobsen thought of her outburst about twins? He had not seen him since that day either. He obviously thought her a complete nincompoop and was keeping his distance.

Yesterday evening, Pamela had told Elizabeth that Mrs Wybrow had received several calling cards.

Calling cards? Elizabeth's insides had instantly started to fizz, as her immediate thoughts went to Lord Bauval. Had he too left his calling card? She had brought her thoughts to an abrupt halt. No, she could not let him invade her mind and her heart day after day. His letter had made his feelings plain. His opinion, no longer mattered, she had to ignore her aching

173

heart. Of course he had not left his calling card at Nimbus Folly. Even so, her stomach had knotted. She knew from what Mr. Wybrow said, that James Bauval was in London for some time, but had since returned. James had not made contact. Nor would he.

Her 'champion' had had his fun of a minor dalliance with an ignorant girl. She closed her eyes to shut out the memory of his rich voice and soft words. *Oh, Jemmy*, her mind cried, in spite of her just-made decision. *Why did you let me come to believe in love?*

Still feeling somewhat wretched, she knocked on Pamela's door to accompany her down to the Nimbus Folly breakfast room.

'Pamela, Miss Chetwode,' Mrs Wybrow beamed as they entered. 'Lady Levana sent us a note paying her respects and inviting us to call upon her now that we are settled here.' She gave a satisfied smile and indicated another card on a silver tray beside her. 'Mrs Smith-Jacobsen has asked if she may call upon us this very morning.' She looked across the table as the girls sat down. 'What do you think of that?' The lace on her head fluttered as she sighed. 'It is a pity Mr. Wybrow is so often away on his lordship's business. He really should be here to welcome our new friends.'

'But Mama,' Pamela helped herself to hot rolls a maid placed before her, 'They are not new. We already know most of them.'

'My dear, think of his position as head of this family. Think how many of our guests will concede to his authority now he is the earl's chosen man?' She nodded to a maid, who poured her another cup of steaming coffee.

Elizabeth silently marvelled at how quickly Mrs Wybrow had adapted to the new luxuries. Like the second cup of coffee at breakfast time, pudding at luncheon and dinner. A welcoming fire in the Nimbus Folly hallway every morning. And extra servants.

'I would like you to make a special effort Pamela, dear. Although our furniture is new, this house is still damp in places, so your turquoise Jacquard frock will be perfect. I think too, that your hair is just a little too headstrong when loose.' She cast Elizabeth a meaningful look, 'perhaps you can arrange some of it in a small topknot, then brush the rest free?' She spooned more sugar into her coffee. 'You will both need to begin getting ready as soon as you have eaten.'

'Mary-Beth,' Pamela whispered even though they were now upstairs and out of her mama's hearing. 'I have an idea.'

Elizabeth raised her brows as Pamela giggled through her scheme.

An hour later some of Pamela's hair was dressed in a most becoming coil on top of her head, while the rest flowed in glossy dark russet waves down the back of her Jacquard gown. She had pinched her lips until they were red, and a silver filigree pendant round her neck completed her look.

Elizabeth was dressed in almost the same way.

Pamela had pleaded with her to wear the deep-aqua damask gown. Pamela then dressed Elizabeth's hair to match her own. Pamela also encouraged Elizabeth to pink-up her lips.

'Ah there you-,' The breath caught in Mrs Wybrow's throat. Her daughter looked every inch as she expected, but Miss Chetwode had copied Pamela's style exactly. 'How becoming you both look,' she muttered archly, 'Miss Chetwode, I do believe you are vying with my daughter.'

'Mama,' Pamela cut in, 'Miss Chetwode has such beautiful clothes I thought she too ought to dress for the occasion.'

It was obvious that Mrs Wybrow was not pleased.

'Well, it is far too late for Miss Chetwode to go and change, as the barouche is outside.'

'This is so exciting,' Pamela whispered as they entered the receiving parlour.

Nimbus Folly, now decorated in all the latest styles, glittered and glimmered with new everything. There were currently fires blazing in all fire-grates in every room to eradicate, so Mrs Wybrow declared previously, any lingering damp. Now she was fussing about where they should all be when Mrs Smith-Jacobsen was announced.

Her hands flapped through the air. 'Pamela, please sit down on the new sofa, and I should like you to remain seated as she comes into the room. Come along dear, and arrange yourself. After she is announced, you will then stand and courtesy in your prettiest manner.'

She glanced at Elizabeth. 'Miss Chetwode, you may take a seat over there.' She pointed to the bare wooden stool underneath the window.

Elizabeth clamped down her irritation. She had to remember that she was only a companion. 'Thank-you Mrs Wybrow.'

'And you are to stand up and courtesy the moment she enters.'

'Yes, Mrs Wybrow.'

Elizabeth felt, rather than heard Pamela's suppressed merriment, and it lifted her spirits.

Dabbs tapped on the receiving parlour door before opening it fully and stepping inside.

'Mr. and Mrs Smith-Jacobsen, Mr. Henry Smith-Jacobsen and Miss Rhoda Smith-Jacobsen.'

As the visitors swept in, it took all Elizabeth's self-control to hide her astonishment.

All of them?

She and Pamela leapt up and curtsied at exactly the same time.

'Mr. and Mrs Smith-Jacobsen, Henry, and Rhoda,' Mrs Wybrow gushed happily. 'What an extreme pleasure this is.'

'My dears,' Mrs Smith-Jacobsen beamed at Pamela and then Elizabeth after the greetings were over, 'how clever of you to dress in like fashion.' She turned to her host. 'Miss Wybrow is the envy of all the girls in the district. They all want a companion just like Miss Chetwode.' She addressed Rhoda and Henry. 'Is that not so my dears?' Twitching a dark brow back to her host, she smiled. 'I believe you have made substantial alterations to this beautiful house.'

It took Mrs Wybrow a second to catch on. 'Please,' she gestured with a wave of her hand. 'Do let me show you around.'

George Smith-Jacobsen, like his son had a fair skin that mottled easily. 'Oh no, dear Mrs Wybrow,' red spots coloured his face, 'it is the children who would love to see the place. Perhaps Miss Wybrow and Miss Chetwode would show them around?'

Due to the time, it took for the younger ones to navigate Nimbus Folly, the visit lasted longer than the accepted twenty minutes. After they left however, Elizabeth sensed that something was definitely amiss with Mrs Wybrow. She was tight-lipped with her, and snappish with Pamela. Why though, when the Smith-Jacobsen family were made so welcomed beforehand?

The dour annoyance continued throughout the morning and during luncheon.

What had gone wrong? What had happened to cause Mrs Wybrow to be so upset? Pamela sensing it too, announced that perhaps an afternoon walk in the brisk September air would be just the thing, and Elizabeth readily agreed.

It would be a relief to be escaping the stifling atmosphere of Mrs Wybrow's ill humour.

They were just stepping through the front door when Pamela squealed with excitement.

'There is his lordship.'

Elizabeth's foolish heart skittered the second she saw James Bauval walking towards them.

He looked exquisite. And, irrespective of her intentions to the contrary, Elizabeth's unruly heart disobeyed her insane mind, as fluttering butterflies sashayed along her spine.

His elegant navy-blue frock coat emphasising the breadth of his shoulders and the slenderness of his waist gave her toes a peculiar sensation. His dark blue breeches tucked into glossy black leather knee boots revealed the muscular perfection of his legs. A simply tied silver-grey cravat fell gracefully over a white silk shirt perfecting the whole look.

He tilted his black steeple hat as he reached the veranda-porch.

'Good afternoon. I am delighted to see you both looking so well.'

Elizabeth's stomach rose and fell in little flurries as his blue-black hair caught the light as his head inclined.

This was the man she loved!

This was the man who stole her heart, only to crush it and throw it carelessly away.

So why then did her whole being react with exquisite pleasure to his presence? Why did her heart thump and bounce?

'Good afternoon my lord,' Pamela responded prettily. 'We are just starting an afternoon walk.'

'Good afternoon, Lord Bauval,' Elizabeth said before Pamela could possibly ask him to join them. 'Pray do excuse us, the afternoons can grow nippy at this time of year, and we do not want to be caught by the mists.' She took Pamela's elbow, to steer round his immense frame.

James gazed at her with indulgent tenderness. She had every right to be angry. He had told her he loved her and wanted her to be his wife, then mad with jealousy accused her of having a lover. No wonder she left the room straight-backed and angry that last evening they were together.

Then in the torment of one who loves too much, and believes too little, he had sent her that dreadful letter. In it he admitted arrogance, over-bearing pride, and autocratic behaviour. He begged her forgiveness and promised to let her go without a blemish to her reputation.

At the time it seemed the gracious thing to do.

Only he was completely wrong, and now despised himself for it.

She did not have a lover.

There were many times, he thought about writing back but decided to face her directly instead.

Now she glared at him now in such a blistering, fulminating manner he felt sick with self-disgust. To let her down with his green-eyed accusation was vile enough, his rejection however was far worse.

He had come to Nimbus Folly to put matters right, on the pretext of informing Mrs Wybrow that her husband had one or two more errands before returning home.

'Would you delay your walk until I have completed my business with Mrs Wybrow?' he cast Elizabeth a swift glance, 'Then I shall be delighted to escort you round the parklands myself.'

Her chrysolite eyes flashed prisms of yellow gold fury, yet her voice remained completely steady.

'My lord, we would not dream of inconveniencing you.'

That schoolmarm, tone! How sweet the sound.

'I understand,' he pursed his lips to hide his childish pleasure. 'In that case,' he schooled his expression to one of polite query, 'may I perhaps entreat you to call at the house? My mother has expressed a wish to meet you both.' He paused. 'She will be delighted to see you.'

Mrs Wybrow had bustled into the hallway.

'Of course, my lord,' she trilled. 'They will consider it an honour to pay their respects to Lady Levana this very afternoon.'

Elizabeth perched on the chintz sofa in Lady Levana's 'pleasant' room trying not to think of the time she was here before. The time she realised that she had fallen in love with Jemmy Bauval and there was no way out. Now, she was destined to love in vain for the rest of her life; to be a slave of unrequited love. Not that she knew it at that time, for she had already begun to believe that he truly loved her.

She had chided herself many times since.

Lady Levana broke the brief silence. 'It is a pretty room is it not?'

'It is the prettiest room I have ever seen Lady Levana,' Pamela agreed happily.

Lady Levana smiled at the sweet-faced, russet haired girl, so full of the joys of life, and who obviously adored this new Mary-Beth.

Elizabeth blinked back her thoughts. Lord Bauval's mother, Lady Levana was an elegant woman in her late fifties. Now as her host's discerning eyes roved over her face, a *frission* of alarm sped down her spine. *Not her too?* 'Yes, I agree,' she managed with quiet composure.

Lady Levana had not really believed it possible that Mary-Jane had had a Mary-Beth too. She sighed within herself. The pact made between the twins so long ago might have been shelved under the circumstances, but true to their childhood vow, each sister had named their eldest daughter after the other.

Mary-Beth.

Mary, after Mary Jane Bauval-Lynes. Beth after Elizabeth Anne Bauval-Lynes. Of course, neither had intended them both to have a daughter of the same name. Only the first-born daughter was to bear that name. The other twin was to call her eldest daughter, Anne Jane, so each twin had a girl named after the other. Yet, unknown to the other, both their daughters had the same name.

Miss Chetwode, though had taken the more formal name of Elizabeth, but Jemmy had told her of his first meeting with Miss Chetwode, and that in her confusion, she almost said 'Mary-Beth' when he asked who she was. He had not exaggerated the likeness either. This lovely child sitting before her, apart from one or two minor differences, was indeed a living image of the sick, spiritless Mary-Beth. Yet, Miss Chetwode was neither sick nor spiritless.

No. There was a fire behind the chrysolite eyes. Her Chetwode eye-colour was the main distinguishing difference between the two Mary-Beths. Levana swallowed the lump in her throat. Mary-Jane found happiness after all. *Oh Mary, why did you swap your gown for Betty's?* her mind railed, *Oh Betty. Why did you do such a dreadful thing to your sister? Why did you not speak up before such a tragedy occurred?*

180

She knew the answer of course. Grandfather Bauval vowed never to forgive Mary-Jane for eloping with the Westernbury rogue. Full of pain and anger, he cut off his beloved granddaughter without a penny and refused to have her name mentioned ever again. What would he have done if he knew the truth? What if he knew it was Elizabeth Anne, their own dear Betty, who planned to run off with that dreadful man? That only hours before the planned elopement, Betty discovered that Westernbury already had a wife and several children in the North somewhere? That in a panic had sent her beloved, and blissfully uninformed, sister into the gardens instead?

Poor Betty, the weaker of the two sisters had fallen for a philandering liar.

But it was Mary-Jane who paid the price.

Did this child now perched on the edge of the chintz sofa, really not have any idea of her real lineage? A blissful pleasure stole through Levana.

After some effort, Finn Chetwode eventually married Mary Jane. How would Betty take that when she found out? Would it give her absolution, or would it only add to the pain? The widowed Sir Finn Chetwode, Baron Filton, was a full twenty-five years older than the twins. But Mary-Jane loved him to pieces. Betty hated him. Hated the thought that such an old man might wed her sister, and that she too might be coerced into marriage with an older man. Betty had plotted and schemed until at last both Mary and Finn thought the other had given them up. A year later, Betty was too madly in love with Westernbury to give her previous scheming another thought.

How the sins of the parents rested on the heads of the children, even down unto the third and fourth generation.

No! Please let it not be so in this case. Please let the sin stop with the death of the late Mary-Beth.

Surely there was such a thing as divine forgiveness?

Levana's heart went out to this new Mary-Beth; this Elizabeth Chetwode who had captured her son's heart. What kind of life had she experienced? Not an affluent one by any means.

Would she forgive the terrible wrong done to her sweet mother? Would she look kindly on Betty and love her in spite of everything?

Levana gazed into the clear innocent face of her own flesh and blood. Because, if this child refused to forgive, then it was better that Betty never discovered her existence at all. On the other hand, Betty needed to be told, and the sooner the better.

Elizabeth drank the offered tea, but could not touch any of the tiny cakes. Lady Levana had given her *that* look. Now, the thought of eating made her throat dry up. Yet Lord Bauval's mother had not looked at her unkindly. It was that assessing look that concerned Elizabeth. Had someone told Lady Levana of the likeness to the other Mary-Beth?

Jemmy? Did that mean he too, noticed the resemblance between them?

A chill nipped down her spine, then was immediately chased away by a searing heat coursing through every vein in her body.

What was the dead Mary-Beth to Lord Bauval that he had to tell his mother of it, and of her? She knew her namesake could not possibly be Lord Bauval's sister, because his mother did not look in the least like her own dear Mama. If not his sister, then what? His mistress?

She drew a steadying breath. Mistress to two men? Is that why the other Mary-Beth was in an unloved grave?

Was that why James had not mentioned her? Did the two men who loved the deceased Mary-Beth expect her to love them also and in exactly the same way?

Lady Levana instantly noticed the sudden flush that followed the pallor of Miss Chetwode's cheeks.

'My dear, are you quite well?' She glanced at the merry fire crackling beyond the hearth. 'Is it too warm in here?' She picked up a bell to summon the maid. 'Let us remove to a cooler room.'

'Thank-you no, Lady Levana,' Elizabeth glanced at Pamela. 'I think we should be going?'

'You must take my carriage.'

'There is no need Lady Levana, it is but a short walk back to Nimbus Folly.'

Anxiety crept over Lady Levana's face. 'I could not bear it if you got a chill.'

Elizabeth's heart quickened. She was obviously thinking of the other Mary-Beth. Lady Levana had loved and approved of the other Mary-Beth? How was that possible?

Elizabeth's heart jumped, but not with anxiety. Lady Levana was a woman she could trust.

'Lady Levana,' she gazed into the gentle blue eyes and took immediate courage from them. 'There is something I must know. A mystery I need to solve.'

The gentle reply came on a thready breath. 'Yes, my dear, I believe there is.'

James sat in his usual place by the fire turning the whole thing over in his mind. Mama was quite right to admit to Miss Chetwode that there was indeed a mystery. He would not have it any other way. She was right too, in asking Miss Chetwode to wait until a more suitable time for the tale to be told.

Just who should tell it though? And how?

There was Lady Bucklow of course, but she was too far away. Mama was a little too involved perhaps to tell it. The time for flimflam was over however. Miss Chetwode needed, and was entitled to, the truth.

Betty? He instantly dismissed that idea. Her brother? No, even he did not know all of it. He sighed. It would have to be him. He would have to acknowledge that his family were guilty of such betrayal as to shame him to the depths of his being.

He loved Elizabeth Chetwode and it broke his heart to tell her what happened. He closed his eyes as the image of her filled his mind. He recalled the way she looked at their first

183

meeting. How a golden twist of hair caught the sunlight, her chrysolite irises, her raspberries and cream cheeks. The swish of the chambray dress as she took those two infinitesimal steps away from him, a move that made him want to take her in his arms and soothe away her racked expression.

The thought of revealing all made him shudder. Would or could she ever forgive them?

Swallowing the last of his brandy, he sighed again. Irrespective of the outcome, it had to be done.

In spite of all the buzzing questions, Elizabeth slept well that night. She much preferred her room at the Folly than the one at Wybrow House. More importantly, there was a lock on the door, with a key on the inside.

'I believe we are in for a fine day,' Mrs Wybrow beamed at breakfast the following morning. 'Probably one of the last we shall see for some time. I still need a few things for the house therefore a ride into Market Overton will make a pleasant change.'

'Mama,' Pamela burst out happily, 'may we take the new carriage?'

Mrs Wybrow nodded smugly. 'Naturally dearest.'

Elizabeth's heart sank. The last thing she wanted was a trip out. She wanted to be on hand in case Lady Levana sent for her.

Pamela had been very curious by the talk of a mystery. Thankfully Lady Levana quickly changed the subject before any questions were raised. Just before they left however, Lady Levana took Elizabeth aside and confided that soon the story would be told.

What story?

Elizabeth looked from Pamela to Mrs Wybrow. Why did it have to be today?

Pamela noticed her dismay. 'Are you unwell Miss Chetwode? I do hope you have not taken a chill.' She turned to her mother. 'Lady Levana was quite worried about her yesterday. Miss Chetwode suddenly went a ghostly white and then flushed most alarmingly.'

Mrs Wybrow took up the eye glass, a recent indulgence, dangling from her neck to peer at Elizabeth from across the table. 'I doubt there is much to worry about,' she dropped the eye-glass. 'However, Pamela, you are right to express concern. Miss Chetwode, I feel you would benefit from a day indoors. I shall have a fire made up in the library, as well as in your room. That way you may go where you please, and still be warm.'

Elizabeth supressed her surprise. Fires to be lit just for her?

'I shall instruct the servants to make sure you have everything you need.'

Elizabeth watched the carriage disappear round the tower of the Folly with amazement. She could hardly believe it. She was being well and truly regarded.

A little thought niggled at her though. Was it anything to do with the Smith-Jacobsen's visit? Perhaps it had something to do with James Bauval? An unreasonable ripple of anger fanned through her.

Even though she felt a sense of freedom at being alone and not having anything to do, Elizabeth still found it hard to settle.

When would Lady Levana send for her? What was the mystery?

Wandering alongside the shelves browsing the books, she trailed her fingers down the spines of one or two the newer ones intending to choose one and settle in a comfortable chair, but abruptly sheered backwards staring with horror at a familiar gold lettering on dull red leather.

That book? The same vile book she found under her bed at Wybrow House. Mr. Wybrow had it brought here in full view of his family? Had he no shame? Twisting around, she rushed to an armchair-back to lean on, and almost keeling over the top, gulped in great gasps of air.

185

Suddenly she was engulfed in a firm embrace.

'My dear Miss Chetwode.' Barely able to comprehend what was happening, Elizabeth found herself being hauled against a wool-coated body. 'My darling,' he crooned, 'when informed that you were a little out of sorts, I had no idea it meant you could hardly stand up.'

Still shuddering, she clutched blindly at the coat.

'My love,' she heard, 'come and sit down.'

Her brain suddenly rallied as her senses returned. 'I am all right,' she whispered into the woollen coat. Then, to prove it looked up and almost collapsed with shame. 'Mr. Smith-Jacobsen?'

His intense blue eyes roved her face. 'My darling, you look as if you have had a great shock.'

She began pulling away from him. 'It is nothing. Now, if I can just sit on this chair, I shall call for refreshments.'

He continued gazing down at her. 'I only came to tell you that I have left a box of plants in the summerhouse. Thank-goodness I did.' His face, still creased with concern, hovered over hers. 'I shall call for a doctor immediately.'

'No. I thank you Mr. Smith-Jacobsen, but there is no need.'

She was a fool to let the book distress her. What harm could it possibly do? 'I am perfectly well.'

'Yes,' he agreed carefully, 'your colour has returned.' His fair lashes dipped to the hollow below his eyes. 'In that case,'

And before Elizabeth could move away, he lowered his face.

'What the devil is going on here?' an enraged voice suddenly struck out.

Elizabeth was not the only one to jump. Henry pulled away with such speed that she nearly toppled backwards. Only the back of the chair behind, saved her.

Smith-Jacobsen spun on a heel. 'Lord Bauval, I have permission to address Miss Chetwode. She is to be my wife.'

James Bauval glared at Henry. 'The devil she is, Jacobsen,' he growled. 'You know very well Miss Chetwode is under my wing.'

Henry faced James with calm assurance. 'You may deem that to be true, Bauval, but I know better. You have no legal rights over her whatsoever.'

James crept forwards like a cat stalking prey, 'You sir,' he grated ominously, 'had better get out before I throw you out.'

Elizabeth, too shocked to move before, now pushed away from the chair-back. 'You will do no such thing Lord Bauval!'

James turned to her, and with slow deliberation asked, 'Am I to believe you are encouraging his suite?'

Elizabeth froze. How could he ask such an appalling question? 'No.'

Henry's face mottled pink. 'What is it to you if she is Bauval?'

Elizabeth faced them both. 'Stop this,' she fumed. 'If neither of you can behave like gentlemen, then you may leave immediately.'

'You heard what she said,' James grated. 'Clear off.'

'You would like that,' Henry returned with forced calm. 'So, the way is clear for you,' he advanced a little closer to James, 'to reject her.'

James moved swiftly. 'Why you-'

'-Just as you rejected my Mary-Beth.'

Elizabeth's hand shot to her mouth. What did Mr. Smith-Jacobsen mean?

Her eyes flicked to the earl's. Had he rejected Mary-Beth? 'Did you?'

As soon as James saw her racked expression his anger evaporated. 'No.'

The full realisation suddenly struck him, and turning to Henry, said, '*Your* Mary-Beth?'

The split-second silence was more frightening than the noise of their quarrel.

Henry's face mottled even more.

Chapter Twelve

Henry Smith-Jacobsen's jaw moved, then, resuming his former calm, he slowly nodded his head.

'Yes,' he said in a clear calm voice. 'Mine. She was always mine.' His voice dropped. 'I loved her.' His eyes closed with his murmured, 'Oh, how I loved my sweet Mary-Beth.'

'Mr. Smith-Jacobsen, I beg you, say no more,' Elizabeth pleaded.

Smith-Jacobsen so lost in his reverie, however, ignored her.

James swung to her. Their eyes met and locked. Those chrysolite irises, so beautiful, yet now so racked, caused a pain to rip through him.

A selfish, greater need, however, spurred him on. He inclined his head. 'Is there more Miss Chetwode?'

Her chrysolite irises sparked. 'There is nothing you need to know.'

Henry heaved in a deep sighing breath. 'Oh, but there is,' he whispered. 'So much more.'

The barren grave seared into Elizabeth's mind. It had to bloom. Whatever the other Mary-Beth did was of no consequence anymore. She reached out and touched Henry's arm. 'Mr Smith-Jacobsen, I beg you, say no more. It is in the past, leave it there, I beg you.'

James took two steps forwards. 'Let him speak.'

Capturing her outstretched arms in his hands James drew her gently to his side. His dark eyes flecked silver as she made a move to protest. His top lip formed a wavy 'm'.

'My love, let him speak.'

The scent of spicy soap and a scent that was unique to him fired her senses. She had so longed to be close to him.

She caught her breath as a tremor flitted through her. How could she still want him? If he asked, she knew she would give herself to him in the same way the other Mary-Beth gave herself to Henry.

No, she must not let such notions overrule her common-sense. How in the middle of all this could he have such an effect on her? How could she feel such love after his behaviour towards her? Had her treacherous heart failed her, or was she just another victim of his charm? Her mind roiled. Like the other *Mary-Beth*?

'She was never 'your love' Bauval.' Henry's eyes were unseeing. 'She was mine.'

Elizabeth wanted to shout over his calm impenitent voice, but her mouth froze.

Her emotions were trapped. Crushed with concern for Henry on the one hand, intoxicated by the closeness of James on the other.

She felt strong and weak at the same time.

Henry's voice wobbled slightly.

'Married?' he murmured as if answering a question. 'Yes.' He turned directly to James. 'Not in the eyes of the law you understand?' He shifted with defiance. 'But enough for us to feel man and wife in each other's eyes. Man and wife in all but law,' he went on without remorse. 'I loved Mary-Beth as a man should love a woman.'

Elizabeth wanted to shut her eyes against the onslaught to come.

The shock on Lord Bauval's face exposed it all. It was as she thought. Mary-Beth was loved by both men.

She gasped. That was it. The story behind the summerhouse mural. The picture of a peacock too proud to see what was in front of his arrogant nose. Beneath him, the two seemingly insignificant brown doves, lovebirds in every sense, yet invisible to his lordship's lofty eye.

189

She glanced at Henry's softly glowing face. There was no sorrow there now.

She dared a look at Lord Bauval's face.

To her surprise she now saw not the anger or pain of a man deceived, but an exquisite gentleness flowing through him like clear melting honey. His onyx irises, now soft black velvet saw something only he could see. And whatever it was, it completely softened him.

Her heart leapt.

This was the man she would love for the rest of her life.

Her heart sank.

This was the man who loved so much, he was able to accept that his beloved loved another.

Henry shrugged. 'Call me out if it makes you feel better Bauval,' he drawled calmly. 'Not that I am any match for you, as well you know.' He sighed. 'My life for hers.'

His chin dipped. 'If only it was possible,' he groaned, 'I would have gladly given all to see her well again.'

'Oh, I shall call you right enough Jacobsen,' James responded softly. 'I think cousin-in-law might be a start.'

Elizabeth snapped from his side. 'Cousin in law?' she echoed in disbelief. 'Am I to understand this Mary-Beth was related to you?'

Bauval did not take his eyes off Henry. 'Second cousin to be exact.'

Oh, what a fool she was not to have realised that the other Mary-Beth was a close relative of James. She was in the family resting place after all.

And she, Elizabeth Chetwode, had not only fallen in love, but she had fallen in love with a blood relative. For, if what she and Henry discussed in the summerhouse about the twins, was true, and the other Mary-Beth was James' second cousin, then there was a possibility she too was related to him.

She hated him! Hated him for loving the other Mary-Beth so completely. Hated him for pretending to love her.

She stared up at his handsome face, crushed to her insides. He had only professed love for her because she looked like the other Mary-Beth.

Glancing at Smith-Jacobsen, she knew that he too, only showed an interest because of her resemblance to the woman he loved.

It was just too much to bear.

'I want you both to leave,' she said. She was shaking, and if they did not leave, she knew she might make a complete fool of herself and start crying. There was nothing wrong with crying, but she did not want to do so in front of either of them.

James looked at her. He could see she was in great turmoil, but her chrysolite eyes did not spark prisms of gold fury. Her skin lacked the pink tinge of indignation. The set of her jaw, the pallor of her skin, and the rigid way she faced them told him she was more than angry. She was desolate and heartsick. He looked at Smith-Jacobsen. What had Smith-Jacobsen done to so deeply wound her?

Recalling how he found them together brought back his own fury, and of course the reason he came.

Turning to her, and covering his feelings by stiff formality, he offered his refusal. 'Forgive me, but I cannot oblige, Miss Chetwode. I have something of great importance to discuss with you.'

He gave Henry a cursory glance. 'Excuse us if you please. This is a private family matter.'

Suddenly it all started up again.

'There is nothing you can say to my future wife that cannot be said in front of me,' Henry declared. Then, without waiting for a response he continued, 'Shall we all be seated?' He motioned to the various chairs in the library.

Elizabeth reeled back, 'Your future wife Mr. Smith-Jacobsen?'

'I think not,' James rallied.

'This time Bauval,' Henry was unyielding, 'there is nothing you can do about the matter. Mama has made some inquiries about Miss Chetwode.'

Mrs Smith-Jacobsen nosing around on her behalf? Elizabeth's stomach churned and the words came tumbling out.

'Inquiries?' she squeaked. 'What right do you or your family have to make inquiries about me?'

Panic stricken she looked from one to the other. What if anyone found out about her drunken Papa? What if anyone found out she had spent her childhood in a respectable, but poorer part of London? What if they discovered Mama worked her fingers to the bone to keep food on their table? That James started his working life in a brewery; and that she had worked as a teacher in a penny school? Worse still, that whenever Papa came home, he demanded they hand over, or pawn anything he considered of value no matter how little, to cover what he loathingly called his expenses'.

James instantly noticed the change and that racked expression sliced through him. Before he could say anything however, Henry turned to her.

'My father is, at this very moment seeking out your next of kin Miss Chetwode. So, you see,' he turned triumphantly to James, 'You are out of the running.'

One look at her ashen face was more than enough for James. He wanted to thrash Jacobsen for his tactlessness. However right now, she needed his gentleness.

'Come,' he said, taking her stiff shoulders and guiding her to a sofa. 'Sit down.' Pressing her gently down he took the liberty of sitting beside her.

Elizabeth needed to be alone and gather her wits. How could she get the two men out of the house and out of her sight?

Illogically, however, Lord Bauval's nearness made her want him to stay. She longed to nestle against the silk of his lemon waistcoat. She longed to feel the soft lawn of his pure white shirt sleeves round her. She craved the scent that was his alone, to fill her space.

'I assure you,' he whispered so close to her ear that his breath sent shivers through her, 'The Smith-Jacobsens have no inkling of your brother.'

The room began spinning. 'My brother?' she echoed faintly.

'Yes,' he whispered. 'The young man I saw you with in the village the day I left for London.'

Suddenly everything fell into place.

It was glaringly obvious that despite her previous denial, James Bauval thought her faithless, and without bothering to find out the truth, instantly discarded her. Tears pricked her eyes. The dull ache she experienced previously was nothing to the pain she felt now. She loved a man who thought her capable of duplicity. Fighting back the tears that threatened to disgrace her, she looked him full in the face.

Her chrysolite eyes so searching, fired his senses.

He wanted her in every way possible.

That tiny bud of tenderness he felt at their first meeting had blossomed upward and outward into a glorious bouquet.

Nothing else mattered except her. Her happiness was his happiness. Her will was his desire. Her needs were his needs. There was nothing he would not do for her. Her command was his to obey.

As the chrysolite eyes ended their search, her chin rose causing her rosy-beige hair to catch the glow of bright autumn sun coming in through the mullioned windows.

James' senses quickened.

The scent of her, the rustle of her dress, her breathing, sent fires roaring through him.

'I want you to go,' she said with soft resolution. 'Now.' She paused, sniffed, and pulled herself together before adding, 'I do not want to see you ever again Lord Bauval.'

Elizabeth, blinking into the night, tried to push that last awful scene from her mind. Yet, no matter how hard she tried, that dreadful moment when she told James Bauval she never wanted to see him again, kept winging back to her. It had dogged her for three long weeks now and would not go away. She had tried to chase the look on his face from her mind's eye a million times and failed. She tried so hard to forget the way he shook his head and raised his palms in utter defeat. She tried to forget the way he agreed, without further argument to leave. At the time, his stunned amazement nearly made her change her mind the very next second. But she remained strong. Self-preservation demanded it. After all, he never really loved her, his true love was the other Mary-Beth.

Now, Elizabeth spent every waking moment and times like this, in the night when she should be asleep, agonising over it until she hurt all over and sleep would not come. Her fists clenched under the bedcovers. She had to get over him.

Millions of women fell in love with men who could not, or would not return that love. The world must be full of unrequited love. Did those people remain broken hearted? No, they got on with their lives as if nothing untoward had happened.

Her stomach churned, and her mouth went dry. Her breath came in low groans, because she knew, deep in her being, she would never get over James Bauval. He would be there in her head and heart forever. After death even.

Her love would last beyond eternity.

Elizabeth knew she desperately needed to sleep. The dark rings under her eyes were becoming more visible each day. She was irritable with Pamela and now dreaded going out and about. She wanted to be invisible, yet everywhere she went, low whispers followed her.

Yet, still, the niggling feeling kept searing back that she had she missed something somewhere along the way. Something important. Every time she thought of it, she also remembered the letter. After all, the letter really spelled out his true feelings did it not?

What was the use of going through it all again? She needed to rest. Tomorrow was the day of the six-in-hand, and although she and Pamela had sewed, embroidered, and made lavender bags for the charity stalls, there was still much to do.

There was also the Mary-Beth mystery to solve. To her deep disappointment Lady Levana had not asked her to visit. Elizabeth, had however, completed the work on the grave. Even that fact brought that terrible afternoon back to her, because after Smith-Jacobsen and James left Nimbus Folly, she dragged herself to the summerhouse where she found a box of the exact plants she ruined, along with two large twine-knotted, wooden crosses for her to place there too. One at the head of the grave, and one for the foot. Her efforts, the rain, and the autumn sun had caused the flowers to flourish already. Yesterday the Violas and Alyssum had opened their heads to the sky, the cream and yellow Stardust were peeping through the gleaming foliage of the Begonias. And the Golden Moss daises were just springing up.

If only he had not sent that letter! If only he truly loved her and not the other Mary-Beth. If only her heart would let go.

Go away! her distressed mind cried.

Her impassioned plea, however went unheeded as her restless brain sought for the answer. Had she not done everything in her power to put it, and him out of her mind?

The Six-in-hand race had kept them busy though. It would also be the last large fair of the year, so the whole county was expected to buy from every vendor able to buy a pitch. There were cakes, jams, and preserves to be made to add to the final prize, and to sell. Anyone who was anyone was expected to contribute, and she, Pamela and Mrs Wybrow too, did their part.

Pamela's cheerful patter had kept her going to a certain extent. Not, that she always felt so kindly about it anymore. Sometimes it got so much, she just wanted to scream. There were shopping expeditions for new bonnets and gloves as Mrs Wybrow said it would be most unseemly to be going about in old tat on such an occasion. To Elizabeth's surprise, Mrs Wybrow had given her an advance on her companion's allowance to make the purchases. Her new bonnet of pink silk had a row of tiny violet rosebuds on the inside rim, and another row at the top of the crown. The gloriously wide ribbon ties matched the tiny rosebuds exactly, and her new kid gloves exactly matched her tan boots.

Why did James, the man she loved, and would always love, send *that* letter? Why did you keep it? another, more sensible voice asked. Anyone else with would have immediately destroyed it.

Now wide awake, Elizabeth sat bold upright staring sightlessly through the moonless room. The answer was to get rid of it right away.

Without another thought, Elizabeth threw back the bed-covers, whisked to the portmanteau and having become accustomed to the dark, was able to find the white envelope easily. Picking it up felt foolish and treacherous, as if she was being disloyal to herself.

Why had she not ripped it up or burned it immediately? Why had she not at least crumpled it up? She was such an idiot.

The feel of the parchment made her fingers shake, and her heart hammer.

Could, she do it? Could she get rid of the only tangible thing she had of him?

Then, with a soft cry of despair, she hugged it close to her, climbed back into bed, and fell, exhausted, into sleep.

The room was warm when she woke and an oil lamp already glimmered on the tiny square lace covered table next to her bed.

The servants now treated her as if she were family; soon, the iron tub behind the curtain would be filled with steaming, sweet scented water just for her.

Something scraped against her white cotton night-gown. The letter. All she had of a forsaken love. A few hours earlier, she thought to destroy it. Now all she wanted to do was cherish and keep it forever.

James Bauval had probably never given her a single thought since, while she, fool that she was, never stopped thinking about him.

As she held it away from her, his neat masculine slant jumped out at her in black bold letters.

Her head began to spin. Her fingers shook, and suddenly the letter was there in her hands. A split-second later, she had slipped it from the envelope and begun to read.

My dearest Miss Chetwode, After, much painful consideration I am prepared to give up all claim on you. I am ashamed to admit that my arrogance and pride got the better of me. In an autocratic manner, I overlooked your feelings completely. This of course, is no credit to me. Be assured that your reputation remains unblemished, and will continue to remain so. Please know that I am still your champion, and shall be at your side whenever you need me. I can only finish by begging your forgiveness for causing you so much distress. Yours ever, Jemmy.

Tears blurred her vision just as they did the first time, she read it. Why was she such an idiot to believe he ever loved her? She blinked down at his signature. Yours ever, Jemmy.

What a liar! He was never hers. She blinked again. There was more.

Postscript. Please know my darling that I love you and that you will be in my heart forever and ever.

Her heart stilled.

How had she missed that postscript?

In his heart forever and ever?

Her insides sang. She would be in his heart forever even after believing she was in love with someone else and, *after painful consideration*, would let her go, without a blemish to her reputation?

What kind of man did that? An unselfish one? A fainthearted one?

James Bauval faint hearted? The very thought made her want to laugh aloud.

James brought the snorting thoroughbred to a halt.

'Well, what do you think Theo?' he asked from his standpoint on the crest of the hogback. 'Enough of a trial?'

Theo pulled his mount up beside Bauval's, and rose up in his stirrups. 'You have certainly exceeded yourself this time Jemmy,' he grinned. 'Any new blood up for the kill this year?'

James scrutinized the landscape. Some of the two-mile course was clearly visible from their position. Some parts twisted right out of sight though, like the unfenced stretch by Rector's Gate; the narrow track skirting the village, and the start and finish line on the north meadow, behind the village.

The newly trimmed grass between the boundaries of recently partitioned-off areas, glistened with the residue of the previous night's rain. The conditions did not matter to him, but they might to a less experienced whip. However, in all the years of the two-mile race, no-one was ever injured, nor was there a horse lost. There were spills and other minor mishaps, but nothing that several flagons of ale could not put right.

A trace smile crossed his lordship's face, before a quick flip of the reins set his horse downwards. 'That would be telling sir.'

A few thundering paces later, Theo panted alongside. 'Do I take it there is a contender for the coveted ham?'

Without losing a stride, James tapped the end of his nose with a gloved finger. 'Let me put it this way, play it safe and hedge your bets. Come,' he called, before Theo could reply. 'Let us take a look at what is going on in honour of the event.'

The stalls set out on the u-shaped green, their oilskin awnings flapping in rhythm with the early October breeze, were already full of local and county specialities.

'Very industrious.' Theo observed. 'Considering it is more than four hours before the start.'

'Indeed, and there is plenty to go around.' Bauval scanned the brightly coloured stalls hoping to catch a glimpse of Elizabeth helping somewhere. Disappointment, however, nipped his insides.

'The six-in-hand is the event of the year Theo. All traders, and craftsmen have the right to have a stall here.' He pointed out a stand. 'The more affluent contribute to the Hooby Alms Society by making things to sell. Tradespeople, make a smaller contribution, by giving a percentage of their takings to the same.'

Had Miss Chetwode's fair hand made a contribution too?

He suppressed a sigh. He had stayed away from Nimbus Folly ever since she told him she never wanted to see him again. During the last three weeks, the whole excruciating episode went around his mind so many times, that he wondered how he kept his sanity.

Why had it gone so horribly wrong? Why did those chrysolite eyes look at him with adoration one minute, and aversion the next? Had he mistaken the adoration? His heart had leapt when he saw that look of love on her face. A love that meant he had not completely lost her after all. It meant there was a chance, no matter how faint, that she cared for him a little.

Enough to work and build when the time was right though? Enough to forgive him for his crass assumption of her character? Enough to forgive the dreadful wrongs his family inflicted on hers?

They were all to blame. Each played a part in Mary-Jane's downfall.

He had unwittingly added to it in the most degrading manner by assuming Elizabeth had a lover.

So, what happened to turn everything round that fateful afternoon in Nimbus Folly library? Was something said or done during the exchange, or after, that caused her outburst? Whatever it was, it gave him no chance to speak of the past, or the future. Now of course, it was up to her brother, the soon to be officially declared, Lord Bauval-Chetwode, to break it to his sister.

A wry chuckle rose into his throat. Against all odds, Finn's son, by his first marriage, died years ago. Unlucky for the older Chetwode, not even forty years old, but somewhat lucky for the much younger half-brother, James. For James not only inherited an original and substantial legacy direct from Finn, but now stood to inherit the Cambridge pile too.

As for Miss Chetwode, Finn's settlement provided for her every need. An immense property in Hertford, with all the necessary funds to run it, a generous annuity with the clause that it was for her own personal use, and a dowry of twenty-five thousand pounds.

What a prestigious companion for Pamela Wybrow to have!

'That chuckle banished your frown, old man. Thought you might remain in a sulk forever.' Theo chortled. 'She must be some filly for you to be so smitten. When do we get to meet the female who has knocked you into a humourless trance?'

James wheeled his mount away from the village. 'Doubt you ever will Kennelly,' he said without looking around. 'She has refused me. Come,' he rapidly changed the subject. 'There is much work to do before the race starts.'

Elizabeth's heart jumped at the sight of the two horsemen cantering away from the village.

One, she did not know.

The other was James Bauval looking so straight backed and powerful in fine burgundy. She doubted whether anything bothered him at all as the two of them were laughing, so obviously he did not have a care in the world.

That frightened her. It had been raining during the night, which meant quagmire conditions underfoot. The wind whistling in from the sea did not help either. Yet, she knew, that whatever the conditions, the race would go on.

And what a race!

Nearly the whole course wired off and wide enough in some parts, for four carriages to pass, while other stretches were almost too narrow for a dog-cart to scrape through.

Mrs Wybrow bobbed her head round the canopy of the new carriage to look over to the village green.

'Thank goodness Mrs Smith-Jacobsen and Mrs Snape have not yet arrived.' The two lime-green feathers on her new mustard coloured hat wobbled as she was helped from the carriage. 'On this occasion being early is to our credit,' she explained to Pamela and Elizabeth. 'It shows how willing, and eager we are to serve the less well appointed, who, you understand need the charity of the likes of myself. To be ardently immersed in benevolence, is extremely gratifying.'

'Does that mean we are now in a similar position to when we lived in America Mama?'

Mrs Wybrow's head jerked to Pamela. 'Hush,' she muttered. 'You know Papa forbade us to speak of the past.'

'But Mama,' Pamela persisted, 'It cannot matter anymore, not now we are rich again?'

A thin white line formed round Mrs Wybrow's mouth. 'Pamela,' she said, her voice hoarse, 'I do not know what has got into you these past weeks while Papa had been away.' She shot a quick glance at Elizabeth. 'I hope you have not encouraged her Miss Chetwode?' Without giving Elizabeth a chance to speak, she added, 'Mr. Wybrow will be back this very afternoon. It is his responsibility to ensure all rules of the Six-in-hand race are followed to the letter.'

An instant icy chill swept through Elizabeth. Being at her employer's mercy again, on top of everything else did not bear thinking about.

The sun breaking through the grey clouds, caused a cheer to go up. With less than ten minutes to go before the start of the race, its appearance was considered a good omen. The growing throng, in lively mood, pressed through the crowds, placing bets, and sizing up the displays. With good natured banter and cheery shouts, others spilled out to the stands on the meadow behind the inn.

'How pretty,' Mrs Smith-Jacobson suddenly exclaimed taking out a piece of tapestry from a box. 'I might buy this for Rhoda. She adores peacocks.'

Elizabeth quickly bustled Pamela away from the stand. She had worked hard on that particular piece, and was not quite sure she wanted to give it up for charity. It was a smaller copy of the one on the summerhouse mural. Perversely it reminded her of true love. She was a fool, because her true love had ended in disaster.

A gloom settled over her. If there was no such thing as true love, then why did each generation encourage the next to believe it existed? Why did poets write, and singers sing of its power?

Why were books so full of the absurd optimism that each man and woman, eventually found their true, one and only sweetheart?

Why did she feel there was a great space inside her? A space often so overflowing with joy that she wanted to race across the hill tops, shouting it out to the whole world. At other times, a space so cold and empty, all she wanted to do, was creep into the tiniest hole possible and hide away forever.

How could one man's simple quirk of a brow, a trace smile, or a fleck of silver in onyx, have such an effect on her? Why did her blood rush through her veins at the mere memory of his touch? Why did she ache, with the need to be near him, and yet dismiss him when he was?

She of all people should know better.

Pamela's voice brought her out of her ruminations.

'Look, Mary-Beth, the brass band,' she waved a dainty gloved hand in the direction of a strong but temporary wooden dais.

They had reached the thronging meadow behind the village without Elizabeth really noticing. Now as she looked up, her gloominess vanished, and she smiled. There was indeed, a fine brass band, getting ready to play.

'Oh, look,' Pamela waved towards the very far end of the meadow. 'There is Lord Bauval.'

Elizabeth's heart thumped at the mere mention of his name. Then, whipping her head up, she spotted him disappearing out of sight.

And gasped.

For perched on a racing phaeton pulled by six greys, making his way to the start line, was Jamie.

'Mary-Beth, if we hurry to the north meadow, we will see the line-up.'

Blinking, Elizabeth gawped at Jamie. How had he managed to find out about the race? What if he won? The consequences did not bear thinking about. Naturally, she did not believe Hooby would be doomed if an interloper won. The villagers however, did, and a victorious interloper would be in danger of their fear.

She turned to Pamela, 'Quickly then!'

The next moment they were spinning through the crowds, Elizabeth grim faced, and a blithe Pamela, one stride behind.

Someone suddenly stepped directly into their path. 'Ah ha.'

The loathsome voice brought them both to a rapid standstill.

'Papa!' Pamela exclaimed.

Walter Wybrow's thin smile covered them both.

'My dears.' His triumphant grin directed at Elizabeth caused her insides to squirm. 'I have been looking everywhere for you.

'I had hoped to catch up with you before now.' Wybrow glanced swiftly round before swivelling his eyes back to Elizabeth. 'I have someone with me.' There was a malicious gleam in his eyes. 'Someone extremely interested to meet the amazing *Miss Chetwode.*' His eyes narrowed. 'Such an enlightening fellow.' He turned to Pamela. 'I believe your mama is looking for you.'

'She said we could look around.'

'Quite so,' Wybrow returned smoothly, 'however, due to Miss Chetwode's special surprise, your mama will accompany you this afternoon.'

A horrible intuition caused Elizabeth look beyond Wybrow and search the crowd. A moment later, her stomach lurched, for, pushing his way drunkenly through everyone, was her father, and there was no way of avoiding him.

Chapter Thirteen

'A Cambridge Chetwode?' Wybrow mocked close to her ear. 'I think not *Miss Westernbury*. A runaway impostor more like.'

Elizabeth instantly skipped sideways, ducked into the crowd and was off, running blindly through the crowds.

James Bauval, seated high on his crane-necked phaeton and keeping careful control of six gleaming horses, glanced over the press of people. A flash of pink silk caught his eye.

He knew instantly who was racing away from the meadow and his insides crumbled. Was she so determined never to set eyes on him again that she had to run away? His blue-black brows snapped together.

'I say Jemmy,' Theo's enthusiasm jarred his senses, 'from your dire expression anyone would think the race lost already.'

'That, or someone's just walked over his grave,' Lawrence grinned, wheeling the six Arabs attached to his lightweight phaeton around on the moist grass.

Lord Rawsthorne moved his rig to face them. 'A bit previous to be talking of death, ain't it?'

Lord Bauval turned and saw the soon-to-be announced baron, Lord Bauval-Chetwode in his position at the far end of the line-up with his high-flyer phaeton and team of Sixers clearly ready for the off.

Could Miss Chetwode be running from her brother and not him? James glanced back through the crowd just in time to see her duck through the trees and disappear.

204

He inwardly shuddered. When she previously attempted that route, she became embedded in mud.

Theo had followed his gaze to the end of the line-up. 'I say, Bauval, that fellow at the far end looks remarkably familiar. Do we know him?'

'Everybody looks familiar in this setting Theo,' Rawsthorne drawled. 'Everyone who's anyone from here to London has turned out.'

'Yes,' Lawrence nodded. 'Play is high this year I believe.'

Suddenly James could not give a fig for the play, the race, or the good of the village. All he cared about was Miss Chetwode and the reason for her flight. His first impulse was to break up from his party to go chasing after her. Her words however, came searing back to him. *I do not want to ever see you again, Lord Bauval.* He closed his eyes to dash the words and the haunted look on her face, from his mind. Whatever the reason for her flight, she would not thank him for interfering. Having made her feelings plain, he being a true gentleman had to accept them. She felt betrayed. His high-handed arrogance had robbed him of the woman he loved. Now, he had to accept her decision, as disheartening as it was to him. He had to endure the unendurable. This excruciating was pain was far beyond anything he had ever experienced in his life. And nothing had prepared him for it! Nobody had told him that the torment of the rejection of the person you loved, was worse than all pain put together. He would not, could not reveal his anguish to anyone. Ever. It was his, and his alone to bear.

Pulling himself together, he turned to the task ahead.

The racecourse ahead, still damp, but no longer waterlogged, beckoned the twelve entrants, with their seventy-two horses between them. Each man poised on his sporting vehicle and eager for the off had waited for the gun to sound and the flag to drop, before careering into action.

The first hundred yards of the track was at least the width of several vehicles. After that, it tapered slightly. Then about two hundred yards later, it narrowed before opening out again, and so on until the finishing line. Those taking part had had plenty of time to inspect the route to each and every church steeple point, by foot or horseback. There was no excuse for anyone to go astray or to start grumbling about the risks.

The dreadful conditions made it an extra risk this year. Glancing at the competitors, James drew a deep breath. In the preceding years, only four or five young whips braved the course. This year however, due the famed race with his second cousin James, at The Caldicot Inn, there were twice as many. This newly-discovered second cousin was his only true rival. For the man who initially introduced himself as James Westernbury, proved himself an expert in hard driving. That evening in the meadow behind The Caldicot Inn, they had raced neck and neck before finishing in a dead heat.

A dead heat? James was astounded. Nobody had ever come close to him in such brilliant horsemanship. That, of course could not happen here, for, irrespective of all his inner distress the last stretch of track was only wide enough for one vehicle.

His!

At last, Elizabeth sank down on the grass, too out of breath to even cry. Now she either had to go the half mile round to the main gate, or cut through the unfenced part of the race track just round the bend, in order to reach Nimbus Folly. The main gate was out of the question because she had neither the energy, nor inclination to run that far.

The race track, although dangerous, was just on the next bend and a much quicker route. She could slip home, collect only her most precious possessions, and head for the main road.

She would be sad to leave, she now realised. She would miss the mixed greens of the fields and the trees. She would miss the openness of land, the lanes, and the wind whisking in from the sea. Noticing the crown of shrubs and bushes bordering this particular area, she felt the wild damp grass beneath her, and slipping off her gloves, ran her fingers through it. Although damp, it was soft and pliable. Yes, she gulped back a sob, she would definitely miss this place. Was there no justice in the world? Was she to be haunted by her past and her permanently inebriated father forever?

The pounding hooves and seething wheels reached a crescendo as the two lead vehicles raced neck and neck. Unaware of the background noises and cheering, Bauval having forced his sorrow to the back of his mind, only had one aim. That was to regain prime position once more! His one challenger had already pulled ahead of him twice and now levelled with him for the third time. He had to get clear before the track narrowed again. Focusing on the next point, Bauval swirled and cracked his whip high above his team without the whip touching them.

A second later his Sixers pitched gloriously into the lead.

A swift governing breath was all that prevented him from whooping into the air like a school-boy as he charged by his rival. It was not sporting to gloat, and besides, his second cousin, now galloping in his wake giving him a good run, deserved better.

It was tough going though, and both of them, well ahead of the rest of the field, meant to win.

Only now did the cheer of the handful of spectators lining the route, register in Bauval's brain. He could not let them down. He had to stay ahead and keep their faith in him intact.

He urged his team onward. This was a proper challenge. Not the half-heartedness of the race in previous years.

Keeping up the thundering pace, he reined his leaders smartly round the curve and into the narrow lane alongside Bauval Park. His mind buzzed with the thrill of each thrust and twist, his whole body alive with exhilaration, plied every single movement by instinct. This part was his. This was ground he knew so well he could do it blindfold. Best of all, his mother had gladly promised to continue the custom of waiting by the break in the fence to cheer him on. Therefore, deftly drawing the ribbons into one hand, he set his other hand high, ready to wave as he galloped by.

This time he could not resist a whoop, as, in perfect one-handed control he neared the bend.

Elizabeth froze at the sound. Surely the race was not in full swing already? And to her sudden horror, realised she was mindlessly sitting on the racetrack, between the two fences. The ground vibrated, and, roused by blind panic, she leapt into action.

James saw the blur of pink bolting across his path the same instant he turned the bend. In one sweeping movement, he tugged on the reins with one hand, and jerked forward to yank the breaker chain with the other.

Elizabeth whirled round just in time to see the two horses nearest to her rear up in terror. Next came a squealing neigh of agony from the two wheelers as the racing phaeton cannoned into them and instantly upended. A second later James catapulted onto the middle shaft with a horrible thud.

The shuddering impact had the six horses plunging forward into a terrified, disordered gallop right off the race track.

Elizabeth, knowing it was her fault, could only watch in absolute terror, as James Bauval slipped between the traces and was dragged helplessly along with them.

She heard a scream, and whipping her head up, was just in time to see another phaeton charging towards her.

'Miss Chetwode!'

Elizabeth sprang toward the voice and was swiftly pulled clear in the nick of time.

'Thank goodness my love,' a relieved Lady Levana held her close as the second phaeton ground to a shuddering halt alongside them.

'What the devil. *Elizabeth*?'

Her brother's voice had her turning in amazement. 'Jamie?'

She heard a gasp from behind her and instinctively spun round.

Suddenly everything within her screamed out in shock. Yet no sound came. Instead, her legs almost gave way; her breath came in short sharp bursts, as she gawped at the woman in modish black. *Mama!*

Her mind rallied. No, that was impossible. The twin. It *had* to be the twin.

The woman's thin trembling hand shot from under her black cloak and flew to her face. Pale blue irises rimmed with smoky grey flickered from Jamie to her, then back to Jamie again. Sparse, gold-tinted lashes fluttered on a groan.

Suddenly everyone was talking at once.

A bewildered, 'It cannot be,' from the twin.

'Aunt Betty?' from her brother.

He knew about the twins?

'My son!' from the pale and wildly gesticulating Lady Levana.

The talking abruptly ceased as they all immediately followed the direction of Lady Levana's outstretched arm.

The runaway horses, unable to drag the upended phaeton any further, had come to a standstill only yards away. Suddenly everyone moved at once.

James Bauval tried in vain to open his eyes. He tried again, but nothing happened. As if in a dream, he put out his hand out in order to lever himself from the most peculiar position he seemed to be in. Just where was he anyway?

Still nothing happened. He heard a low moan of someone in deep pain. But who? His head throbbed with the effort of trying to fathom it out. His whole body hurt. He strained to do something. Anything. Was he in a dream that his body refused to wake from? He hated dreams that made him feel totally incapacitated.

He tried to call out, but his throat would not move and his feeble efforts to wake up were countered by a mind-blowing pain that made him want to give up all together.

Someone began to whisper. Was this too part of the dream? If not, he hoped whoever it was, would wake him and free him from his paralysis. The whispering became urgent.

'Jemmy! Jemmy!'

His mind quickened. He was being summoned. Did they not know he was in a sleep so deep it needed more than words to get him out of it?

Wake me up, his brain shouted. A low groan merely mocked his puny effort.

'Begging your pardon milady, me and Turner will steady the team, while,' Mills having seen the mishap, and come to the master's aid, now stared at Jamie with shock, 'you free him from the shaft.'

James Bauval narrowed his eyes against the sea of faces peering down at him. What the devil was the matter with them all? Was he naked or something? The absurdity of it made his body vibrate with silent laughter but groaned at the pain ripping through him.

His mother's face loomed close to his. 'Be still,' she ordered softly. 'The doctor has been summoned.'

James tried to shake his head to let her know that he did not need the quack. All he needed to get him going was a good shake.

'You took a tumble,' she explained in a whisper. 'Just stay still my love, and try not to talk, or move.'

He wanted to move and be up and off to complete whatever it was he was doing before all these silly people sent for the quack.

A deathly pale face framed with pink lowered into his line of vision. He stared in helpless fascination at the loose golden hair sliding over her shoulders.

A surge of joy lifted his spirits. 'Boadicea.' he murmured.

Elizabeth gazed down at the man she loved more than anyone else. Her heart slammed against her ribs. She had brought him to this. She had caused this calamity. Her hairbrained actions had nearly killed him. Her stomach knotted at the realisation that he still might die of his injuries.

His lower left leg, twisted at an awkward angle, was almost certainly broken. His right leg, lacerated and bleeding, had obviously scraped along the ground. His body, apart from his torn clothing, was, thankfully, in one piece. Even so, there was no telling what damage lay beneath.

His arms, although close to his sides, were limp, and powerless. One large hand, as ripped as the leg, bled profusely. The other curved softly inwards to his body. But the worst of all, was the pale stillness of his face.

He groaned making the wavy 'm' on his top lip shoot up into two defined tips.

Elizabeth blinked back her tears. That first groan, such music to their ears meant he was alive. Now her heart ached for him, because his subsequent groans meant acute, relentless pain.

'Thank the heavens Bauval,' her brother sang with brittle cheer. 'I thought you a gonner for sure.'

The sound of his rival's voice parted the fuzz in his brain. James knew he could not win the race now, but his second cousin could.

Summoning his strength with an iron will, he forced his lips to move. 'Go,' he directed his voice upwards. 'Save the village,' he rasped. 'Win the race!'

'Damn the race!' Jamie countered wildly.

Onyx irises sparked silver with the effort of the command. 'Go and win the race!'

Elizabeth loomed over him. 'My lord, my brother cannot possibly save the village.'

Betty swooped on her. 'Oh, do not say so my love. A Bauval *must* win the race. It is a matter of safety.' She turned to Jamie, who, although kneeling on the moist grass beside Bauval, still kept a firm hold on his team's reins. 'Please,' Betty urged, 'for all our sakes.'

Lady Levana swept her face up. 'Betty is right. A Bauval must win.' She glanced back to the track, 'I can hear the others. Please, I entreat you, get back on course while you still have time.'

Elizabeth's gaze flew from one to the other. 'No!' she gasped in alarm, as her brother stood up and began pulling on hardy leather gloves. 'He is an outsider.' The swirling mass of dangers whirled in her mind's eye. Panic washed over her. 'He will be lynched.'

A gentle hand touched her shoulder. 'Everything will be all right.'

'Bauval will need splints,' Jamie threw out, deftly mounting his phaeton. 'Wood, sticks, strong straight branches, anything. And something to secure them if possible.' With that, he drew his team round, urged them into a canter and dashed back onto the track.

Elizabeth stared after him in silent trepidation.

Lady Levana stood up. 'He is right. The surgeon will have everything of course, but it will do no harm to have extra on hand.'

'The coppice,' Betty started upright. 'There are plenty of fallen branches there.'

'The coppice is too far away.' Elizabeth jumped up. 'There is some wood in the grave-yard that might be suitable.' She looked briefly at the man she loved. The man who could never, would never, be hers. Her stomach knotted, but she managed to stop her breath coming in sharp bursts. 'Twine too,' she managed with control, darting her eyes over his limp helpless limbs. Suddenly she turned, and with a graceful leap was off. Running like a hare towards the cemetery where two wooden crosses defined the head and the foot of the other Mary-Beth's grave.

It did not take her long to reach the now flower festooned grave. She glanced only briefly at the effect her hard work had had, knowing that some of the plants would continue flowering year after year because of her. She leaned to the viola surrounded cross.

'Gotcha!' Westernbury's voice suddenly slurred the instant his scrawny hands gripped the top of her arm.

Panic washed over her. 'Let go! Please!'

Acting on instinct Elizabeth brought her foot smartly against his thinly hosed leg.

Yelling, he released her, before she had time to duck however, Wybrow grabbed her.

'No, you do not!' His rich tone slid icily down her spine. 'The fraud is over. Your distraught Papa has come to take you in hand.'

Although she really wanted to scream, Elizabeth calmed herself enough to face them. 'No, you do not understand.'

Ignoring her plea, Wybrow began dragging her away from the grave. A moment later he was half marching, half dragging her out of the cemetery.

She kicked out.

Wybrow's bony hand moved even faster, and he struck with full force across her cheek. Momentarily startled, she stilled at the ferocity of his assault. Less than a second later he had spun her round, yanked her hands behind her back and forced her into a stumbling walk ahead of him.

'A Cambridge Chetwode indeed,' he sneered, into her ear through the new silk bonnet.

She held back the tears spiking her eyes. 'I never said I that.'

'My dear wife told me all about it in her letters.' He marched her through the cemetery gates. 'You had them all fooled.'

His humourless laugh caused a chilled feeling to filter through her veins.

'Even the Smith-Jacobsens' championed your cause.' He sniggered. 'Imagine that? Henry Smith-Jacobsen asking if he might address you? The absurdity of it. The lure of being attached to a Cambridge Chetwode made complete idiots of the lot of them.'

'The money is mine,' slurred Westernbury from behind her. 'Mine by right.'

Elizabeth's stomach balled. Not only had she lost James, she had lost her reputation and the means of supporting herself too.

The law was always on the father's side. And irrespective of Mama's money being left to her, in her name, her father had a legal right to control it all until she was of age.

Control? Bitterness welled up inside her. Every penny would go on drink.

The lock and key that made her feel so secure previously now turned and clicked from the other side of her new bedchamber. She was a prisoner.

Wybrow's last gloating words danced like ragged ghouls in her brain.

'I hear Lord Bauval has turned you off too. Now you have no one to protect you.' His emphasis on the word, 'protect' left her in no doubt regarding his disgusting thoughts on the matter.

Elizabeth dashed back the tears. Crying would not help, and thankfully she was not tied up, so, she wandered aimlessly over to the windows.

The whole place was deserted. Even the cemetery seemed extra silent.

She gazed in the direction of where James Bauval might still be lying and, worse, dying. She groaned; she had misled him in so many ways. Now he was at death's door and she would never have the opportunity to explain.

Oh, why had Mama wanted her to change her name anyway? Being Elizabeth Chetwode brought nothing but deception.

A Cambridge Chetwode? It was almost laughable! Whoever they were, they appeared to be *haute monde* and well respected by polite society.

She shivered. The fire, left low during the morning now smouldered gently. Wybrow implied that as she was less than a servant, she had to brace herself for the cold and whatever else the future brought.

With slow despondency she removed her violet spencer and pink bonnet, then gently brushed them clean with her hands before putting them away. Forlornly eyeing her frocks in the wardrobe, she knew her father would sell them, and everything else too.

She groaned again. All that money, more than enough to buy a house and some land in the country-side and give her a decent annuity for life tossed down his throat within a couple of years.

Above all however, was the loss of James Bauval. She could bear the loss of good clothes and a decent future just to know he would recover.

If he did not, it would be her fault. She was to blame for his dreadful accident.

Suddenly she was crying. She had caused serious injury to, or the death of, the man she loved.

The soft knock brought Elizabeth out of a doze. Having thrown herself on her bed crying, she had eventually fallen asleep.

'Miss Chetwode,' Pamela whispered from the outside of the room. 'May I come in?'

Elizabeth sat upright and blinked, because the afternoon had now faded to dusk. Shivering, she saw that the fire had gone out.

Then it all came back to her.

Her father had come to claim her and all she had.

'Mary-Beth,' came Pamela's worried voice. 'Please? I promise not to stay long.'

Elizabeth did not want to see anyone, nonetheless, despite her unhappiness she slipped from the bed and walked to the locked door.

'Of course, you may come in,' she replied softly. 'However, my door is locked.'

Almost before she finished, the key turned, Pamela then opened the door and tiptoed through.

'You are not a prisoner,' Pamela frowned, 'Papa says you are not well, and not to be disturbed, but,' her voice trailed as she looked anxiously into Elizabeth's face. 'I just had to come and see you.'

Elizabeth's spirits lifted at Pamela's innocent concern. Caution, however, made her wary. 'You will get a severe scolding.'

'They are both out,' Pamela said. 'However,' her face brightened. 'There is something I must tell you.'

Pamela followed Elizabeth to the bed where they both sat down.

'A rich relation?' Elizabeth gasped once Pamela had finished her story.

The satin counterpane rustled as Pamela moved closer to Elizabeth. 'Yes, a distant uncle of Papa's.' Then, dropping her chin, and setting clasped hands on her lap, she added dutifully, 'Of course, although we never knew of his existence, it is terribly sad that he is on his deathbed.'

'Of course,' Elizabeth gulped.

Pamela her gaze still serious, sighed, 'We must be thankful though. Fifty-five thousand pounds is a considerable sum is it not?'

Elizabeth's mind reeled, 'It is.'

A glimmer of hope flickered through her. Perhaps she would be allowed to leave on her own now Wybrow was going to be rich?

Pamela's face glowed. 'I am to have two thousand pounds for my come-out in two years-time, and five thousand pounds is to be put aside for my dowry. Just think?' she tripped out. 'A dowry?'

A dowry? The words echoed through Elizabeth. That was what Mama wanted for her. She choked back her tears.

'My chances of a good marriage will be so much better. Mama is beside herself with joy. Oh,' she stopped abruptly and put her hands over Elizabeth's, 'Mary-Beth, please forgive me. I have over-taxed you.' She jumped up. 'May I get you some water?' She gave a small wail. 'Papa will be furious if he finds out I have come here, and overtaxed you.' She wrung her hands as she hurried over to the jug on the dresser. 'Oh dear,' she murmured, filling a glass with water from the jug then hurrying back to Elizabeth. 'Mary-Beth, please do not tell him I disobeyed his orders.'

Elizabeth took a sip of the water.

'He says the money will not be available if I dare to visit you.'

Elizabeth looked up at Pamela. 'Whatever do you mean?'

Pamela lashes fluttered as she began hastily backing away. 'N-nothing-,' she stammered, retreating. 'O-only that if you find out, y-you might put a stop to it, b-but,' she edged to the door. 'I-I know you would not be so unkind.'

With that, she twisted round and fled in some kind of terror, pausing only to lock the door behind her.

Elizabeth stared at the closed door trying to make sense of the last few moments. Was Pamela's startling news so wonderful that she had remained seated throughout the encounter without trying to make a run for it? Worse still, she had sat listening to Pamela without asking after Lord Bauval.

She leaped towards the door. 'Pamela!' she called, 'Pamela please, you must tell me what happened to Lord Bauval?'

Silence.

'Miss Wybrow!' she almost screamed in desperation 'If you tell me I will promise to do, or not to do, anything you ask.'

Pamela's door opened, and a moment later Elizabeth heard the floorboards creaking outside her own door.

'He,' Pamela started to whisper, then, 'I think someone is coming up the stairs.' The floor creaked again as Pamela fled back to her own room and closed the door.

Elizabeth dived for the chair, sat swiftly down, and set her hands demurely on her lap. Wybrow was back, and she was ready for him.

The fumbling of the lock brought a nervous flutter to her stomach though. Determined not to let it show, she remained perfectly still.

The door burst open.

'Ha!'

The very last person she wanted or needed to see, stumbled into the room.

Her father.

'Did you think you could get away from me so easily?' He shook a wobbly fist not quite in the air as he stumbled to stand directly in front of her, 'I have a right to the money,' he slurred, leaning over her.

In spite of her fear and revulsion, Elizabeth slammed to her feet to face him head on. 'Get out!'

The smell of alcohol her feel sick. She swayed, and realised she had not eaten for several hours. Even so, she still managed to brush past him. He was quicker. He turned on her, grabbed her arm, and wrenched her painfully back into the chair.

'Sit,' he ordered in slewed fury. 'You will not get away from me this time! The money is mine!'

'Mama left the money for me and Jamie.'

Charles Westernbury drew his face level with hers. His ghastly odour disgusting, and the diminishing light making him look fiendish.

'Fifty-five thousand pounds.'

Elizabeth managed a contemptuous laugh. 'Fifty-five thousand pounds?' She swallowed with relief as the smell of alcohol receded as he drew back. 'There is nothing like that amount.'

'Liar,' he sneered. 'What about the Hertford estate *and* the twenty-five, thousand-pound dowry?

'Think I would not find out what the old man left?'

Who was he talking about, and what tied Mama to him for so long if she had had family all this time?

More than family. An instantly recognisable twin too. What had happened to cause a lifetime rift?

Suddenly lunging forward again, Westernbury snorted.

'Whoever heard of a woman managing her own money? It is mine to do with and manage as I please. The whole fifty-five thousand.'

An unease crept through Elizabeth. Why was he talking about the exact sum Pamela mentioned? Was it coincidence? Or something far more sinister?

She knew with mutinous contempt that the only way to calm him was to use the same pacifying methods Mama had used.

Gritting her teeth in order to crush all the rebelliousness from her tone, while at the same time hating her weakness, she gave what she hoped was a placatory shrug.

'I see there is no moving you Papa,' she sighed dramatically. Then forcing a sweetness, she did not feel, added, 'Yes, very true, you do have the legal right to manage my finances in whatever way you see fit.' She took a composing breath before delivering what she hoped would be a discouragement, no matter how small, of some sort. 'However, I too have legal rights. I have the right to put the money in trust until I am of age.'

Lady Betty Interton paced the pleasant room. 'I wish I had not met my dear Mary's daughter for the first time under such terrible circumstances, but now that I have, I am extremely concerned. I really think we should go to Nimbus Folly and find out what happened to her,' she said worriedly. 'I am quite sure she meant to return with wood for the splints. Oh,' her tone dropped to a groan. 'I hope she has not with an accident.'

Lady Levana sighed and drew a hand over her tired features. 'Betty dearest, I have to stay here, just in case.'

'It could be days before Jemmy regains consciousness, and,' Betty pivoted to look down at her cousin reclining on a *chaise lounge*. 'I feel so uneasy.'

Something snapped inside Lady Levana. She had helped and supported Betty for years. Surely her cousin could do the same for her this once?

'Uneasy?' she sat up. 'You spend your existence in unease,' she gave a derisive sniff. 'I have never known you to be anything else, cousin.'

As soon as the words came out, she regretted them, but it was too late. Betty paled, put a limp hand over her mouth to fight back the tears, and fled.

Lady Levana stared unblinkingly into the cheery fire for a moment. Why had she said such a horrible thing in such a horrible way? There was no knowing what Betty might do in a moment of despair.

What had she done?

She sprang up, 'Betty, please,' she called, hurrying rapidly from the room after her dearest friend.

A maid met her as she reached the stairwell. 'His lordship is awake milady.'

A moment later Lady Levana rounded the curve of the stairs, and sped silently along the landing to her son's room.

Chapter Fourteen

Trying not to reveal how relieved she was, at thwarting him, Elizabeth drew a calming breath.

'You are too late,' Westernbury sneered. 'It is all being taken care of this minute.' His head lolled back as he gave a satisfied grunt. 'Your good employer, now my legal agent, Walter Whatishname is doing the honours. Got the papers signed for me, and is, at very this moment setting everything in order.'

His head rolled forward to meet her horrified expression. 'As soon as he returns, everything, the house, the land, the dowry,' he smirked, 'and your personal annuity will be in my hands.' His head jerked back. 'The whole lot.'

His drunken gloating made her spine prickle. Much worse though, was the connection between her supposed inheritance and Wybrow's recent windfall.

Fifty-five thousand, pounds?

In Pamela's own words, a considerable amount.

Pamela had mentioned a dying relative though. Papa was not related to the Wybrows, nor was he on his deathbed.

Or was he?

'Are you ailing Papa?'

His head rolled forwards. 'Vixen!' he spat, 'I am not ailing, so you can put any thoughts of my untimely demise from your nasty little mind.'

A shadow appeared in the doorway.

'Very cosy.' Mr. Wybrow's rich voice dripped sarcasm. 'A family *tete a tete*.' He swept metallic eyes over the scene before resting his gaze on Elizabeth. 'Being filled in I, see?'

'Papa?' Pamela had followed him in without anybody noticing. Her eyes slid to the drunken man, 'Uncle Charles?'

Wybrow rounded on her. 'Get out!'

Pamela turned and fled.

Wybrow turned to them with smug satisfaction. 'You see Westernbury,' he smirked rubbing his hands together. 'How much easier life is when one's child instantly obeys?'

He walked purposefully to stand behind Elizabeth's chair and put his hands on the back. His odd sickly-sweet smell combined with rancid sweat was as bad as the smell of alcohol of her father.

'This child of yours,' Wybrow mouthed silkily, 'has much to learn.' Then bending down so his mouth almost touched her ear he whispered goadingly, 'Instant obedience is something I shall demand of you, my dear.'

Aversion and terror ripped through her. The situation was far worse than she imagined. Not only was her father the dying man and the benevolent uncle, Pamela so innocently mentioned, but she herself, was part of the vile plan.

She looked up and saw her father take his flask from his pocket and toast Wybrow before guzzling the remaining contents.

Wybrow let go of her chair, strolled over to her father and gave a thin smile.

'A top-up is in order, I think. There is plenty more where that came from,' he grinned with false cordiality.

Her father's face shot up to meet the metallic eyes.

'Got the papers ready Wybrow?' he suddenly demanded.

His unexpected coherence surprised both of them.

Wybrow's brow creased, along with the swift reply. 'Yes, of course.' The skin on his balding head glistened disgustingly in the fading light. He cast Elizabeth a quick look as if assessing her reaction.

Elizabeth controlled an outward shudder and willed herself into composure. Her insides though, trembled with the reality of her situation.

'In that case,' Westernbury's sour breath shot through the air, 'we had better get down to business.'

Putting a bony hand over his mouth and nose Wybrow spluttered. He was as repelled by her father's inebriated state, as she was.

'Then you had both better come with me,' Wybrow croaked. He turned to Elizabeth with a brusque, 'Come along.'

Her father grinned, then turned to her. 'Better get your cloak.' His self-satisfied tone sent chills through her. 'It is going to be a long, cold trip.'

'Betty dearest?' Lady Levana peeped into the room her cousin always occupied when staying at Bauval Park.

Lady Interton's maid came out of the dressing room shaking her head. 'She has gone milady. She grabbed the pelisse I had just finished smoothing, and hurried off.'

Lady Levana felt terrible. 'Did she say where she was going?'

'No milady.'

Lady Levana suppressed a shudder. 'Thank-you.' She had a vague idea where Betty might have gone. Her only option now, was to send someone after her or go herself.

'I have to go out,' she informed the maid. 'Lord Bauval has regained consciousness, and although he is still weak, I believe he is on the mend,' she said with relief, 'I will just look in on him before I go.'

Elizabeth tried to pull her arm from Wybrow's grip. He responded by digging his bony hand further into her flesh. Wincing, she then pretended to trip on the moss-coated cobble path, but he pulled her up with a painful jerk. Pride and fury prevented her yelping. Besides, she needed to save her strength for an escape.

'Where are we going?'

His thin smile mocked her. 'A place only I know about.' He twisted behind him to her father. 'Keep up Westernbury.'

Elizabeth used his momentary lapse of concentration to strike. In one swift movement she whisked her chin down and bit the back of his hand.

Wybrow screamed.

She bared her teeth again, but as he snatched the bitten hand aside, she brought a booted foot up hard against his shin instead.

He released her instantly.

'Vixen!' he rasped out as he stumbled.

Quick as a flash Elizabeth hooked her foot round his other ankle and sent him crashing to the ground.

He swore, but she had already skipped sideways and was racing round the uneven dimensions of Nimbus Folly before he managed to get up.

Thankfully, she knew where to hide too.

Several breathless moments later she burst through the ramshackle door of the summer-house and closed it quickly and quietly behind her.

The half-light filtering through grimy windows gave the place an ethereal feeling. She shuddered, then blinked to get used to the gloom, then picking her way carefully to the bench in front of the mural, she shivered again but thought better of sitting down where she might be seen by anyone looking through the grimy windows. She looked around her with an odd appreciation. This *Belvedere*, this almost sacred place, beloved by the late Mary-Beth and very-much alive Henry Smith-Jacobsen was now her refuge.

Their paradise and haven, now, her sanctuary.

Moving with care, she approached the mural. Then creeping slowly along the length of the wall she tried to imagine the glory it once was, and as *they* once were. The two seemingly insignificant love-birds so devoted to each other, but with so little time left.

She traced gloved fingers along the length of the mural, letting them hover for a second over the beautiful peacock too proud to see what was under his nose.

Oh Jemmy.

The mural came to an abrupt end at a recess in the wall, and trailing her fingers round it, was surprised to discover a door that was very slightly ajar.

Lady Levana looked down into her son's face. 'I have to go out for a while,' she whispered gently smoothing wisps of damp blue-black hair from his brow. 'The doctor left some laudanum for you, should you need it.'

James tried to shake his head and immediately regretted it. He did not need medicine. He needed to be up and about, not lying on his bed like an invalid. His mind was crystal clear, so why would the words not come? Why could he recall the accident in precise detail and know exactly what his brain was saying, but when trying to speak, only hearing an incoherent mumble.

'Do not try to talk dearest.'

His mind dashed her hand away; his arm remained still. *What about Miss Chetwode?*

'Be still my love,' his mother soothed. 'I shall come to you the moment I return.'

With that, she pressed her lips to his forehead, and tiptoed softly from the room.

Do not go, his mind cried. *What of Miss Chetwode?*

Vance appeared. 'My lord,' he began firmly, 'you are still in shock and need to rest,' but his eyes twinkled under greying brows. 'You are a hard man to floor my lord. A lesser man might not have survived.' He flashed a look along the bed at Bauval's inert body. 'Trampled, gashed, and broken, and still worrying about who's done what, if I am not mistaken.' His eyes narrowed as James tried to speak. 'What is it my lord?'

Groaning with pain James forced the sentence. 'Is Miss Chetwode safe?'

Vance frowned. 'Miss Chetwode, my lord?'

Yes! he wanted to bark. The adorable, beautiful, fleeing Miss Chetwode, whom I narrowly missed. All he did, however, was swallow in incoherent frustration.

'That particular young lady has kept well away,' Vance sniffed. 'Good job too from what I hear. Damned near killed you.'

Hell fire! *He would damn near kill someone if he could.* 'Where is she?' he croaked desperately. *Not with Wybrow, please not with Wybrow.*

Concerned, Vance hovered over him.

'My lord,' he said as if soothing a recalcitrant child, 'there is no need worry about her. I expect she has gone down with a dose of shame.'

'Damn you,' his body went into spasms of pain at the effort. 'Aghh!'

Vance was immediately alarmed. 'Be still, I beg you.'

James refused to quit. His Boadicea was in serious peril. Whatever she had done; whatever she thought of him, she did not deserve the vile fate Wybrow had in store for her. Yes, his new manager had been warned off, but was he to be trusted now there was no one to stop him? James suspected not. Miss Chetwode was definitely on the run when he last saw her. His Boadicea had felt danger, and whether real or imagined, she needed his help.

'Get me up,' he demanded hoarsely.

His valet snorted. 'Certainly not.'

Jittery, yet relieved she had managed to push open the stiff door just enough to squeeze through it, Elizabeth wiped the clinging cobwebs from her face before pushing the door as far-closed as possible, back into the slightly ajar position again. She turned around, and once her eyes had adjusted to the gloom, saw she was in a tiny room.

To her right, at the end of the short wall, a hazy bubble of mote-dusky-light, meant there might be a window there. The ancient musty smelling straw scattered over the floor that was probably crawling with vermin dried her throat, and the thought of shuffling through it turned her stomach. However, she needed to see if the source of the light was a possible escape route or whether the door was the only way out again.

How long would Wybrow and her father search for her? Her head ached with fear. Fear that Jemmy had died beneath the traces of his phaeton. Fear that she would be found by her father and Wybrow. Fear she would never get away.

Heaving in a shuddering breath, and wrapping the cloak that Westernbury suggested she put on, more closely round her, she calmed herself. Fear was not going to get her anywhere.

The source of light turned out to be a tiny square window caked in dirt on the inside and almost blocked with overgrown foliage on the outside. So, taking up one edge of her cloak, she wiped the grubby glass surface inside and peered through.

She had expected to see an unkempt tangle of weeds and bushes stretching as far as the eye could see, so was astonished by the neat grassy area beyond the immediate shrubs round the window. More astonishing was, that to the left was the track of a well-trodden path leading to somewhere behind the summerhouse. Slightly to her right was an overgrown hedge that concealed the front view of the summerhouse from the back view of the summerhouse.

Momentarily forgetting she was in the summerhouse for protection, Elizabeth drew away from the window and began feeling her way left, along the back wall.

If there was a path directly outside, then there might be an exit. Gingerly staying close to the wall, she began inching her way to where it might be. Just as she thought she felt a door lintel, she heard a sharp voice.

'Did you honestly think-?'

Suppressing a squeal, Elizabeth swung to the direction of the summerhouse.

It was Wybrow.

'-That I ever intended to become a lackey to a drunken sop?' His humourless chuckle followed the slam of the summerhouse door. 'Not a chance, Westernbury.' Elizabeth heard scuffling, that was followed by a dull thud. There was cruelty in Wybrow's rich, sneering tone. 'Look at you,' he scoffed. 'You are not even in a fit state to defend yourself.'

Elizabeth froze. Would Wybrow notice the door in the summerhouse?

'And do you know what? Nobody will miss you. Not even that so-called daughter of yours. It is obvious there is no love lost there. She cannot stand the sight of you any more than I can.' He snorted with chilling derision. 'If only she knew the truth about her real father.'

Elizabeth let out the breath she was not aware of holding in until then.

'You would not then have stood a chance of setting yourself up as Pater. Not that you ever played the doting parent. Why she never guessed is beyond me.'

His sneer cut through her.

'Naturally I shall make it my business to inform her of her true sire,' he chortled with sickening glee.

'After I have shown her who is master of her and of all she owns. Then,' his voice dipped so Elizabeth had to strain to hear, 'it will be too late for anyone to come to her aid. Now,' he continued with a slick and utterly false amenability, 'I have to go and look for the inconsiderate chit. She cannot be too far away. However, if I take a long time, please do not worry your woozy head. I shall be busy enjoying the heady delights that The Right Honourable Miss Chetwode will not willingly offer.'

Elizabeth heard the ramshackle noise of the outer summerhouse door opening.

'I shall put you out of your misery later,' Wybrow called out with vile, self-assured glee. The door slammed leaving only an eerie silence in its wake.

Eerie, because even her father was quiet.

Elizabeth's heart quickened.

Westernbury not her father? Every hair on her back stood on end. Did that mean her father really was a Chetwode? Warmth flooded through her.

A true Cambridge Chetwode after all?

In a fit of jubilation, she flung herself away from the wall then stopped mid-step.

Oh no! None of it made any sense, because if Westernbury was not her real father, why had she been brought up to believe he was? Her jubilation turned to crushing disappointment. It obviously meant one thing. She was a baseborn Chetwode. She smothered the sobs that rose in her throat.

Filia populae! Base-born. Was that why Mama never mentioned she was a Chetwode?

The shame of it. Her mind swirled as the enormity hit her. She was no-one. A woman of no consequence, a nothing in the sight of everybody. Even her father, she instantly corrected herself, even Westernbury had no claim on her.

She gasped. Especially Westernbury.

Did Mama tolerate Westernbury because he knew her secrets? Furthermore, was he blackmailing her? That meant that the man who imposed his parentage was nothing more than a cheat. He was no more entitled to 'look after' her interests than Wybrow.

A feeble shuffle from the summer house brought her back to the immediate situation. If what Pamela said was true, then Westernbury, having handed some kind of authority over to Wybrow, now stood to lose his life. She shuddered. Even he, with all his contemptibility did not deserve such treatment. What could she do though? From the sound of him, he was not in a fit state to stand, let alone walk or run. Then there was a chance of Wybrow showing up and putting a heavy-handed stop to any means of escape for them both.

She held her breath listening for further sounds.

Nothing.

Tip-toeing to the still ajar door, she stood still and listened. Still nothing.

Carefully dragging the door open a little more, she peered into the gloomy space of the summerhouse.

The stench of stale alcohol reached her as she spotted him lying in a senseless huddle on the floor close to the bench. He was not only drunk but in some kind of pain too.

She crept over to him.

'Can you hear me?' she whispered.

He seemed lifeless.

Squatting beside him she shook his shoulder.

He gave a low moan and tried to shrug her off.

'We need to get out of here before Mr. Wybrow gets back.' She shook him again. 'Do you understand?'

This time there was no response at all as he seemed to have drifted into a mindless world of his own.

'Do you care about what he is going to do to you? Or me for that matter?' she hissed furiously.

Still no response.

His apathy both scared and infuriated her. If Wybrow appeared, she would be as helpless as he was. Her sibilant, 'Get up!' had no effect on him whatsoever. In a fit of panic, she grabbed his legs dragged him over to the door of the secret room.

'Come Betty,' Lady Levana mouthed, gently tapping her cousin's arm. 'Elizabeth is not in here dearest. She must have left, just as Mrs Wybrow said. Let us go downstairs and thank her for allowing us to come up here.'

After much soul-searching, she and James had eventually sat Betty down, and told her about Elizabeth. To their surprise, she whispered, 'Yes, I know. I saw her.'

'Levvy,' Betty's gaze shot to a shadowed picture on the wall in Elizabeth's bed-chamber, 'Look.'

'Dearest-'

'-Hold the lamp closer Levvy.'

With a sigh, Lady Levana slipped over to the wall and held up the lamp.

'Oh,' Betty gazed through the flickering halo at the picture of the two little girls. A sob cracked in her throat. 'My darling

Mary-Jane,' she murmured reaching up to trace a finger over her sister.

The flame in the lamp flickered wafting a flare of light over the portrait. It was the first time since that dreadful night, all those years ago, that Betty had uttered her twin sister's name.

A tear-stained face met hers. 'Levvy,' Betty whispered, 'Miss Chetwode must be in some kind of trouble to leave this behind.'

A tremor ran through Lady Levana. Supposing Betty was right and Miss Chetwode was in trouble? She lowered the lamp and looked into her cousin's ashen face.

Oh, dear dear God, please, I beg you, let the child be safe, her mind pleaded. *For all our sakes.*

Elizabeth heaved the unresisting Westernbury into the secret room. Then between panting breaths she stood still and listened in case Wybrow had returned.

All was silent, so, pushing the door back into position again, she went back to him.

All she had to do now, was somehow get them both out of the summerhouse where Wybrow could not find them. Hopefully, Wybrow had no inkling of the hidden room.

She cast frantically about for the door she thought she had felt, but all she could see through the deepening greyness, was the lighter grey rectangle set in the wall. Not much good in the circumstances.

Westernbury suddenly snorted. 'He plans to kill us.'

His abrupt coherence always startled her; his chilling comprehension sent waves of terror through her.

'It is you he intends to kill,' she snapped, 'he has other plans for me.'

Controlling her fear, she felt her way along the back wall to where she had previously felt a door lintel.

Maybe there was a way out after all.

The sky although darkening, still held a grey gloom, so when the flambeaux skittered back and forth it illuminated, then shadowed, the immediate area both in front and behind.

Mills walked ahead of the two women holding one aloft while Felton, Bauval's chief man in the field, did the same behind them.

'Mrs Wybrow was most insistent about the direction Elizabeth took,' Betty said, keeping as close behind her cousin as possible.

They were feeling their way round the curved back wall of Nimbus Folly.

The hem of Lady Levana's dress caught on yet another untamed shrub. She tugged it free. This was worse than a nightmare. For a start, the night would soon draw in quickly, natural for the time of year of course, but inconvenient, that they now had to rely on lamps and flambeaux. Moreover, she did not believe that Mrs Wybrow was telling the truth, because why would a young girl take the back-way round, when the front was so much easier? Also, as Betty pointed out, would Elizabeth really leave the painting behind?

Levana shuddered, recalling that dreadful night nearly twenty-five years ago.

Betty's painting was a gift of promise.

Betty, so in love with Charles Westernbury had wrapped it up and given it to him as a token of her affection. Proof too, of her intention to elope during their coming-out ball. Several hours before the intended getaway though, she discovered that Charles was already married and in a fit of panic, Betty, sent Mary-Jane out instead. Poor Mary-Jane had gone out into the night completely ignorant of the facts.

And never returned.

The front torch dipped, bringing Levana back to the present and their current predicament. The path seemed to go on forever, and try as she might, she could not remember where it led to.

'I simply cannot imagine why she took such a wild route.'

Mills spoke up, 'Rector's gate leads directly onto the lane milady.'

'Rector's Gate?' Lady Levana echoed in surprise. 'That has not been used for years.'

'His lordship had it opened up.' Mills said.

With a flash of memory Levana suddenly recollected where the path went. Not just Rector's Gate. It passed the back of the old summerhouse and then alongside the cemetery.

No! They could not go anywhere near either of those two places. Betty's mind would not take the strain. She had already talked of bedlam recently, and for her to see either the summer house or the cemetery might push her over the edge. The summer house was where she and Westernbury arranged their infamous rendezvous. The cemetery, harboured the wild unkempt grave of their dear Mary-Beth.

She stopped so suddenly that Betty cannoned into her. Then with a quick twist, Lady Levana turned. 'We ought to go back.' She paused. 'Did you hear that?'

'Oh, Levvy,' Betty murmured, her tone now laced with sympathy. 'Of course, you must be desperate to keep vigil by poor Jemmy's bed.' She sniffed, 'You are right, I have been so selfish for years. I am so sorry. Poor Jemmy.'

Elizabeth, having managed to push ajar what turned out to be a stable door, pushed Westernbury through, then stepping onto a path, stilled as she heard voices.

'Vigil?'

'Poor Jemmy?'

People only kept a vigil at night on the dead. In that one frenzied moment, Elizabeth had lost everything. She had lost the man she loved.

Jemmy! Jemmy! her mind railed. *If only I told you I loved you!*

If only she had begged him to her make his. If only she had trusted in him more. Loved him more. Now he lay alone; cold and dead. And it was all her fault.

She could just about see the group now, two women with the two men, one in front and one behind, holding their flaming torches aloft as they dodged in and out of the trees. The little procession giving her a glimpse of the area and her bearings. She now realised that the back of the summerhouse was close to the rear of Nimbus Folly and that the path just beneath the grimy tiny window in the secret room led directly to the cemetery.

She took a juddering breath. A peculiar notion told her they were looking for her. Yet guilt and fear made her think it was to punish her. She was the cause of Jemmy's death. She was the reason he needed a vigil. As she closed her eyes, shivering at the consequences of her recent thoughtless actions, she could see him, in her mind's eye, lying alone, pale and still.

Due to her cowardly deceit, the man she loved was dead.

She deserved all the blame.

Her stomach rose and fell in bleak waves, she needed to be sick, but she could not even retch because all her muscles were twisted up like knotted string.

She had lost everything.

Nothing mattered anymore.

Knowing his family would not allow her to her take a turn by his bedside in penitent silent prayer as she so badly needed to do to make her peace with Lord Bauval, she made a swift decision. She would go to him right now to whisper her heartbroken sorrow and confess her fraud. She needed to tell him of her everlasting love and that there would never be anyone else for her. She needed to be by his side one last time.

To do that, however, she had to take the risk of running into Wybrow, for if he caught her before she reached Bauval House, even her love for James would be worthless.

She would be worthless.

Cold fear chilled her inside and out as the string knots froze into position.

It was a risk she had to take.

James turned his head from Vance's hovering form.

'No,' he muttered with more doggedness than was good for his pain, 'I have told you I will not take any of that stuff until I know Miss Chetwode is safe.'

Vance shook his head at the perversity of it. Even under these conditions, Lord Bauval was his own man. 'My lord,' he countered calmly, 'The doctor says you must rest.'

Pain, not bad manners prevented James from turning as he spoke. 'Then I shall do so without it. Take it away.'

The stringent, 'very well my lord,' was followed by an undertone of, 'However, if on my return, you are not resting, I shall personally pour it down your throat.'

If he had not been in such physical and emotional pain, James might have laughed at the man's insurrection. Acute pain, and fatigue prevented him from doing so.

Elizabeth, wet, weary and deflated looked up into the stern face of Vance. 'Please,' she had begged. 'I need to see him.'

Seeing Miss Chetwode, there in front of him, bedraggled and miserable had softened his resolve. Besides he knew that turning her away went against his master's wishes and having reluctantly taken pity on the Elizabeth, had agreed.

'You may have five minutes Miss Chetwode,' Vance huffed ushering her into Bauval's suite.

Once inside the dimly lit room Elizabeth hardly dared breathe. A single oil-lamp threw out a vague light, its glow barely reaching the large bed where the inert Jemmy lay, and although she felt numb all over, every inch of her ached.

Tiptoeing to the bedside Elizabeth perched herself on the edge to face his stillness.

She groaned.

'Jemmy my darling, I love you. Please forgive me.'

Her voice came to him as the healing balm of angels singing and soaring with soft plumes of solace through his world of pain.

His body began to thrum as her sweet fresh-air scent abruptly set all his senses quivering in spite of his pain.

A terrifying thought suddenly came to him. Was his beleaguered mind imagining her? Were these angels singing his way out? Was imaging Elizabeth Chetwode beside him to be his last fevered thought? Ever?

'I-I never meant this to happen. I did not s-set out to deceive, I only wanted to do as Mama wished,' she sniffed. 'I never ever w-wanted or even expected to fall in love.'

She was real, and all James could do was mutely and profoundly thank that divine choir for bringing her to him. As she tried and failed to stifle her sobs, her misery, however whorled through him. He wanted to reach out and hold her close. He wanted her to be happy.

He heard her voice again.

'Please know my darling, that I love you so much.'

She loved him?

The desolation in her sigh however, made him more desperate to reach out, take her in his arms and comfort her.

Forever.

'My darling, how can I live without you? I would do anything.' She gulped down a sob. 'Anything.'

He felt her head drop onto his chest and he could only listen in helpless silence as her muffled sobs vibrated softly through him. He felt her hands clench underneath her chin by his side.

He could not bear it. Her desolation overrode his own excruciating pain so that by sheer strength of will he blocked off his agony enough to reach out and close his hand over hers.

Elizabeth felt not only the touch, but the abrupt beat of a heart too. He was alive?

Her startled gasp forced the sobs to a juddering halt.

Every part of her shouted in silent elation. Every nerve ending glistened with dazzling joy. Every inch of her wanted to leap and dance.

'Jemmy?'

Her transformation from despair to joy combined with his utter helplessness pitched him into self-reproach. Why had he not put everything right before now? Why had he allowed the dreadful misunderstanding, his misunderstanding, to go on for so long?

He forced his eyes open. 'My love,' he rasped. 'Forgive me.'

Her head rose to meet his flickering gaze. 'I thought I had caused your death.'

Caramel lashes glistening with tear drops fluttered over chrysolite irises. Her tongue slid across the glossy contours of her tear-jewelled lips. Tenderness and longing seeped into every part of him.

'I-I,' she faltered sliding her tongue across her lips again, 'thought I had lost you forever.'

Although just the mere crease of his brow caused him pain, he wanted to laugh. Not at her, but at his own helplessness at being able to express his happiness.

Then his mind whirled.

Anything?

'You are cold and damp,' he managed to murmur. 'Come under the blankets and warm up.'

Elizabeth rallied in surprise. What was he asking of her?

Chapter Fifteen

His soft plea was so irresistible, that Elizabeth slid carefully beside him.

The moment the length of her body nestled against his, his body surged with a reviving euphoric power. At last, he had the means, fair or foul, to overcome her refusal to marry him. Besides, just moments ago, she had said she loved him and would do anything.

A tiny bud of tenderness began to swell within him; growing and expanding until it filled him with the blossom of unselfish love. It ruled his head, his heart, and his body as the urge to cherish and protect her rose within him. 'My darling,' he whispered.

The warmth of his voice on her cheek sent fluffy apple blossom fluttering through her. She would do whatever he wanted regardless of the consequences. She would become his; the same way the other Mary-Beth became Henry's.

'I love you, Jemmy.'

James knew it was more than an affirmation of love. He knew from her tone that she really was prepared to do anything to prove it. This time she would not, could not refuse him. Very soon, she would be honour-bound to marry him, just as he was honour-bound to expect it.

A few seconds later they were both sound asleep.

Elizabeth blinked, not recognising her surroundings at all, then gasped in stark horror as something shifted beside her. Lord Bauval?

She was in his bed.

A large bed too, yet, anyone seeing them crushed together as if on the edge of a precipice, would think the very worst. His reputation, his honour, and his integrity at stake all because her imagination had run wild with foolish thoughts.

Not just her imagination either.

For, when she overheard the conversation between Lady Levana and Betty the previous evening about keeping vigil, all that mattered was getting to his bedside. Without another thought, she had covered Westernbury with her cape and charged off into the dark. She had squeezed through the hedge to the front of the summer house and ducked into the shadows before making straight for the safety of the coppice. The moisture of the trees drenched her. Being wet and weary to the bone had not deterred her. She was desperate to see Jemmy. She needed to beg his forgiveness and look at his face one last time. She thought to keep watch over his body for a while. Except, to her joy he was alive! Then what had she ended up doing? Making a complete fool of herself that was what. She had wept, and told him she loved him. As if that was not enough, she had promised the man who loved another, anything.

He stirred again now, and his arm tightened round her waist. 'My sweet love,' he murmured drowsily before drifting off again.

Her mind blazed with the knowledge of what her being in his bed might do to his reputation.

She had to get out before anyone saw them.

Moving him was impossible as his arm encircled her waist, so she began moving as gently as possible to disentangle herself from him.

James felt her movement because the delicate feel of fabric guarding the contours beneath, shifted him from blissful sleep to heavenly wakefulness. He half opened his eyes and from the height of his pillows, silently watched her.

Trying not to wake him, Elizabeth was attempting to slide his arm from her when the bedchamber door opened and Vance walked silently in and up to the bed.

'Miss Chetwode,' Vance began with solemn courtesy, 'Lady Levana has asked if you would like breakfast brought up? Would you like bacon and scrambled eggs?'

Elizabeth gaped speechlessly up at him. Then, her stomach grumbled.

'Breakfast for two please.'

A thread of a smile crossed Vance's face. 'Certainly, my lord.'

Elizabeth face snapped to Bauval's. 'You are awake?'

'I am awake?' James echoed ingenuously reaching out and touching her cheek. 'You are not a dream?' he added guilelessly.

How long had he been awake?

Her first impulse was to dash his hand away, the next, to nestle into the gentle touch.

She resisted doing either. 'No, I am not a dream.'

He was still in terrible pain, yet her presence made it more bearable. 'Can we go back to how we were just before Vance interrupted us?' He raised a dark brow. 'Just to ensure neither of us is dreaming.'

The expression on her face instantly changed to a racked expression. And his heart tumbled.

Why had he behaved so tactlessly?

'Miss Chetwode,' he tried to draw her close to him, but she resisted and remained firmly where she was.

Elizabeth's stomach lurched. She had deceived him for too long. Now she had to be honest.

'I,' she drew a shuddering breath before plunging on, 'am not entitled to be called that.' She lowered her gaze. 'It was Mama's wish. Jemmy and I presumed it was so Papa could not find me. We had no idea that that was our real father's name.' She twisted away from him in anguish. 'I,' she added raggedly, 'am base-born.' Swallowing back the tears she waited for his onslaught.

His breath wafted gently over her neck.

'My darling,' she heard him breathe as his gentle fingers caressed her hair. 'You are no more base-born than I am.' He tipped towards her. 'Finn Chetwode married Mary-Jane.'

He knew about the Chetwode connection?

Snapping her face to his she raised her hand. 'Please stop,' she begged.

James suppressed a yip of pain as he reached out. 'My sweet darling,' he whispered, pulling her stiff body close to him. 'You should have been told,' he rested his cheek against hers, 'a lifetime ago. The truth is, we all should have been told. Me, you, and Jamie.'

Elizabeth heard regret and shame lacing his tone. What caused such anguish? She gently placed her hand on his cheek.

That simple gesture gave him hope. Perhaps she would forgive them after all?

He took a deep breath, 'My sweet love, it is a sad tale.'

Elizabeth listened in total silence as the story unravelled. The story of twins, so alike, no one could tell them apart.

'Except Finn Chetwode that was,' Jemmy said. 'He was somewhat older and wiser than Betty or Mary, and was not deceived when Betty went out to meet him that last time pretending to be your mother. He knew the truth but when challenged, Betty told him Mary never wanted to see him again and had sent her out to tell him so. The following year Betty fell in love with the already married Westernbury. And Westernbury *was* deceived by the wrong twin. He really thought the woman eloping with him in the moonlight was Betty. Westernbury's real intention was financial. He planned to blackmail grandfather Bauval into keeping it quiet when he sent her back in disgrace.

The old man, refused, and cut Mary off completely. He went so far as to put a notice in every paper in England, saying he never wanted to see or hear of her again.'

He sighed, before drawing in a ragged breath.

'Mary struggled alone for a couple of years before she met Finn again. He was ailing by this time, and his son hankering after the title and all that went with it, resented Mary's intrusion and the shame attached to her to such an extent that he swore all kinds of mischief against them. So, Finn, a widower for years, married your mother in secret. They had you, then James, and Finn died soon after. Not before he settled his affairs though.' Bauval whistled softly. 'The young new baron was livid. He threatened your mother with everything under the sun. Eventually, however, after consulting his lawyer, and for the sake of the family name, promised to keep it a secret at a price. Your mother had to promise never to bring dishonour to the family. In return, she received a small allowance. If the merest breath of scandal reached him, the new baron vowed to drag her through the courts and get custody of you and James. He said he would have his father declared too mentally unfit in his last years to have married anyone. That of course would make you and James illegitimate.'

Elizabeth broke her silence. 'Then what was Westernbury's hold on her?'

'He threatened to cause trouble, and said he would swear under oath that she was his mistress all along.'

'He blackmailed her?'

'Yes.'

'Why?'

'Money and revenge.'

'Revenge?'

James took a breath. 'Do you recall me telling you my father was killed when I was very young?'

'In an accident in the North?'

'Yes,' James replied quietly. 'One of grandfather's mines blew, wiping out half the village including my father, and Westernbury's eldest son. As his son was not the bread-winner Westernbury received some compensation, but he wanted more. He vowed to get his money one way or another and set his sights on Betty.'

'Betty,' Elizabeth hissed out the name. 'My mother suffered because of her betrayal.'

The previous evening Lady Levana had squeezed Betty's arm as they neared the Bauval cemetery. 'You are sure you want to do this, my love?'

Betty remained steadfast. 'I know what I saw Levvy.'

'Surely it was too dark for you to see anything?'

'Why will you not believe that I saw sprays of colour as I looked down from dear Elizabeth's window?'

It was, Lady Levana realised later, the reason Betty so readily agreed to give up the search for Elizabeth. She believed that the grave being in bloom, was proof that her sister's child was safe and well. Thankfully, and unknown to them at the time, Miss Chetwode was, by then fast asleep in her son's bed.

They had reached the iron gate.

'Look,' Betty had pointed. 'There. See?'

Lowering the flambeaux, a little, they all gazed down at the closed flower heads on the grave.

'Her favourite flowers too,' Betty had whispered in awe. 'When I come to see them tomorrow, they will have opened and will be in full bloom.'

Levana had closed her eyes. *Thank-you Jemmy.*

'Miss Chetwode's choice I believe,' came a masculine voice behind them.

The two women had turned.

Henry Smith-Jacobsen's steeple hat reflected the glow of the light as he tipped it.

'The stardust will be rather pretty in daylight.' His normally pale face mottled pink in the flambeaux flames. 'Ah, I see you need an explanation.'

James, still holding Elizabeth close, inclined his head to a small table Vance placed within their reach.

'Breakfast,' he ordered softly.

His breath on her skin, and the slight burr of his unshaved chin, sent the familiar velvety butterflies fluttering through her. 'Yes,' she agreed on a whisper.

243

'Marry me?' he asked. 'Please?'

It was mid-afternoon when Elizabeth sitting alone by the window of Lady Levana's pleasant room went over the events of the last twenty-four hours.

She and Lady Levana had talked before luncheon with Elizabeth describing the events of the previous afternoon and evening again. She had left Jemmy's room just after breakfast, and as he was still resting, had not seen him since. Lady Interton had returned to her own home just a few miles away.

It was so peaceful now that everything seemed like a bad dream. Except it was not.

Her whole life revealed in a few hours.

Betty's betrayal, her real father, her brother's new title and inheritance, and her inheritance.

Why then, did she feel so numb?

A familiar voice broke into her thoughts. 'Miss Chetwode please may I come in?'

Elizabeth turned a weary face to Pamela hesitating in the door way.

A Wybrow.

Although she never wanted to see any of that family again, she nodded. After all, none of this was Pamela's fault.

Pamela sidled right up to where Elizabeth was sitting and lowered herself, grey-eyed and pale, on the banquette. 'I,' she gulped, 'am so sorry. I truly believed Papa's promise that he would not do it again.'

Elizabeth blinked at Pamela in astonishment.

'Mama says it was all grandfather Wybrow's fault for re-marrying,' Pamela explained. 'We were so rich and happy in America. When grandpapa died, however, we discovered he signed everything over to his new wife and their son. Papa took it to law, but everything was in order so there was nothing he could do. He spent every last penny on fees and things. We got nothing.' She shivered. 'He threatened to kill them, so, when their mansion burnt down, he was accused of carrying out his threat.' She looked into Elizabeth's face. 'He

244

did not do it, but we were outcasts. Mama's brother, Uncle George, gave us the money to come to England and start a new life. Uncle George also gives us a small annual allowance, but Papa never got over the humiliation. He demanded the sort of life a wealthy gentleman can expect, as recompense.' Her lashes fluttered up. 'He threatened to leave if Mama did not agree. Poor Mama had no choice. It was awful. Mama said that Papa was the perfect husband before it all happened.' She groaned. 'My previous companion Henrietta, took his fancy. She hated his attentions and tried to fend him off.' Pamela fought for composure. 'She became with child and was sent away in disgrace.'

Elizabeth rapidly pieced the fragments together, then stared at Pamela in horror. 'You should have warned me!' she flung out bitterly.

'I tried, but he seemed to genuinely like you. I was so relieved that you also had the earl's patronage. Besides,' she added softly, 'he promised.'

Elizabeth closed her eyes as another sharp edge of betrayal sliced through her yet again. 'You should have told me all the same.'

'I promised never to tell.'

'Did you know about my inheritance too?'

Pamela gulped again. 'No. Mr. Westernbury told me and Mama just before he left. He said you saved his life.'

Did they know Wybrow planned to kill him?

'He told us that he was drunk, and that you put your cloak over him. He would not have survived the night otherwise.'

Relief washed over Elizabeth. He had gone.

'He said Papa was a wicked man, but it is not true.' Pamela's eyes filled with tears. 'I know Papa would not have hurt you. He promised.'

Her hands twisted in her lap. 'He has gone too. Vanished,' she finished on a whisper.

The numb detachment of before was as nothing to the cold chill of betrayal now. It seemed as if everyone she loved had deceived her. Mama, Bauval, who knew the whole story weeks ago, but never told her, Jamie, Lady Levana, Lady Betty, Pamela, and Mrs Wybrow.

'There is something else,' Pamela muttered. 'Gossip in the village.'

Gossip? Elizabeth could not care less about gossip.

'That the man who won the race is really Lord Bauval's secret younger brother. A base-born.'

Elizabeth's stomach lurched. She had not given the winning of the race a thought since the accident. Even so, she knew Jamie would have won, and immediately rushed to his defence.

'That is absurd Pamela. Lord Bauval's father died when he was three. My brother is twelve years younger than him.'

'Your brother?' Pamela gave a strangled cry. 'Then the village is in terrible danger!'

'I think not Miss Wybrow.' Vance came soberly toward them with a tea tray which he then set on an occasional table near them.

'Miss Chetwode's brother is a Bauval through their mother's line. The late Bauval's granddaughters, Levana, Lady Alstoe; Elizabeth-Ann, Lady Interton; and Mary-Jane, Baroness Chetwode, were expected to, and given the right to continue that name. So, the village is not in danger at all, because they all bear the Bauval name.'

His sanguine tone annoyed Elizabeth, 'He could have been lynched before anyone realised.'

'No Miss Chetwode,' Vance continued with a smile, 'Lord Bauval had it all arranged beforehand. His friends knew exactly what to do if the new Baron Chetwode was declared the winner. I hear your brother fulfilled his obligations perfectly. Baron Chetwode presented the flitch of ham and other winnings to those in need. Will that be all?'

Elizabeth gave a dazed nod.

'I must go,' Pamela sighed. 'I realise that we can never be friends again, and am truly sorry for that.'

Pamela was right. Recent events had spoiled their friendship.

Pamela sniffed. 'Good-bye,' she sniffed. 'I hope that one day you will find it in your heart to forgive me.'

Elizabeth watched as Pamela walked noiselessly to the door. Poor friendless Pamela who usually managed to mask her unhappiness with bright cheeriness, now so downcast by disasters not of her making.

It was so unfair. The burden belonged to her parents.

The words on a tiny stone blurred into her mind, '*the sins of the parent*'.

Pamela was paying for the sins of her father.

'Pamela,' Elizabeth called softly. 'Come and have some tea.' Pamela stopped and turned around. 'When I go to Hertford, I'll need a com,' she chuckled, 'a friend. I shall be honoured if you agree to be that friend?'

Pamela's eyes glittered with tears. 'Oh, Mary-Beth,' she breathed, 'thank-you.'

Elizabeth avoided telling Lord Bauval of her decision. Firstly, she wanted to be sure he was on the mend. Secondly, she had to be sure that she really did have a house in Hertford.

Lady Levana had insisted that Elizabeth stay with them until everything regarding her house in Hertford and her inheritance was settled, and Elizabeth, knowing she could not go back to Nimbus Folly, agreed.

Although she had not spent any more nights in Jemmy's room, he had talked of marriage several times since, when she visited him. Due to his weakened state, Elizabeth was able to steer the subject to other matters.

Now, sitting beside the *chaise longue* James rested on during the day, with a maid just outside his bedchamber door, Elizabeth drew a deep, silent breath. She had to be strong.

His blue-black brows were arched. 'My love, why do you need a companion? You will have me. Is that not enough?'

Elizabeth slid her gaze away from him. She was too close to him. She should have taken the chair by the fire-place. Being too close might melt her resolve.

She loved him and always would.

Marriage though, was completely out of the question. There was so much she wanted to do. Besides, how could she and Jemmy be happy when she would always despise Betty, the aunt who should be a source of comfort and love for her? Betty, would of course expect to be included in everything connected to Jemmy.

She knew it might not matter at first. How long would it take for the cracks to appear though? How long before Lady Levana's sweet understanding turned to hostility at a daughter-in-law's lack of forgiveness? How long would Jemmy tolerate the situation? Then what?

A family torn apart by divided loyalties that's what. Besides, she knew that even if they accepted the uncomfortable situation, there might come a time, when she could not. There might come a time when all the hurt might spill out in bitter recriminations.

No, she was better off sticking to her original plan. If a Season as Mama wished, was not possible, she would retire straight to Hertford. Although there was enough money for a season and enough to live on afterwards, those who considered themselves Quality might reject her. It that happened, then there was no point going through the ritual of it all in the first place.

She looked down at him now, although still in pain, he was freshly shaved, immaculately, but comfortably dressed, and smelled of soap and his own delicious scent.

'No,' she said with more determination than she felt. 'It would not work. Betty will always come between us.'

'My darling.' He winced as he reached out to her. 'I am sure you will forgive her in time.'

Elizabeth frowned. 'Do you not see? For Mama's sake I cannot.'

Funnels of the late afternoon sunlight poured into the room making his dark hair glint. His onyx eyes flecked silver sparks. 'Surely for your Mama's sake you must?'

Elizabeth drew back just out of his reach, and lowered her voice. 'Do you know what Mama went through because of Betty and Westernbury? Have you any idea?'

His expression changed.

'Do you think I can just let you turn tail, and disappear, my darling Elizabeth, without trying to win your heart and your trust? Do you think I can ever forget how much you mean to me?

Besides,' he added with a slow smile, 'I believe as your oldest male relative, I am your legal guardian-?'

'-What?' Elizabeth's stomach jolted as she then lost her voice and stared at him in stunned disbelief.

Was he really her legal guardian and therefore prepared to compel her into submission? 'You beast!'

With that, she flung out of the chair and pivoting away from him, stalked furiously from the room.

What was she to do now? Cast herself on Jamie's charity until she became of age? No, she simply could not. She scowled to herself.

After all she and Bauval had been to each other?

Her champion?

She was such an idiot to be taken in.

Again.

Flinging herself along the galleried landing away from his room, she flounced down the stairs to inform Lady Levana of her decision straight away, *I will never be able to repay your kindness Lady Levana, but I have to leave immediately*, she rehearsed again and again.

She would not be beholden to any man, even the man she was in love with. No man would treat her with anything less than equal respect. No man would behave in a high-handed manner towards her.

No man. Not even Jemmy.

249

Still simmering, Elizabeth swept toward the pleasant room in a tide of anger, skidding to a halt outside the slightly open door.

'Betty my love, do not expect too much too soon,' Lady Levana was saying. 'The poor girl has had much to overcome.'

No, she would not go in while Betty was there.

'Oh, Levvy I know that,' came Betty's tearful voice. 'But the flowers on the grave mean that *Mary-Jane* has forgiven me.'

'Dear Elizabeth however, has not,' Lady Levana replied sadly.

There was a pause, and as Elizabeth turned to go Lady Levana sighed, 'If only she knew the whole of it.'

'No,' Betty cried out. 'No,' she resumed on a softer note. 'It is past and gone. Elizabeth must never know of the circumstances.' Her voice shook. 'It is enough that she despises me without losing faith in poor Mary-Jane.'

'What if she knew about the dresses?'

Betty sighed. 'Whatever happened with the dresses is past and gone. It is of no consequence whatsoever.'

'It is of no consequence?'

Elizabeth heard the astonishment in the reply.

'It is nothing that in a fit of jealousy Mary-Jane, exchanged her gown with yours? If she had not worn your gown, Westernbury would have known he had the wrong sister, and would not have carried her off.'

Betty sounded weary. 'Levvy, I have gone over it a thousand times in my mind. What is a gown between twins? She wanted the one with the blue-ribbon trim.' She gave something between a wry chuckle and a sigh. 'In the portrait of us as little girls, she wanted the dress with blue trim too. Do you not remember?'

Elizabeth nearly stopped breathing. The portrait belonged to her, not Betty.

'I believe I do,' Lady Levana mused. 'I was about eleven,' she paused. 'You and Mary were about five.'

'Grandfather ordered us to use to the same colours for our coming-out gowns so he could compare the come-out portraits with earlier ones and know who was who.'

Elizabeth's mind flew to the portrait of the two little girls and of all those childhood years looking at it and never knowing what it really meant.

'Naturally,' Betty continued, sighing, 'dearest Elizabeth must have Mary-Jane's picture too. I am not entitled to it now.'

Elizabeth was stunned. There were two portraits?

Mama, her mind railed. *Why did you not tell me there were two of you?*

'And who knows?' Betty added wistfully, 'Although she will never come to love me as I love her, she may see it in her heart to forgive me one day.'

Elizabeth could see it all now. Especially the portrait. That portrait was the last thing Mama laid eyes on before she died. Elizabeth's heart sank at the recollection of those last moments of dear Mama's life as Mama's smoky-grey eyes rolled to the painting. 'Please,' she had implored, *'forgive her.'* Her weak voice had trailed. Her once lovely eyelashes had fluttered. *'I beg you-'*

Elizabeth's heart started bouncing as the meaning of those very last words slammed into her. *Forgive.* The word reverberated through her body filling her mind, her heart, her skin, her space.

Yet she could not. To forgive was to forget, and now knowing the truth she knew she could never forget.

James groaned at her obstinacy. Why, after all they said and did, during the last few days, did she still reject him? She said she loved him, and he certainly loved her. The forgiveness bit needed a little more time, but it was resolvable.

He turned it over in his mind. He had done everything in his power to convince her of his total love. Protected her. Rescued her. Nurtured her. Protected her. *Loved her.*

Just the memory of her nearness sent tenderness through him.

No woman had ever had this effect on him before. Even before and after Mary-Beth, if a woman had no interest in him, he just moved on. Why, oh why could he not do the same this time? Why could he not forget this wonderful Boadicea?

The pain in his heart was far worse than the pain in his body.

He rang for Vance.

Elizabeth was still outside the door of the pleasant room as Vance came hurrying by.

He stopped, 'Here allow me,' he quickly pushed the door wider before she managed to protest. 'Miss Elizabeth Chetwode,' he announced.

Elizabeth had no choice except to walk sedately towards the two women seated by the cheerful hearth. As pale blue eyes rimmed with smoky grey, met hers, Elizabeth's stomach lurched. That was how Mama looked the last she saw her. Elizabeth's stomach lurched again.

And suddenly she cared!

Really cared about her mother's twin.

Please do not let Betty be dying too.

Betty extended a thin white hand. 'Come and sit beside me,' she murmured, indicating the chair nearest to her.

Elizabeth faltered. This was the woman who came between herself and her world.

Betty noticed the uncertainty. 'Please?' she implored softly.

The gentle voice so like Mama's made her spine prickle, not with anger, or fear, but with the dulcet familiarity of it.

A lump rose to her throat.

'Mama,' she whispered, 'You are so like Mama.'

The thin cool hand reached out as Elizabeth sat down. 'And you are so like my darling Mary-Beth.'

'But I am not your Mary-Beth. Jemmy loved *her*-'

'-Yes,' Betty cut in softly. 'Jemmy loved her, but,' she sighed. 'Not as a man should love a woman. I knew, deep down he only loved her as a sister.'

Elizabeth's stomach fluttered. Then something warm inside her began unravelling. Jemmy loved Mary-Beth only as a sister? Jemmy was not in love with the other Mary-Beth after all?

'He proposed to her when she was dying, but had she lived, we would have discouraged the match.' Betty's hand trembled, 'She was in love with,' her voice wobbled.

'Smith-Jacobsen!' Jemmy suddenly flung out.

All three veered to the voice.

'Aghh! Dammit Vance,' Bauval grated through gritted teeth from a decrepit wicker bath chair. 'Are you out to kill me?' He grimaced and groaned as his leg, held out at an angle in front of him, jarred with every twist and turn of the contraption's ancient wooden wheels.

Vance gave a martyred sigh and continued wheeling the chair towards them.

There was a flurry of voices from Betty and Levana, but Elizabeth hardly heard as James and the dreadful conveyance advanced. He looked far too large for such a broken-down vehicle. And quite preposterous too, sitting there with a grimacing grace the bath chair did not merit.

She wanted to laugh. She wanted to cry.

As Vance halted the chair right next to Elizabeth, James felt his heart give a thump as her chrysolite eyes roved his face. How could he have behaved so high-handedly? How could he have issued threats? He was no better than the absent Wybrow or the permanently inebriated Westernbury. Yet, there was tenderness in her roaming look.

He held out his uninjured arm and took her hand.

His gentleness caused every part of her to glow.

Onyx eyes flecked with silver, met hers.

Her heart soared. He was never in love with the other Mary-Beth.

Jemmy loved her.

An intense relief surged through Elizabeth. Thank goodness they had not grown up knowing one another. For if they had, she stilled at the thought, *if* they had grown up together, then they too would only love as brother and sister. Love as she and Jamie loved each other. As Betty and Lady Levana loved each other. As the twins loved each other.

As the twins loved each other?

Tears of shame began to rim her eyes.

'My darling,' James whispered, 'I am sorry for my high-handedness, and have come to ask you to forgive me.' Her hair flashed rosy beige as she moved. Her cheeks pinked; her delicious rosebud mouth parted. The caramel lashes fluttered.

Tenderness seeped through him.

Elizabeth sighed. 'It is I who should beg for forgiveness.'

She turned to Betty.

'Can *you* forgive *me* Aunt Betty?'

It was sometime later James held her close to him.

'Are you sure you want to marry me?'

'Oh yes,' she whispered. 'I knew it the day I met you in the field and saw how your men respected you helping with the harvesting.'

Then, he dipped his chin and brushed her mouth with his.

The touch sent fluttering velvety butterflies sashaying along her spine and gliding into every nerve of her body.

This time, his lips did not merely brush hers. He kissed her properly. His kiss firm, yet sublimely gentle caused an inner cry to go through her. *Soon!*

Soon, his inner voice echoed in thought. *Soon, before the last autumn leaf falls.*

A little about me.

I have always enjoyed words, writing, and I love and appreciate history.

I am the family genealogist, and take great pleasure in looking up the births, marriages and deaths of my ancestors and wondering what they were like, how they lived, and so on. As a result, I have a considerable and diverse family tree.

The Two Mary-Beths©, came about, due to discovering how alike in looks, character, and talent, even distant family members are.

In some families, the siblings hardly look related, yet put one alongside a second cousin, or a second cousin once removed, and hey! Almost twins!

Thank you, dear readers for reading The Two Mary-Beths©

I hope you enjoyed reading as much as I enjoyed writing it.

Look out my next Regency Novel. The Little Nun©

At fourteen, two years after her darling Mama's death, Franny's Papa announced they were going on The Grand Tour.

Less than four months later, just after arriving in Spain, however, the war between France and England broke out again and Franny's father, Sir John Huttingstone, fearing for her safety, left Franny at the convent of Our Lady of Humility nestled at the foot of the mountains, east of the Basque Country, until he was able to return.

He never did.

Carlos Roberto, on a dangerous mission, did not need or want a travelling companion, especially a naïve but beautiful

French nun. Sometimes, however, doing the right thing, overcomes needs, and wants, and, danger.

The Little Nun. ©

'Frances Magdelina, have you come to a decision?'

Franny shook her head, 'No Holy Mother. Not yet. Please?' she cast a hesitant look round the small austere cubicle that served as Mother Superior's advice centre as well as her penance room. The walls, so badly in need of white washing, leaned inward. It was obvious the antiquated but well-loved convent's foundations were either slipping, or crumbling, or both. The simple wooden chair the Holy Mother occupied creaked every time she moved her slim ancient body. A prickly straw mattress covered with threadbare ticking was airing under the open window, where the morning sun already blazed through. 'Please, may I wait just a little longer?'

The Holy Mother shook her head. 'It has been six years child. Six years is more than we have ever allowed anyone.'

Franny's voice cracked. 'But Papa promised to return.'

In a rare display of emotion, the Mother Superior shook her head sadly. 'My child, anything could have happened to him. The war wreaked havoc all across the continent.' She crossed herself softly. 'He might not have survived.'

'No, please do not think such a thing.' The wrenching of her insides caused Franny's face to contort in anguish. 'He is alive, I know he is.'

'My child,' a gnarled work-worn hand slipped across the bare wooden table in a consoling gesture, 'perhaps this is God's will.' Her eyes rimmed with compassion. 'Perhaps this is His way of telling you to do His work.'

Franny swallowed and blinking back her own tears she dipped her chin to stare sightlessly down at her hands resting demurely on the coarse grey cotton of her novice's habit.

Was the Holy Mother, right? Was she destined to spend the rest of her life cloistered up here in the Basque area of Spain doing good works, and never speaking to a living soul once she had taken her vows?

'You may go into the Most Sacred Bower,' the Holy Mother continued softly, 'nobody will disturb you there.'

The Most Sacred Bower? This was privilege indeed.

The Most Sacred Bower was where only the most honoured went to pray and meditate, and where it was whispered, prayers were answered and miracles wrought.

The Holy Mother put her fingers to her lips, and Franny knew here of all places the vow of silence remained.

How long had she got? An hour? A day?

The Holy Mother drew her hand in a half arc.

Until midday.

A few short hours to decide whether to take her vows, or face the world outside the confines of the convent.

'Promise,' the Holy Mother whispered, 'that if you leave us, you must not to reveal your true nationality or identity until you reach home shores?'

'My true identity?'

The old nun's eyes glistened under the glow of the candles. 'For your safety, child. Speak only what little Spanish you already know, and French when you need to. Moreover, tell no one that you have not yet taken the vow. Behave like a holy sister at all times.' Her tone heaved with feeling. 'It is the only way you will survive.'

Franny's brow creased in the candlelight.

'My child,' the Holy Mother's voice wobbled, 'just promise. Here,' she drew a leather-bound bible from a shelf, 'make an oath on the Holy Book.'

Placing her hand on the book, Franny made the promise.

Carlos Roberto whipped his sombrero from his head and stared.

Bile from the pit of his stomach rose to his throat. He retched. Letting go of his mount's reins he staggered to a patch of newly turned soil, leaned over and vomited.

How could anyone commit such a vile act? What sort of humans could wipe out an entire order of nuns in so a barbaric manner?

Flies, attracted to the smell of dead flesh, were buzzing round the carcasses of the mutilated grey-clad bodies.

Wiping a large dusty hand across his parched mouth Carlos blinked. Some of them had obviously been labouring in the dusty vegetable patches. The blood splattered gardening tools discarded lay as unnerving silent monuments on blood splattered ground.

Someone had to do the decent thing and bury them.

He ground his teeth, scanning the seemingly deserted hills. He turned, straining his eyes to catch sight of movement on the road below him. Nothing but the reflection of the sea just over half a kilometre away, shimmied on the landscape. Even the fishing village beside it, had an aura of stillness about it.

He pulled his long, lean, six feet two, frame upright, and walked with leaden steps to the door of the dilapidated whitewashed building. He studied the plaque on the wall next to it.

The inscription was in French as well as Latin. His stomach lurched with shock and disgust. Innocent nuns massacred just because they were a French order? Had enemies, claiming to be patriots in the cause of good against the evils of French rule murdered a convent of innocent women?

He shuddered and swallowed back more bile.

'Senior!'

Carlos wheeled round, instinctively drawing his pistol at the same time.

'No, no Amigo!' The tiny Spaniard gesticulated wildly.

'Amigos?' Carlos spread his arms wide as several other men scrambled into sight.

'Guerrilleros,' The tiny Spaniard spat with disgust and pointed to the hills beyond.

Carlos understood immediately. These men bore no weapons; they were not the murderers.

The tiny man shouted to his men to get to work and bury the dead.

Carlos Roberto nodded and picked up a discarded spade. 'I will help.'

The perspiring men, including Carlos Roberto threw down their tools and then crossed themselves.

'It is done Amigo.' The leader of the group looked up at Carlos Roberto's rugged tanned features.

'It is.' Carlos murmured, relieved once again, that his Spanish was almost perfect.

The men gathered round him as if expecting something.

'What is it?' Carlos felt like a giant peering down from on high.

Silence.

He shrugged. 'Well?'

'Senior,' the leader took a tentative step forward, 'the Inner Sanctum might still be intact.'

Carlos drew his dark bronze brows together; his tanned fingers automatically stroked his chin. 'Inner Sanctum?'

'Senior, every convent has one. It is where the Pontiff, the Holy Father,' the little man reverently crossed himself, 'is received.' He shuffled. 'Should he feel inspired to do so. It is full of riches.' His eager face glowed, 'sacred riches that should be placed in safe keeping until such time they are required.'

'Of course,' Carlos Roberto nodded.

'We have your blessing, Amigo?'

'Blessing?' Carlos echoed.

'You are a Caballero?'

A Caballero was a man of superior rank and authority. He raised his head to the heat of the sky and drew in a long slow breath. A denial would disappoint them, anger them even. He bowed his head to them again. 'Yes,' he replied smoothly, 'you have my blessing.'

The men whooped.

'Come,' the tiny Spaniard ordered. 'We will search the building.'

Carlos watched them scatter. Sacred riches indeed. They would soon have the whole lot whittled down as booty for sure.

Franny opened her eyes and inwardly groaned. She ached all over. Then she stretched out on the hard stone floor and blinked, suddenly remembering where she was and why.

Did God answer prayers to those who fell asleep during them? Only one candle remained alight and that was slowly ebbing. She eased herself into sitting position. How long had it been?

She winced, drew up her knees and stood up. Her feet were numb so it took some effort to lean over to the one flickering candle and prise it from its golden stem. Then, holding it aloft she set herself toward the door willing her reluctant feet to move.

She still had not come to a decision. What was she going to tell The Holy Mother?

'This is it!'

Franny did not even have time to think another thought before the Inner Sanctum door flew open and several men with blazing flambeaux whooped through.

The leader stopped abruptly. The cries of jubilation died. Every mouth quieted as each man jostled to an astonished halt.

Franny's feet still refused to move.

The leader sank to his knees. 'The Blessed Virgin,' he mouthed in awe.

'The Blessed Virgin,' came the fearful chorus as several more prostrated themselves before her.

Confused, Franny slowly lowered the candle so that it glimmered just above their dark heads.

The men still standing muttered oaths, edged backward.

Franny managed one step.

'The vision moves,' someone said.

'She is coming for us,' another cried. 'Get out!'

Franny's toes tingled as she took one careful step unable to force her numb feet to move any farther.

'She is giving us time!' came a relieved cry.

The men scrambled to their feet practically falling over each other in their frantic bid to escape, and fled.

Carlos Roberto walked over to the well he saw while they buried the dead. With wearied and heartsick effort, he turned the handle and let the bucket down until he heard the soft splat as it hit the water below. The sound revived him somewhat.

'Senior! Senior!'

Half a dozen men with faces as white as the building, charged out and circled him. 'We are cursed!'

'Cursed? Why so?' He pulled the bucket up.

'She has come for vengeance.'

Carlos calmly balanced the bucket before unhooking it from the shaft. 'Vengeance?'

'We heard,' one gasped.

'And did nothing,' added another.

'The Blessed Virgin has come to avenge the blood of her Sisters.'

Carlos shook his head in bewilderment, cupped his palms, and scooped up a handful of cool water.

'No!' one cried. 'It is cursed.'

Too late. Carlos had already slaked his thirst and was tipping the remaining water over his head and body.

'Quickly!' Several other whey-faced Spaniards appeared and gathered round him. 'She is coming.'

7

Carlos set the bucket down with defined deliberation, before pulling himself up to tower over the little men. 'Have you all gone mad?'

'No, no senior, we have seen a vision-'

'-In the Inner Sanctum-'

'-Waiting for us-'

'-With a candle-'

'A vision?' Carlos Roberto although a man of little faith knew better than to ridicule outright whatever it was, they thought they saw. 'You must be holy men indeed,' he said curbing all mockery.

'We are all cursed.'

'Blessed I would say,' Carlos Roberto inhaled as he cast his eyes over the men. 'A vision of the,' he cleared his throat to quell all scepticism, 'Blessed Virgin must surely represent good fortune?'

'Glory be Amigo.' The leader suddenly threw his head back and chuckled with relief. 'Why did we not think of that?'

'Why indeed?' Carlos murmured. Unless you were up to no good, he added silently.

'Take heed of the Caballero,' the leader begged. 'A vision can bring us only good fortune. Who will come back with me to the Inner Sanctum?'

Vivid cobalt eyes began to twinkle with amusement as Carlos watched the men haggle between themselves. Some nodded, but most shook their heads.

'Come,' the leader coaxed. 'Take courage. Listen to the Caballero.' He inclined to Carlos. 'He will come with us. He is not afraid.'

Several expectant faces turned to Carlos.

Carlos not scared, but not interested in looting the Inner Sanctum either, drew a silent breath. He needed to be away. He had spent too much time here already.

'It is beyond the wine cellar.'

Carlos suddenly grinned. The wine cellar? Hard unpalatable riches of a holy place did not tempt him. A wine cellar however, was a different matter. He ran a hand through his rapidly drying hair. 'Come, I should like to see this vision.'

The men stood back to let him pass.

At that precise moment, Franny stepped out from the convent into bright sunlight and immediately shielded her eyes with her the back of both hands.

'Señorita?'

The rich baritone voice sent shards of tiny quivers splintering through Franny.

In spite of the glare of the sun, she raised her hands slightly to look at the owner of the voice.

All she could see however was a lean structured body through a white, shamefully translucent, shirt. His flesh, though taut, moved with muscular vibration as he spoke.

To her utter mortification, Franny felt herself blush. Everything about him radiated strength and power.

Overwhelmed and somewhat shocked by his internal reaction and completely unexpected admiration of the woman standing before him, Carlos Roberto, could not stop himself. 'A vision of incomparable beauty,' he gushed.

He reached out, gently took her hands in his then placed them by her sides. 'Now I can see you properly.' His touch sent a soft tremor cascading through her. Then he smiled, and her unruly heart bounced. Although she lifted her face to his, she was still acutely aware of all of him. Her blush deepened and it took every ounce of will power to drag her eyes from his. Her breath crackled somewhere between her lungs and throat as her eyes involuntarily rolled down to graze every inch of his mystifying torso.

The top of his shirt was open to reveal the golden tan of his skin and neck.

She blinked as if to banish him from some dream she seemed to be in. His jaw moved drawing her eyes instantly up to lips curved in languid humour. Her heart, that seemed to have stilled, now skittered. Her breath shuddered as her eyes met his cobalt gaze. Was she dreaming? Was he something her anguished mind had dredged up? She swallowed, willing herself to composure. Then with as much control as she could muster, she drew a tremulous breath and blinked.

He was not as nearly tanned as most Spaniards she had met, but was a light honey-gold like the ancient Greeks in her history books. Her spine flooded with rich warmth as if the honey of his skin had somehow saturated her and become trapped there. Another soft tremor cascaded through her again.

His eyes, that reminded her of the hue of English lakes under uncertain English skies, poured over her. Her heart skittered again as his gaze shifted slightly. Then as his mouth curved to a slow smile, she thought again, of honey, and again, for some unfathomable reason, home.

'Forgive me,' he murmured gravely.

His words, rich, and deep, flowed through her. It was like being in a dream where every detail is sharp and exquisitely clear, yet the reason for it is totally incomprehensible. She felt her lips dry as he ran a tanned palm through glistening, damp, dark brown curls. There was something about him that reminded her of home. Something unfathomable, deep and mysterious.

She blinked up at him realising immediately that she could understand his Spanish better than most.

He brought his sun-bronzed hand down to touch her shoulder. She felt the comforting strength penetrate her grey habit like an aura of spun gold. 'Are you alright?' he pressed gently. 'Did they hurt you?'

She rolled her eyes to the men now huddled silently together, slowly shook her head and frowned. Why did he think these good men would hurt her?

He read her thoughts. 'Not them.' His eyes were glinted with icy-grey specks. 'The others.' She followed his gaze to the hills in the distance. When he turned back to her, he added, 'The Guerrilleros.' His white teeth flashed.

Franny drew her face back to his, confused at the change in him. He whisked his hand away from her shoulder. 'They murdered your sisters.' He indicated the mound of rocks and earth. 'We buried them over there.'

Murdered? Her stomach jolted, but she made no sound.

'She has taken the vow,' a Spaniard muttered.

Franny flicked her eyes to the man then back to the honey-bronze face above her.

From the first moment he saw her, Carlos had a scorching desire to put his arms around her perfectly shaped, slender body and pull her close to him. Another longing took him by surprise too. He wanted to kiss away the look of wide-eyed confusion and promise her the world. It took all his self-control to resist. 'Is that true? Have you taken a vow of silence?'

The Holy Mother's last words sprang through Franny's disordered brain. *Speak only what little Spanish you know.* 'Si,' she nodded, glimpsing again the expanse muscular flesh glistening beneath the translucent shirt. Her heart gave another foolish, excited mystifying skitter. She felt the colour rise to her cheeks again. Oh, how could the sight of a mere man have such a ridiculous effect on her? As nuns, they had cared for the sick, so she had seen men's flesh before. What made this one so different?

The spokesman skipped forward. 'She must be French as this is a French order, but it has,' he quickly crossed himself, 'had,' he corrected, 'a mixture of nationalities.' He shook his head sadly. 'They were good women.'

Carlos looked down to the top of Franny's starched wimple. As his gaze slid down to her high, unlined forehead and over her face, something tight gripped his insides. The lure of her was almost too much. Had the sun and the heat gone to his head? He silently cursed himself. Was he a mere greenhorn to be so influenced at the sight of a female?

Her dark-blonde eyebrows meant that she was probably fair-haired, and a sudden vision of golden untamed locks flying out behind her caught him totally unawares. Drawing a quick breath, he checked himself. Her head would be shaved.

A dull pain of sorrow, so strong that it almost took his breath away dropped through him.

Then as large amber eyes blinked at him under golden lashes, his whole body began pulsating with a lush evocative rhythm. Something he could not explain touched his soul. Sharp, like a knife point, yet soft and yielding like the petals of a rose. Dragging his eyes from hers, he grazed the high perfectly contoured cheekbones; the tip of her prettily tilted delicate nose, and the full well-shaped warm pink rosebud lips. Here his examination ceased. Stopping abruptly in mid-study, so transfixed by her untainted loveliness that his heart lurched. His muscles flinched to control the impulse to slip his fingers under her chin, lift her face up and kiss away the distress. He drew in a swift governing breath.

She was a nun; she was out of bounds.

'Amigo,' the leader hissed, 'she is not safe here. She must leave immediately. If anyone finds out she has survived the massacre,' his voice trailed.

His decision was instant, but that did not prevent the anguish from going through Carlos. 'Then she must go with you. You must give her sanctuary in your village.'

'No, I do not agree with the murder of innocent women,' the Spaniard crossed himself. 'Nor do I support the French cause, but to harbour a French woman, even a nun would be considered treachery.' He wrung his hands in despair. 'The whole village would suffer.'

A murmur of agreement ran through the men.

Carlos spoke through clenched teeth. 'How do you know she is French?'

'Her skin is fair and she speaks with a foreign tongue, the Spaniard said.

Carlos considered this for a moment. The man was right. An almost paralysing pain gripped him. 'Then you would leave her here at the mercy of the murderers?'

'No, Amigo. She must go with you.'

Regret ripped into his body and tore through his soul. 'Out of the question.' The little nun blanched and Carlos immediately remorseful at having spoken so roughly, mouthed on a softer note. 'I cannot take a nun with me.'

The leader motioned to the silver-grey mount, nibbling at the sparse vegetation. 'You are a merchant traveller. Surely, you can get her to the French border where she will be safe among her own?'

With a deep sigh, Carlos relented.

Printed in Dunstable, United Kingdom